THE RISE OF DELILAH

MEAGAN DUX

First published by Making Magic Happen Academy, 2017
Copyright © 2017 Meagan Dux
Cover design by Orlando Media
Edited by Georgina Gregory

National Library of Australia
Cataloguing-in-Publication data:
The Rise of Delilah/Meagan Dux
ISBN: (sc) 978-0-9954104-6-6
ISBN: (e) 978-0-9954104-7-3
Young adult – fiction

Making Magic Happen Academy books may be ordered through online booksellers or by contacting:
www.makingmagichappenacademy.com

Find Meagan online at www.meagandux.com

Dedication

To my parents, Barry and Nicky. Without them, this novel would still be sitting on my laptop. Thank you for encouraging me to chase this dream, it's because of the two of you that this novel happened.

To my two brothers, Jason and Mitchell, and my grandparents, Les and Maureen. Thank you for everything, I love you.

And to my guardian angel, I did it. I hope you're proud.

CHAPTERS

Dedication

Chapter One: Remember When   7

Chapter Two: Past and Present   21

Chapter Three: Wishful Thinking   35

Chapter Four: The Waiting Game   47

Chapter Five: Dreams vs. Reality   58

Chapter Six: Breaking Free   74

Chapter Seven: Sydney Shelter (Part one)   87

Chapter Eight: Sydney Shelter (Part two)   108

Chapter Nine: Back to Reality   118

Chapter Ten: Riptide   134

Chapter Eleven: Perfection Perception   150

Chapter Twelve: Sweet Sixteen   157

Chapter Thirteen: New Beginnings   169

Chapter Fourteen: Surprise City   182

Chapter Fifteen: Back to Basics   194

Chapter Sixteen: Too Good to be True   209

Chapter Seventeen: Broken Hearts   225

Chapter Eighteen: Falling from Grace   241

About Meagan Dux   253

Acknowledgements   254

CHAPTER ONE

REMEMBER WHEN

I look into my father's eyes.

"Daddy, you'll always be my friend, won't you?" He laughs as a smile creeps onto his face.

"Of course, Delilah. I'll always be your best bud and I'll always love you. Don't ever forget that."

He hugs me and picks me up, before gently placing my feet on the ground, putting his hands on my shoulders and kissing my forehead. Without saying another word, he turns around and starts to walk away. I run after him, but he turns and shakes his head.

"Delilah, don't follow me, please."

I start crying. *Why is he leaving me?*

I suddenly wake up, jolted by the sudden ending of my dream, or my nightmare. I'm not even sure what it is anymore. I've had the same dream for the past eight days, and every time it has ended the same: with my father walking out on me. I sit up in my bed and look over my shoulder. I smile when I see my boyfriend, Cameron, who is fast asleep. I grab my water bottle from my bedside table and take a sip, allowing the now room temperature water to soothe my incredibly dry throat. I put the bottle down and grab my phone to check the time; it's 3:00 a.m., and another Monday has begun.

It's the middle of summer in Perth and there's a storm raging outside my window. The thunder has intensified and the rain is hammering against the roof. The lightning floods my room, showing every inch of the objects neatly placed around me. I turn my phone light on and open the top drawer of my bedside table. I pull out an old envelope and open it, carefully taking out the letter encased in the delicate paper. I open the letter and begin to read it, with the same sense of sadness I always get. That doesn't stop me from reading it anyway:

"You were never the reason I made the decision to leave. You deserve better and only your mother can give you that. Don't try to find me. When I feel I can be your father, I will find you. I will always be your father, and I will never stop loving you, even if you hate me."

Tears pool in my eyes; before I know it each delicate tear begins to escape. I try to wipe them away, but they keep flowing. I stop reading the letter, gently put it back into the envelope and replace it in the drawer. I close it and put my head back against the pillows. Cam rolls over and pulls me into his chest.

"It's okay. I love you."

He kisses my forehead before rubbing my back; he knows that helps to relax me. Before I know it, I'm fast asleep again.

I hear my alarm going off. It feels like I've only just gone back to sleep, but it's no longer 3:00 a.m. It's 9:00 a.m., and I've got to get up and get ready for work. Cam is already up and getting ready to go to university. He's twenty-two and in the final year of his journalism degree. He wanted to follow his heart instead of following his family's dream of him being a physiotherapist. And I am proud of him for that.

Cam and I adore his family. His older brothers, Ethan and Gavin, own and work at the family physiotherapy business they started together a few years ago. It is incredibly successful and both boys are passionate about what they do, but working so closely to your family can often be a recipe for disaster. When you're as close as Cam is to his siblings, problems are bound to arise, and that's what he wanted to avoid. Cam knew he didn't want to mix family and work. He liked that he kept those two elements of his life separate. Although Cam's parents were pretty pissed when he told them he was changing his degree a year into it, but when he explained his reasons, they understood and were happy to support their son on his new journey.

I personally think Cam was able to calm them down with the help of his younger sister. Since Nia is the only girl in the Collins family, his parents, William and Anna, usually listen to her over the boys, especially when it comes to things like that. She knows how to approach her parents and how to diffuse situations when they get tense and that's exactly what she did for Cam and funnily enough, she still does it now.

When I first started dating Cam I instantly connected with his family, probably because I'd grown up around them. They accept me as one of their own and they treat me with love and kindness. It makes me realise something I've been fighting against for most of my life: I've never believed each person has another person who they're meant to be with. I mean, how can two people actually be made for each other? The whole 'soulmate' thing just didn't add up, at least not to me. Even when Cam and I started dating, I never believed we were soulmates, two people made for each other. But as time went on, I realised maybe we were.

We'd grown up together, but when we were young we didn't really get along. Cam's mum, Anna, met my mum, Deidra, when they were pregnant with us. They were both health conscious and they were always at the gym, so when they saw a mothers' club starting there, they joined and soon became best friends. The rest is history. Both our mums had children around the same time; I think they secretly planned it, although they won't ever admit it. I know they were ecstatic when they found out they were having a boy and a girl a few months apart. They both wanted their kids to be best friends, and while my siblings and Cam's siblings were close, I always kept my distance.

Since we grew up together I was sick of him by the time I was seven, especially when we went to school together. He was always full of confidence, even when we were little. He was the class clown, always getting into trouble and making everyone laugh along the way. I, however, was the opposite. I was shy and quiet; I was always one of those people who liked to be on their own. Even now I'm the same. I like to explore and relax, and everything in between, mostly by myself. I've grown up around a lot of people, especially since I've got a big family, so sometimes being by myself is what I prefer. When I'm alone I'm able to explore the ideas and thoughts I'm having. It's not always good, but how are you ever meant to deal with things if you just avoid them? Sure, I have things I've tried to avoid, but eventually time catches up to you, and running from things suddenly doesn't become an option.

In saying that, I also thrive on being around people, especially my two best friends, Hadley and Rosie, who mean the world to me, and I can always count on them for anything and everything. Having friends is pretty much essential to every human, but there's also no shame in wanting to be alone. Of course that was pretty much impossible when Cam and I started seeing each other.

During primary school we were the best of friends outside of class. When we were in the comfort of our own homes we got along like a house on fire and loved being around each other, but at school it was a completely different story. We both acted differently at school and we pretty much avoided each other. It wasn't because we were embarrassed; to be honest, I think we both knew from a young age that we were going to end up together, but we were opposites. I wasn't confident like he was. He became even more popular as the years went on, and I didn't care for any of that, so I stayed away from him.

I met Hadley and Rosie in Year Four, and that's when Cam and I really drifted apart. As our friendship deteriorated, I found comfort in my new friends. Hadi, Rosie and I instantly connected. We'd always been in different classes before then but from the first day we met, we knew we were going to be best friends. We spent the rest of primary school and all of high school together. We had sleepovers and movie nights, we discussed boys and dating, and we spent countless days at the beach, laughing and enjoying life. We were pretty lucky to have the friendship we had. We always talked about our friendship slowly drifting apart when we graduated from high school, but it didn't; in fact, it did the opposite. We continue to grow closer and we are always there for each other. That kind of friendship is hard to find, especially these days. We know how lucky we are to have each other. I certainly wouldn't have made it through four years of high school without them, especially when Cam and I finally got together. Another time I don't think I'll ever forget.

By the time we left primary school, Cam and I were no longer friends. We hadn't spoken in years; he stopped coming to my house with his mum and sister, and I stopped going to his house when my family went over. Although going to different high schools was actually the best thing for our friendship. In due time, we started connecting again, we became friends and talked all the time. We even talked about seeing each other more; things were going perfectly. Then Cam moved to the same school as me, and our friendship quickly took a sour turn. The distance we had had was what had helped our friendship blossom again, but suddenly being thrown back into being around each other almost all the time wasn't what we needed.

Within his first week, Cam became one of the most popular boys in school. He excelled in sport so he always had people watching him when we had sport class, and he was the class clown again. Everyone loved him. For some reason, we lost our connection. He was focused on being popular, and he loved the attention, whereas I was getting into my music more. I've always wanted to be a singer. Writing songs and singing is my passion. So, during that time I distanced myself from everyone, including my two best friends. My relationship with Cam was pretty much non-existent over the next two years, but when we got into our second last year of school, everything changed.

One winter night, Cam's neighbourhood lost power. Anna called my mum who invited them over. Twenty minutes later Anna arrived with Cam, Nia, Gavin and Ethan in tow. My mum put on a movie for us in our living room, she made us hot chocolate and prepared dinner while Anna made sure we all had blankets. For some reason Cam wanted to share my blanket with me. At first I didn't understand why, but halfway through the movie, Cam suddenly grabbed my hand under the blanket. I looked over at him and he smiled. I felt happy - really happy - and that scared me.

I wasn't used to feeling like this, although if I'm honest I think I've always known I liked Cam. I just never allowed myself the chance to explore those feelings. After that night we began texting again. We spent the next two months getting to know each other again. We had both changed more than we realised since the last time we were friends, so it was almost like we were getting to know each other for the first time. We connected in ways we'd never connected before, and we both knew we wanted something more than a friendship. We were at that point in our teenage years where we were both ready for a relationship, and that's when we both realised we wanted to be with each other; we were just too afraid to admit it.

After months of texting and spending quality time together, we decided to go on our first official date. We went to my uncle's house. He has a farm with a few acres of land, so he drove us out into the middle of one of the paddocks and opened the back of his ute. He put a mattress, pillows and blankets in and set up a picnic for us. He told us to be careful, not do anything we weren't supposed to do (talk about awkward!) but most importantly, he told us to have fun. He knew Cam, and he knew he could trust him, so he was happy to make our first date one to remember. After he had set everything up, he headed back to his house, leaving Cam and me alone.

We spent most of the night talking about our futures. We discussed all of our hopes and dreams and we talked about where we wanted to be in ten years. After our conversations died down, we snuggled up. We looked up to the sky and gazed at the stars. Time seemed to stand still; I was overcome with peace. After spending what seemed to be forever in silence, watching the stars, Cam and I decided it was time to sleep. Just as I was drifting away, Cam asked me a question I didn't think I would ever hear him ask.

"Delilah, I can't fight these feelings anymore, and I don't think you can either. Sometimes in life two people are meant to be together, no matter how hard they try to deny it, or fight it. I think we're two of those people." He took a deep breath before continuing.

"With all of that being said … ummm … I was just wondering if … uh, well … I was wondering if you'd want to be my girlfriend?"

I smiled, before remembering we were in the middle of a paddock, at night. Cam could barely see my smile, which was probably a good thing. I must have looked like the goofiest sixteen-year-old in the world, and the heat had risen to my cheeks again. I snuggled up higher on Cam's chest; I could hear his heart beating. Suddenly he interrupted my thoughts.

"Um, Delilah, you haven't answered my question."

I laughed before answering him.

"Do you really need to ask? Like you said, we're meant to be."

We both fell asleep almost immediately. The next morning, my uncle drove us back to my house, which wasn't too far away. Anna was over to take us to school as she and my mum took it in turns taking us and picking us up. We got ready for school before joining our mums for breakfast. When we sat down with them we decided to tell them the news. They both hugged each other before telling us they'd always wanted this.

Somehow I think they were more excited about our relationship than Cam and I were. Suddenly my mum blurted out something I was not prepared to hear.

"Oh this is amazing. I can't wait until you two get married and have kids!"

My eyes darted towards her.

"Shit, Mum, calm down! We haven't even been dating for twenty-four hours and you're already talking about kids. I don't even know if I want kids."

Anna, Cam, and my mum turned to face me, and I felt the force of having three pairs of eyes looking at me so I awkwardly laughed.

"Firstly, don't swear. It's not ladylike. And secondly, you say you don't know if you want kids because you're young. In a few years you might feel differently."

I felt the heat rising in my cheeks again. I swear I knew this feeling all too well. I checked my phone for the time; thankfully it was time to leave for school. Anna gave my mum a hug as we piled into the car. Cam and I sat in the back as our silence filled the majority of the trip. Anna kept talking about how excited she and my mum were now that we were dating.

After the fifteen-minute drive we finally pulled up to the drop-off area at school, and I suddenly got really nervous. I'd never been one to care about what people thought about me, but today was different. I felt self-conscious and scared. What was happening? Cam noticed, and he grabbed my hand as I faced him.

"Everyone's going to find out eventually; we may as well get it over with now. Don't worry about what anyone thinks. We both like each other and we both want to be with each other, that's all that matters."

I knew he was right, but the butterflies in my stomach intensified despite his comforting words. He kissed my forehead and we got out of the car. This was it, everyone was going to find out we were together, and there was no turning back. We walked into school holding hands; I could feel everyone looking in our direction. Everyone, and I mean *everyone,* knew Cam. I don't know how many people knew me, but suddenly I felt incredibly uncomfortable. I could see people whispering and pointing; I needed to get out of the situation immediately.

I let go of Cam's hand. He looked at me and before he could get a word out I told him I needed to go to the music room before class. I gave him a quick hug before retreating to my sanctuary, the only place I felt completely comfortable. I sat there for the next fifteen minutes, watching as the time passed by. Suddenly the door opened and my best friends walked in. They saw the look on my face and raced over to sit with me. Rosie quickly grabbed my hands.

"Delilah, are you okay? You look pale."

I looked up at my friends, noticing the look on their faces. We didn't have class until second period, so I spent the next forty-five minutes filling them in. I told them about our date, all the nice things Cam had said to me, and how I had a little panic attack that morning. My friends were nothing but amazing. They comforted me and helped me find ways to deal with everything. They made me laugh and I instantly felt better. I won't lie, dating the most popular guy in school was hard, but my friends helped me deal with everything that I struggled to cope with, and they helped pick me up when Cam and I had one of our worst fights.

Cam and I were a year into our relationship. It was our final year of high school and we were a month out from graduating; it was an exciting time. I had worked on my confidence and allowed myself the time to transition from being Cam's girlfriend to actually being known, and recognised, as Delilah. My popularity had soared, and suddenly I was a part of the 'cool' group. Not that I really cared. I split my time between Cam and his friends, and then my friends, although I made them sit with me whenever I was with Cam. They didn't care about popularity either and they often hated sitting with Cam's group - who had a habit of being overwhelming, especially when all the boys got together- but they did it for me and I appreciated that.

Anyway, the day of our first big fight I decided to spend

some time by myself. It was lunchtime and I headed to the music room. I was working on a new song and I wanted some alone time to go over it and figure out all the little errors. Cam asked my friends where I was, and when they told him he made his way to the music room to find me. I was in the middle of the song when the door to the music room flung open; I was sitting on a desk as Cam strolled towards me. He gently took my guitar out of my hands before placing his hands on either side of my legs.

"Come have lunch with me. I feel like I haven't seen you much this week."

I picked my guitar up and placed it back on my legs. For some reason I was annoyed at him. I wanted this time to myself and the last thing I felt like doing was dealing with his friends. I looked at him and snapped.

"Cam, I don't care about being popular. I want to live a meaningful life and meaningless gossip, getting drunk and partying every weekend isn't going to help me achieve that."

He looked at me with a mad look on his face before he snapped back.

"What the hell? Where did that come from? Jesus, I only wanted to have lunch with you, not get a bloody lecture! And I don't get drunk every weekend."

I took a moment to calm myself down before continuing.

"Cam, ever since the date was announced for our graduation, you and your friends have been partying and drinking. God knows how, since you're all underage, but I'm trying to focus on my music. No offence, but your friends are a distraction. I get that it's the rage when you're this age. We're about to graduate and that's exciting. But for me, *this* is what's exciting. I don't care about all of that other stuff, so please just let me be."

Cam didn't reply. He turned and stormed out of the room, slamming the door behind him. I tried to concentrate on my song, but I couldn't. I felt bad for snapping at Cam. Between his job and his friends, his time was limited. I'd hardly seen him, and even when I did see him he was always talking about what his group of friends were planning to do that weekend. It became so frustrating. I wanted him to want to spend quality time with me and it seemed like he didn't care. I knew I should have spoken to him about it in a nicer way. I guess my frustrations had boiled over.

I decided to go and find Cam. I felt bad, really bad, and I wanted to apologise. Before looking for him I found my friends and told them what happened. They agreed to help me find him, so we headed to their usual hang-out spot. Sure enough, there he was. Suddenly Hadi stopped and turned to face me.

"Hey … um … let's go and get some food first. I think you should eat. You look pale, you're probably hungry."

She was acting weird, like she was trying to distract me. I looked past her and saw why. Cam was standing with another girl, and I knew who she was straight away. It was Heather, one of the most popular girls in school, who had always had a thing for Cam, and she looked pretty content. He had his arm around her shoulder. I knew what he was doing. This was his way of getting back at me. He saw me and smirked. I watched him as he began to flirt with her. I could feel myself getting angrier, but I refused to allow him the satisfaction of knowing he had gotten to me. I casually walked up to him. I smiled at Heather before I turned to Cam.

"Can I talk to you?"

Without looking up, he said, "I'm busy."

I felt myself crumbling. I wanted to yell at him, but I knew he had reacted like this because I snapped at him. I never meant for this to happen, and I wanted to apologise, but he had taken it too far. I turned around and without saying a word I started to walk away. Tears welled in my eyes and when I reached my friends Rosie whispered, "Don't cry, it's okay."

We started to walk off when Cam chased after us.

"Delilah, wait."

He stepped in front of me and noticed the tears that had escaped my eyes.

"No, don't cry. I'm sorry, I didn't mean to hurt you. I just lost it when you said those things to me."

I bit my lip before looking up at him.

"I came to apologise for what I said. What you just did, well Cam, that's just not the actions from someone who is supposed to love you."

I didn't allow him to answer; I pushed past him and went back to the music room. Thankfully we didn't have any classes together for the rest of the day, so I easily avoided him. When the final bell went, I decided to catch the bus home instead of getting a lift with Cam. I wasn't ready to face him and I certainly wasn't ready to talk to him.

Once I got off the bus, I put my headphones in and started the five-minute walk to my house. Music was my relief; it got me through everything. No matter how I was feeling, there was a song to describe it. When words failed, music spoke. That's the beauty of music; it never lets you down; it's *always* there. I was blasting Vance Joy, one of my favorite musicians, as I walked up my driveway. I checked the letterbox and took the envelopes out. I started shuffling through them when I felt I was being watched.

I looked towards the front of my house and noticed Cam leaning against my front door with a bunch of flowers in his hand. I knew I had to face him at some point, but it was the last thing I wanted to do. I tried to walk past him, but the door was locked. I took my headphones out of my ears as I fished my keys out of my bag while Cam started talking.

"Are you really going to ignore me?"

When I didn't respond, he continued.

"Look, I'm sorry. I think we were both in the wrong. I know I took it too far. I was just hurt by what you said, and then when I went back to my friends Heather started talking to me. I saw you and your friends approaching us, so I threw my arm around her. It was stupid of me, I'm sorry. You know I love you, right? I mean, I wouldn't have gone and gotten you flowers and stood here for twenty minutes waiting for you to get home if I didn't. I don't know what else to do other than to say I'm sorry. When you're ready, text me and we can talk."

He put the flowers next to the door and turned away from me. Just as he was about to walk back to his car I thought to myself, *Do you really want him to leave thinking you don't love him? Stop being stubborn!* I grabbed Cam's hand and threw my arms around his neck. He welcomed my hug, putting his arms around my waist. I let go of him and took a step back. I looked at the ground as I began to talk.

"I'm sorry too. I haven't told you this yet, but I've been feeling like we're drifting apart, and you're always with your friends. You know I don't, and won't, ever stop you from hanging out with them, but even when it's just you and me, you seem like you're more interested in texting them or talking about them. Sometimes I feel like I'm not good enough for you. I mean, you're popular and everyone loves you, and well, I'm kind of shy and I don't like being popular."

Cam pulled my chin up.

"Don't look at the ground; look at me. You can be honest with me. That's what you're supposed to do. I'm sorry I made you feel that way. You've never stopped me from seeing my friends, and I appreciate that. I didn't realise I was too consumed with them. We're so close to graduating and then we're all going in different directions. I know I won't be friends with half these people when this is all over, so I just want to enjoy these last few months with them. I promise I'll make more of an effort. Don't you ever think you're not good enough. You're more than enough for me. I don't care what anyone else thinks. You're all that matters and I love you, and only you. I always have."

I smiled. *Wait, 'always have?' What did he mean 'always have?'*

Suddenly my curiosity peaked. I leaned against the wall and in my most inquisitive, yet cheeky voice, I said, "Always had a thing for me, hey? Well, aren't you just full of surprises!"

Cam laughed.

"Do you really have to question it? It's pretty obvious I've always had a thing for you. Why do you think I focused on being the class clown? It's a great way to get the attention of the girl you like."

I laughed.

"Well, you didn't need to be the class clown to get my attention."

We spent the next hour sitting out the front of my house, watching the clouds pass by. I knew then and there that this was the person I wanted to spend the rest of my life with. I had no doubt about it. For the first time in my life, I believed in soulmates.

Chapter Two

Past and Present

My thoughts are suddenly interrupted.

"Babe, I've got to go to uni, and you've got to get your butt up and get ready for work."

I check my phone; it is now 9:30 a.m. Wait, Cam's class started half an hour ago. Why is he still here? Just as I am about to ask him, he answers my question.

"Class got cancelled. Next class isn't until eleven o'clock, but I'm going in to meet Marc. He's got a new girlfriend, and he wants to tell me all about it. Hopefully he can keep this one longer than two months!"

I giggle. Marc is Cam's best friend; he's actually the only person Cam stayed friends with after we graduated from school. I like Marc. He is the only guy I connected with in Cam's group of friends during our school days. He's always been a great friend to us both but he isn't so good at holding onto a girlfriend for long, mainly because he always goes for girls who want to settle down, something he isn't ready for.

"Well, I can't wait to hear all about her. Tell him I expect you two to plan a dinner date so he can fill me in."

"Will do. I'd better go. Call you later?"

I nod, then he kisses my forehead before leaving my room. I listen as he makes his way down the stairs. I hear my sisters and brothers saying goodbye to him as I jump out of bed and head down the stairs. Cam is saying goodbye to my mum as I reach the bottom. I quickly hug him and head into the kitchen. Breakfast is usually a crazy time in the Walker household, especially if all five kids are home. It isn't unusual to walk into the kitchen and find my uncle, aunty and cousins here too. We are one big family. We usually have family dinners every Sunday night, but we are so close that it is unusual not to see each other before then.

I live in my house with my mum, Deidra, who at forty-five looks better than ever; probably one of the perks of owning a yoga studio. My oldest brother, Dylan, is now twenty-five and he is enjoying life as a successful real estate agent for one of the most successful companies in Perth. He sells luxury places in the city and throughout the northern and southern suburbs too. He has recently moved into his first house with my other brother Declan, who is only nineteen.

Declan is a talented soccer player, but he is pursuing his dream of being a sports scientist, which he excels at. Dylan offered one of his spare rooms to Declan in exchange for him maintaining good grades while he works steady hours each week. My brothers are pretty close. When Dylan started working more hours he wasn't home as much, so Declan felt a little isolated, especially in a house full of girls. So, moving out has done wonders for the boys, and their relationship as brothers. My mum doesn't like her two boys not being home as much, but she still has three girls at home, and we are usually enough for her to handle.

I have two sisters, Dakota, who is Declan's twin, and Darci, who at fifteen, is the baby of the family. Dakota and Declan are extremely close, which I imagine most twins are. They don't fight and they're always happy to see each other. My sisters and I are close too, but I am ridiculously close to Dakota. She's an aspiring model; well I guess she's not aspiring anymore since she's always travelling. She's growing in popularity, often flying to Melbourne and Sydney for castings and photo shoots. Companies are fighting to work with her now, and she's getting herself established while she's young. She knows it might not last long, so she wants to take advantage of every opportunity while she can.

I remember a day when she was back in Perth. She'd been away in Sydney for a modelling job, so we decided to have a sister day. We went shopping and got our nails done while catching up on everything that had been going on. We spent the whole day laughing and talking, the way we used to before she started to travel. That's what I dislike the most about her job. Don't get me wrong, I'm incredibly proud of my sister, but she's always away from home. Seeing her and talking to her is now done through text messages, the occasional e-mail and a ton of Skype or FaceTime calls. With technology these days it's easy to still be connected, but I miss going into her room with cups of tea and spending the afternoon talking about our boyfriends, and life in general.

Dakota's boyfriend, Justin, is often over. He misses her when she is away, so he comes over for dinner twice a week. I think being around us helps him deal with her being away so often. We've all become pretty attached to Justin, and my brothers love having another male in the family. I still remember the day they met, which was the same day Dakota and I had spent the day together. We were on our way home when we stopped at a set of lights. A blue ute pulled up next to us. I looked over and saw a rather attractive guy, so I told Dakota and she looked over too.

"Oh my God, he is stunning!"

Suddenly she wound down my window and started waving her arms around to get his attention. When he finally noticed her, he laughed and wound down his window too.

"How's it going?" he said.

I thought it was so weird, not to mention embarrassing. They were chatting each other up in the middle of the road.

"Dakota, seriously. The lights are going to change any second now. Let me wind the window up."

"Hang on, Delilah. Geez, I'm just trying to get his number!"

Before I knew it they had exchanged numbers. The lights changed and we continued on our way home as if nothing had happened.

"Talk about stranger danger. You have no idea who that guy is, Dakota. How safe do you think it is to yell your number across to him in the middle of a main road?"

She laughed.

"Delilah, you know I go with the flow. I'm all about the *you only live once* lifestyle, and that was definitely a YOLO moment. Plus, he was so cute, I wasn't going to miss the chance to get his number."

I sighed.

"Dakota please don't use 'YOLO' again. And you know there's more to a person than the way they look, right?"

"Of course I do. I'm not that shallow. But why are you with Cam?"

I could sense the sarcasm in her voice, so I answered in a way that Dakota would.

"His great butt, of course!"

Dakota and I started giggling before bursting into fits of laughter. A little sister time was just what I needed, especially after a long week of working. After that night, Dakota and Justin started texting. They were always on the phone talking into the early hours of the morning and, before we knew it, they were officially a couple. I had never seen my sister that happy before; everything had worked out the way she wanted it to. She had her dream job and she had the man of her dreams. Everything in her life was just as it was meant to be. Right before she left to go to Sydney for her next photo shoot she came into my room.

"Delilah, mum's taking me to the airport now. I know you've been feeling a bit down lately, but you're amazing. You have a beautiful voice. I know how lucky I am to be living my dreams, don't be afraid to chase yours too. You've got what it takes to be the next big thing, and I'm not just saying that because you're my sister, I genuinely mean it. You're so talented and I don't want you to miss your opportunity. I'll help you any way I can. When I get back, let's sit down and find a way to get you to the next level, okay?"

I smiled and got up from my bed. I walked over to my sister and hugged her. "Thank you. Have a safe flight, I love you."

She smiled.

"I love you too. See you in two weeks!"

She waved at me before closing my door.

~

To this day, that is one of my favourite days. I'm glad Dakota is home again, even if it's only for a few days. Plus, I know my mum loves having her kids home. She's always had a thing for names that start with 'D'. This started from my nan. Although her name is Patti, all three of her kids have names beginning with 'D'. There is my mum, who is the youngest, my aunty Debbie, who is now fifty, and my uncle Derek, who is the oldest at fifty-five. The 'D' tradition was only carried on by my mum with the five of us though. My aunt has three kids, Adrienne, Georgia and Robyn, and Derek has two boys, Cooper and Thomas. My aunt Debbie proudly shares her last name, Cornwell, with her three kids, but my siblings and I have always had our mum's maiden name, Walker. When my mum married my dad she didn't change her last name, and when she had us she refused to give us his last name. I guess she always had a feeling he would leave one day.

My mum and aunt Debbie own a yoga studio together, while my uncle Derek owns and runs a music business. My family as a whole are pretty successful, which I always feel pressured by. I mean, all of my siblings are doing really well, my mum and her siblings are successful and my boyfriend is on the path to success too. Meanwhile, I can't decide what direction I want to go in. I love music, I love singing and writing songs, and I know it is something I want to pursue. I just don't know how, and when the right time to do it will be.

Whenever I feel overwhelmed by everything, I usually talk to my uncle. I can always confide in him and I know I can trust him unconditionally. We share an incredible bond, as well as a love of music. He is an amazing drummer, so he and his wife, Kelly, decided to open a recording studio. My uncle and I often spend time there, playing music and helping aspiring bands to reach their full potential. He always encourages me to get in the studio and record a demo album, but I've never been able to find the confidence to do it. One day I told him about my fears of failing, and I remember him telling me:

"Whether we like it or not, life has a plan for us. We can't control that. And whether we're ready for it or not, it'll happen. You can either run with it or run from it. That, my love, you can control. Just remember, every setback is a set up for something better. Chase your dreams. You've got an incredible talent. It would be a waste if you didn't show the world what you can do."

I smile at that memory; my uncle always knows what to say. My mum always makes sure we know how important family is. When my dad left, my grandparents, my uncle and my aunty all came together to help my mum look after us. My mum always tells us that family is the one thing that won't ever let you down. I used to get angry when she said that. If that's true, where is my dad? Why isn't he here? I can feel myself getting annoyed all over again, so I decide to distract myself. Once I'm done with my breakfast, I head back upstairs and get ready for work.

It is the middle of summer and business is booming for Boom Clap music store in Cottesloe. I am three hours into my five-hour shift, and this is the only kind of day I dread being at work. The storm is long gone, replaced by the shining sun. It is a beautiful forty-degree day, summer is at its peak and I am ten minutes away from one of the most popular beaches in Perth.

My sisters keep sending me photos from the picnic they are having in the middle of the packed beach. I long to be there with them, but I remind myself that I love this job, and the beach will still be there at half past four when my shift ends.

I sigh and leave the storeroom, taking the box of new guitar picks and microphone cords towards the display I am setting up. As I start walking, I'm suddenly jolted as a customer runs straight into the box, hitting it with such force that I drop it. I jump back to avoid the collision, watching as the box hits the floor, splitting the bottom wide open. The guitar picks go in all directions and the microphone cords fall into a lump on the floor. The customer is flat on his face. Everything happens so slowly, yet so fast. Suddenly I snap out of my moment of stillness. I lean down and help the customer up.

"Are you okay? That was quite a tumble you took."

He laughs, shaking his body as he gets up.

"I'm fine. Sorry about your stuff. I should really watch where I'm going. Let me help you."

His friends are close by, laughing at what has happened.

"Your friends seem to think it is pretty funny. Obviously they don't care about your safety."

He looks over his shoulder to see his friends watching, still laughing.

"Oh don't worry about them. That's pretty standard behaviour for me, I'm pretty clumsy. Plus, I'd do the same if it was one of them."

I look at him and fake a laugh. I bend down to pick up the guitar picks, and suddenly he is right next to me.

"What's your name?"

He is inches away from me. I am able to see every line on his incredibly structured face. He has the most beautiful green eyes, which complement the colour of his skin: lightly tanned, another perk of Perth's summer heat. His brown hair smells of the beach and he has a smile unlike anything I've ever seen before. I feel the heat rising in my cheeks. *Oh God, he's going to notice I'm blushing, and why am I looking at his features like this? I've got a boyfriend, who I love very much.*

I look back to the floor to hide my now flushed cheeks.

"Delilah. You?"

I pick each guitar pick up and put them into a container that my manager, Hayley, has put next to me. She winks before walking off. I'll have to ask her what that is about once I've finished cleaning up.

"I'm Ryan. Nice to meet you, Delilah."

He extends his hand to me, I grab it and we shake hands. I immediately feel something different about Ryan, like there is more to him. It is almost like he is hiding part of himself. I start finding myself questioning why, before realising I am still holding his hand. Ryan has a funny look on his face. I quickly pull my hand away and continue to gather the guitar picks up off the floor. Ryan bends down to help me again. Once we are done, he helps me up.

"Thanks. Are you sure you're okay?"

He laughs.

"Yeah, I'm fine. Um, I know this is random, but what are you doing after work? My friends and I are heading to the beach soon and we're thinking of having a barbecue. You should join us."

I look over his shoulder. His friends have stopped laughing and they are now watching us closely. I feel slightly uncomfortable, and I suddenly feel the need to tell him about Cam.

"Oh, um, I have to meet my sisters, and then I'm going to dinner with my boyfriend."

I say *boyfriend* protectively, and in a way that sounds rude, something I immediately regret. Ryan looks as uncomfortable as I feel.

"No worries. Sorry. Um, have a good day. Maybe I'll see you at the beach?"

I smile, feeling the need to make sure Ryan feels a little more comfortable.

"Thanks for the invite. It was really nice to meet you. Who knows? Maybe I will see you at the beach."

I smile again and watch Ryan awkwardly walk away. Before leaving the store, he turns around and waves. He has a goofy smile plastered on his face. I laugh and wave back at him before turning around. I can feel the heat returning to my cheeks. *Not again!*

After Ryan has gone, Hayley approaches me. I've been working at the same music store since I was sixteen, and I'm now twenty-one. You'd think that after five years I'd be sick of working at the same place, but I love my job.

Hayley leans against the counter with a grin on her face.

"So, surfer boy was cute, and it seemed like he was interested in you."

"Oh yeah, he seemed really keen when I told him about Cam."

I suddenly think about setting Hayley up with Ryan.

"Don't even think about it," interrupts Hayley. "He's not my type."

How did she know what I was thinking? I laugh before I go back to work. The next few hours of my shift fly by and before I know it, there is only five minutes to go. I clock out, grab my bag and head out towards my white Suzuki Swift, which is parked perfectly in the shade. Not that it would make a difference; the sun has been burning brightly all day so my car feels like the inside of an oven. It is one of the things I resent about the heat. I love summer: the long nights, the beach, sitting outside for dinner. It is the perfect time of year, but hot cars, well, that's not so nice.

Once I find a parking spot, I get out and head towards the sand. I throw my shoes off and head into the crowd of people. Everyone I pass is smiling, and almost everyone says hello to me. I finally make it through the sea of people. I instantly find my sisters and the three of us sit down, talk, dip our feet in the water and watch the sun make its way down to meet the ocean as the day draws to a close. After spending a few hours at the beach, I decide to leave. I hug my sisters and say goodbye to them before I head to Cam's house.

Cam and I enjoy a nice dinner with his family, discussing our day with each other. After helping clean up I climb into Cam's bed and rest my head on the pillow as I look up at the ceiling. Cam climbs in a few minutes later. It is too hot to cuddle, so we both decide to keep a safe distance. That's another thing I resent about the heat: the excruciatingly hot nights, when you are lucky to sleep without sweating.

I lay there, thinking about my job, and how much it has changed my life. I have an incredibly strong fondness for music. It has helped me get through the toughest moments of my life. When I have wanted to give up, music has saved me. I picked up my first guitar when I was seven, I wrote my first song when I was thirteen, and I got a job at a music store as soon as I could find one that was hiring. My uncle always told me I could have a job with him, but I like the variety and opportunities I get at Boom Clap. Since then I've continued writing songs. My family and Cam's family always tell me I have a beautiful voice, one that needs to be shared with the world, and I know at some point I want to pursue a career in the music industry. However, I always let my fears get the best of me. I know that is only part of the problem.

The biggest part of my problem? Trying to come to terms with my father, who walked out on his family. My dad made a selfish decision to leave my mother to raise five children by herself, and since then he hasn't made one single attempt to find us, and to try to fix the damage he has caused. There's a life I always knew, but never had; a life with my dad, a life he took away from all of his children. All I have is a few photos and a letter he left in my room before he disappeared. The same letter I read over and over again, trying to make sense of what happened, trying to piece together why he left us, why he left me.

I was seven years old when he left. I remember we were inseparable; we did everything together. I was always closer to my dad than I was to my mum. We bonded from the moment I was born, and wherever my dad was, chances were I was right behind. He was an only child and both of his parents passed away after he married my mum and had kids, but he was so happy - at least that's what I thought. In the letter he left me he tried to explain things, but he didn't do a good job at it and he certainly didn't convince me that he loved me or that he was making this decision for us. I think he was making the decision for him.

I don't know if my siblings got letters from him too. I've never asked since my mum doesn't like us talking about him. I used to find comfort in the last piece I had of him, but now that I'm older, it just makes me mad. How could he leave us? How could he leave me? I needed him. I *still* need him. All my friends and cousins are so close to their fathers, Cam and his three siblings are close to William, and me? Well, I'm just an observer, an onlooker who has no idea what it's like to have that kind of relationship, to have a father present in my life.

William and my uncle do their best to shelter me from not having a father. They've done their best to step up to the plate and fill the void that I've been left with, but it's not the same. I love and appreciate them for doing what they've done, but I *need* my father. His words echo through my head every single day. No matter what I do, I can never stop hearing them, and when they hit, I always try to make sense of what he meant and it's all I can do to stop myself from bursting into tears.

"You were never the reason I made the decision to leave. You deserve better and only your mother can give you that."

What was he on about? How could our mother possibly be the only one who could give us a better life? We were happy with him, at least I thought we were. He loved us. I never thought he would hurt us, yet he did.

"Don't try to find me. When I feel I can be your father, I will find you."

Why wouldn't he let us - let me - find him? Why couldn't we try to bring him home? He was never going to come home; he knew when he left that he wouldn't be back.

"I will always be your father, and I will never stop loving you, even when you hate me."

He's lying, but maybe he will never truly be my father, because a father who loves his children doesn't just abandon his family. Part of me hates him, but all of me still loves him, I just don't know if I can ever forgive him for walking out on us. I have all these questions for him, and I don't know if I'll ever get any answers. Was he going through something we never knew about? Did he just become too overwhelmed? Having five kids when you're only thirty-four is pretty intense, but we loved him. Why would he leave that behind? I don't know if I'll ever get the peace I'm searching for. I don't know if I'll ever get my father back.

~

I remember the night he left; I don't think I can ever possibly forget it. As I begin to think about everything, I fall asleep. Suddenly, I am seven-year-old Delilah. *Oh no, not another dream, nightmare, or whatever these things are!*

I can hear my parents, but it is just muffled sounds. I can hardly make out what they are saying. I can see things I haven't seen before. My dad is overwhelmed. He is trying to deal with his addiction to drugs and alcohol. He is selling the family's most prized possessions. He is willing to sell the house just to keep his addiction going. My mum knows he is going to get himself killed - or worse, get the family killed - so she gives him an ultimatum, hoping it will wake him up to what is really at stake. It doesn't make a difference. He makes the decision to leave and he never looks back. I hear them arguing, and I go out to see what is happening. I see my dad sitting down, yelling at my mum. Then suddenly, I hear her screaming.

"Get out! Leave and don't you ever come back. You're abandoning us. Don't you ever think you'll get to see our - I mean *my* – children ever again. You're pathetic. You can ruin your life, but you will not ruin theirs too."

He stands up and looks into her eyes.

"You can't stop me from seeing my kids. They're all I've got."

She takes a step towards him and lowers her voice.

"Over my dead body! You will not see your children if you don't stop. I told you that if you continued down this path, you would ruin this family. So help me, Tony, you will not get these kids involved in your shit storm. Now make your decision."

He takes a step away from her.

"Fine, I'm leaving."

He puts his hands in his pockets and heads towards his bedroom. When he sees me standing in the corner, he suddenly stops dead in his tracks.

"Oh my God."

My mum looks up.

"For God's sake, what now?"

She follows my father's gaze, noticing me too. She gets up from the couch and starts to approach me.

"Delilah, what are you doing up? Let's get you back to bed, missy."

I can sense something is wrong. I hate my mum for yelling at my dad, so I look at her and yell.

"No, Mummy, I don't want to talk to you!"

I run towards my dad. He picks me up, turns to my mum and begs her to let him tuck me in.

"Please, Deidra, one last time?"

She sighs and nods. My father hugs me tightly before taking me back to my room. He gently helps me into my bed and tucks me in.

"Delilah, I don't want you to worry about that. Everything is fine. I love you. Go back to sleep, okay? I'll see you in the morning."

A tear escapes his eyes. I lean up and hug him.

"Okay, Daddy. We can go to the park. I love you."

He smiles.

"Okay, kiddo. Goodnight."

He kisses my forehead and leaves my room. I fall asleep and when I wake up the next morning, he has gone. Where did he go? No, he can't leave me, not again. *Please, not again!*

I wake up; I can't take these dreams anymore. I get up and get myself a glass of water. I sit at the kitchen table and drink the cold water while trying to process my dream. After all these years I finally remember everything. For once in my life I know what I need to do: I need to find my father.

Chapter Three

Wishful Thinking

I have been getting up early in the morning and going to bed late at night, constantly going back and forth on the decision to find my father. I want to find him, but I am scared of what will happen if I do. I know I would regret not trying to find him, so it's pretty obvious what I have to do. I have to find him.

I have decided not to tell my family about my decision. I don't think my mum will approve, and I doubt she will let me find him. She always said he'd left for a reason, but I know I need to find him and hear his side of the story. I know that finding him means I can get the peace I am desperately searching for. I also know there is a chance it could take a sour turn, but I am willing to take that chance. I mean, surely my own father can't push me away, especially if I make an effort to find him.

"Please don't try to find me."

I shake off the familiar words I've read over and over again in his letter. I focus my attention back to my starting point, although I'm struggling to find what my starting point is, and I feel the need to talk to someone about the mess inside my head. I know if I tell anyone in my family, they'll tell my mum. Even my best friends would tell her. I know they would do it for my safety. For some reason my mum asked my friends to let her know if I ever talked about finding my dad. Maybe she's feared this day since he left.

There is only one person I know I can talk to, and that person is Cam. I take my phone off charge and head downstairs. I check to see if anyone is home, but thankfully I have the house to myself. I sit down at the kitchen table, find Cam's number and press the call button. After four rings an excited voice answers.

"Delilah! You have to come over. I got a dog! Oh my God, this is the best birthday. He is so cute, I'm in love, his name is…what? Oh yeah, sorry."

Suddenly Nia's voice disappears and Cam's voice echoes through the phone.

"Sorry, she's been desperate to tell someone she's got a puppy, *finally*."

I laugh.

"It's her birthday. She's allowed to be excited. Tell her I'll see her soon."

Cam passes on my message, and Nia yells at the phone.

"I can't wait!"

Then Cam starts talking again.

"I'm glad you called, it's been too long. Every time I try to reach you I can't get through to you, other than a few texts, you've been ignoring me. Is everything okay?"

I sigh. I know Cam has tried to see me over the past seven days, but I wanted time to myself to think about what I was going to do and how I was going to approach the whole situation. Now that I know what I want to do, I know I have to tell him the truth about why I've been avoiding him for the past week.

"I'm sorry. I know I've been a bit distant. I've just had a lot going on, and I needed some time to myself to figure things out. That's actually why I called, I need to talk to you. It's nothing to do with us as a couple - we're fine – but there's something I have to tell you."

It feels like an eternity before he finally responds.

"Should I be worried? I don't like the sound of this."

I don't know how to reply without telling him the truth, but this is something I don't want to tell him over the phone. I want to tell him face-to-face.

"No, please don't be worried. It's kind of exciting, actually. I've got to go; I'll see you tonight."

There is another pause before Cam answers.

"Okay, I'll see you later. I love you."

I smile, although I sense Cam is still worried about what I have to tell him.

"I love you, too."

I hang up and put my phone on the bench. A few seconds later my mum walks in with my aunt Debbie.

"Oh hi, love. I didn't know you were here. I thought you'd be at Cam's."

I look up from the bench to answer.

"Nope. I'm going over there soon but I'm going to take Jessie for a walk first."

I get up from the table to get Jessie, our six-year-old Golden Retriever, when my mum comes up to me, getting closer than I'm expecting.

"What are you hiding? Something's up. I can tell by the look on your face. Are you pregnant? Oh my gosh, that would be so exciting! Although I don't know if I'm old enough to be a grandmother. I guess that's the rage though these days, you know? Young grandmothers are in!"

She laughs along with my aunt, and I feel incredibly uncomfortable.

"Mum, seriously. Personal space. I'm not hiding anything, and I'm *not* pregnant. Shit, I'm still not ready for kids. I'm just tired."

My mum is still looking at me like she knows I'm hiding something. I feel the my level of comfortability getting worse. I have to get out of the kitchen before she questions me anymore. I am already anxious enough knowing that I'm lying to her, but having her look at me with her doe-eyed expression makes it a million times harder. I quickly say goodbye to my aunt and mum, before grabbing Jessie's lead and heading out to the backyard.

Jessie is fast asleep in her bed, but when she hears me close the door, she wakes up. And when she sees me with her lead in my hand, she charges at me. She jumps on me for a quick cuddle before I attach her lead to her collar.

"Come on, girl, let's go for a walk."

I smile at her as we head for the gate. I unlock it, let Jessie through, follow her and close the gate behind us. We head out the front of the house and begin our walk. It is just past 4:30 p.m., but the sun is still shining. It may still be summer, but today is one of the days when the weather isn't overwhelmingly hot. It is in the high twenties, which brings more people out of their air-conditioned homes.

After our first lap around the local park, I put my headphones in and start listening to my favourite songs. Jessie and I spend the next forty-five minutes walking before I sit down by one of the trees. Jessie sits next to me and we allow the cool breeze to float over us. I look over at Jessie; she has the biggest smile on her face. To most people she is just a dog, but to me she is so much more. My mum rescued her as her previous owner didn't want her. She'd been put in a box by the side of a main road. My mum was driving home one day when she noticed Jessie's head sticking out of the box. She picked her up, put her in the car and took her to the vet. After the vet cleared her, my mum officially adopted her and brought her home. We instantly fell in love with her. She was our little miracle puppy and we were determined to give her the best life we possibly could. She is one of the happiest dogs I've ever seen. I think she knows her life has been saved and she is just elated to be a part of a loving family.

No matter what the weather is like, I always take Jessie for a walk. I know it is something simple I can do for her and she loves it, so it's always worth it. Plus, the fresh air always does wonders for me. I smile thinking about all the times we've spent with her, from taking her camping to taking her to the beach. She is just happy to be with us, and my mum always tries to take us on adventures where she knows Jessie can come too. Mum hates leaving her at home, and if we ever have to leave her behind, we take her to my uncle's house. He has two Labradors, and she is always happy to chase them around the paddocks. She doesn't cope too well with being left alone for longer than a few hours, so we do our best to minimise that. If there is ever a day I can't walk her, someone else does it. She never misses out, and we make sure we provide her with as many dog treats and toys as we can.

We know she had a rough start in life and we want to make the rest of her life the best of her life. As I remember all the memories I've shared with her, she looks over at me. I pat her head as I start to confide in her. I know I can tell her anything without being get judged, and that is a comfort to me.

"Jess, I don't know why, but I feel like the time is right. I have to try to find my father. I'm scared to tell Cam and I certainly don't think I can tell my family. I don't think they'd understand why I need to do this. They'll probably try to stop me and tell me I'm making a mistake. Even if it is a mistake, it's a mistake I have to make on my own."

Jessie suddenly puts her paw on my leg, like she is trying to tell me to follow my heart. I smile and give her a hug.

"Dogs really are the best therapists! I love you, my not-so-little miracle puppy. Come on, let's go home before it gets too late."

Jessie gets up and barks, and I laugh as her tail goes a million miles an hour. We run home and I open the gate for her. After making sure it's secure, I lock it and fill up Jessie's water bowl. I give her another pat before I head inside. My mum is in the kitchen, carefully curling Darci's hair.

"Delilah, for goodness sakes, where have you been? We have to go. Are you driving yourself or are you coming with us? Anna is expecting us at half past six."

"I'll drive myself. I've got to feed Jessie, and I still have to shower and get ready, so I'll be there by seven."

After giving Jessie her dinner, I head upstairs to shower and get ready. I close the bathroom door behind me, turn the faucet on and wait for the water to become warm. I throw my long, blonde ombre hair into a bun and secure it on top of my head. As the steam fills the room, I throw my clothes into the washing basket, which I remind myself to empty in the morning. I step into the shower and pull the shower curtain closed. I check the temperature of the water with my hands before standing under the showerhead. I allow the hot water to run all over my body as I put my hands together and watch the water create a little pool in them. Once there is enough water in the cups of my hands, I throw it over my face. I repeat this action a few times before rubbing my face, making sure it is completely clean. I use my favourite body wash, one that smells just like fairy floss, before turning the water off. I grab my towel from the towel rack and step onto the shower mat that is placed neatly on the outside of the shower. I wrap the towel around my body and stand there, feeling too lazy to dry myself.

I start thinking about how I am going to tell Cam about my grand plan. I certainly don't know where to start, let alone how to tell him the full truth. I love Cam more than I can even begin to express, and I trust him with my life, but I don't want him to tell my mum. The last thing I want to do is upset her, but this is too important to abandon. I've made my mind up, and I have to find my father, no matter what. But I also need to talk to someone and get advice. If it isn't going to be Cam, who can it be?

I start to think about who else I can talk to when there is a knock at the door.

"Delilah, Mum and I are going now. Are you sure you don't want to come with us?"

"Yes, Darci, I'm sure. I'll meet you there. See you soon. Tell Mum to drive safely."

She giggles and runs downstairs, repeating what I said. I hear our mum come to the bottom of the stairs.

"Very funny, missy! Get a move on. It's half past six, and you're going to be late!"

I can't help but laugh before opening the door. I stand at the top of the staircase and look down at her.

"Oh no, I wouldn't want to be late … says the woman who is meant to be there already" I say, as sarcastically as I can manage.

I look back at Darci, who is now laughing as much as I am. My mum can't help but laugh too.

"I'll let you get away with that one, but we are leaving now. Get ready or you'll be really late. See you soon. Love you."

"Love you too. See you in thirty."

I watch as my mum and my sister go through the front door. Once I hear my mum lock the door, I head to my bedroom. I walk into my walk-in wardrobe and look through my pile of clothes, trying to decide what to wear. I'm five foot seven, and I'm in pretty good shape. I always try to wear clothes that complement my body shape. I don't have wide hips, a big butt and big boobs, I am however, proportioned perfectly. I've always been comfortable in my own skin, and I like the person I am. I think that shows through my personality and how I treat those around me. At least I hope it does.

After sifting through the pile of clothes, I settle on a pair of jean shorts and an oversized, thin cardigan, which I throw over a black singlet. I throw on a pair of sandals and head into the bathroom. I decide to keep my hair in a messy bun, and I put on a light coverage of makeup. My blue eyes sparkles as I apply a bit of mascara. I throw some mint lip balm onto my lip before I grab Nia's present, my phone and my keys before heading for the door.

~

After a ten-minute drive, I pull into Cam's driveway, which is full of cars. I can hear the sound of people chatting away as I approach the door. I'm close enough to Cam and his family that I don't have to knock anymore, so I open the door and walk in.

Before I even shut the door behind me Nia comes charging around the corner.

"You're here, you're here, you're heeeeere!"

I laugh as she hugs me, although she embraces me with such force that I stumble back.

"Nia, calm down. Let her in."

Cam joins Nia and me at the front door as I hug Nia back.

"Happy birthday, princess. Here's your present. Take it into the kitchen and open it with Darci, and then you can show me your puppy, okay?"

She smiles before running off.

"Okay, thanks, Delilah!"

Once the coast is clear, Cam and I share a kiss and a hug. He looks at me like he's worried. I know he's been thinking about what I want to talk to him about. I hook my left arm around his neck as I step closer to him before I look into his eyes.

"Don't worry. I'm not pregnant, and we're not breaking up. Unless you're pregnant and breaking up with me? Then that would be totally awkward."

I see the worried look disappear, and his beautiful smile takes its place.

"That's better. Pregnancy suits you."

Cam laughs, then I hear Darci and Nia giggling. I peer over Cam's shoulder, and sure enough, our sisters are standing six feet away.

"Delilah, boys can't get pregnant!"

I look right at my sister.

"Are you sure? How do you think you were born? Oh, wait, no, we adopted you from the zoo."

The smile disappears from her face.

"That's not funny, Delilah."

Suddenly her smile reappears.

"We all know I was adopted from the panda sanctuary. How else do you explain my clumsiness?"

We all burst into another fit of laugher before we head into the living area, which joins onto the kitchen. After saying hello to everyone, Nia shows me her puppy. She got to pick one from the pound, and she has settled on a German Shepherd that she has proudly named Rocky.

Once Nia has shown me all her presents, we sit down for dinner. Anna has gone all out, making Nia's favourite dinner: roast chicken. After everyone serves themselves, Anna hands me a glass of Moscato. I'm not a big drinker, but I don't mind the odd glass or two on special occasions, and while I'm not generally a big fan of wine, I do like the Moscato Anna has. It is pink and has the most amazing taste: crisp yet sweet, and the perfect kind of drink on a summer's night. I grab the glass and drink it appreciatively.

I then look at my food as I push it around the plate. I feel too nervous to eat; I have this looming feeling hanging over me. My anxiety over telling Cam has taken control of my body, and my emotions.

"Hey, what's up? Why aren't you eating?" Cam says as I look at him, noting the same look of worry that he had when I arrived.

"Sorry. I just got lost in my thoughts."

I pick up a carrot and slowly chew it. I suddenly realise how hungry I am, so I try to relax and allow myself to enjoy the dinner and the company. We spend the next hour and a half talking and laughing. Being around Cam's family always makes me happy. They are as close as I am to my family, and having members of my family here as well makes it even more special. After the conversations die down, Anna decides it is time for cake, which her sister-in-law has made. The red velvet cake is delicious, and Nia says she has had the best birthday ever.

~

After Cam and I help Anna clean up, we head towards the door that leads to the backyard. On our way through, we stop to look at the photos that Anna proudly displays on her walls. I look at a family photo of William, Anna, Gavin, Ethan, Cam and Nia. It was taken about ten years ago, and despite the time that has passed, Cam looks pretty much the same. He still has the same blonde hair, his blue eyes still stand out, and he has the same beautiful smile. The only real difference is the stubble he has now acquired. I smile. He still looks just as happy now as he does in the picture. Suddenly, he grabs my hand and leads me outside. We head towards the pool, where we sit on the pavement that surrounds the water. We sink our feet into the cool water and listen to the sound of crickets. I notice that Cam still hasn't let go of my hand. I look at him and I know it is time. I have to tell him about my plan to find my father.

I look at the water. It is crystal clear, there isn't an ounce of dirt or algae. I take a deep breath and look back at Cam, who is now watching me intensely.

"So, what is this thing you want to talk to me about?"

I take another deep breath.

"Come on, Delilah. You've got me so worried. I can't take another minute of trying to figure out what it is."

I laugh, but after seeing the serious look on his face, I stop. I try to ignore the lump that has now formed in my throat as I begin to tell him everything.

"It's nothing to do with us. I said it wasn't, and it isn't. I'm telling you this because I trust you. I am telling you this with the expectation that it doesn't go beyond the two of us. Promise?"

"I promise. Tell me."

I take a third deep breath before explaining everything.

"I'm jealous of you, your siblings, and my cousins. My siblings and I have always been denied something that every child should have. We have had to live our lives without our father. I am so grateful I have your dad and my uncle, but I want … no, I *need* my father, Cam. I am desperate to have the relationship I had with him. I want that back."

Before I can continue, Cam cuts me off.

"You're going to find him, aren't you?"

"Yes, I'm going to *try* to find him. This is something I have to do for myself. I'm ready, and I think it's time."

Cam looks at me and starts talking softly.

"I promised your mum I wouldn't let you do this. I can't let you go down this path. I know you miss that bond and your relationship but, Delilah, the time for that has passed. Don't you think that if your dad wanted to be a part of your life, he would have come back by now? It's been fifteen years. He's not coming back."

I look at him, stunned by his reaction. How can he say something like that to me? This is not the reaction I was expecting. He has crushed me. I feel two feet tall.

"Cam, I don't care what you think, and I don't care what you promised my mum. This is *my* decision, and I'll be damned if you're going to stop me."

The truth is, I do care what he thinks. I want him to support me, but he isn't. He won't even let me explain why I need to do this. He is meant to be on my side. Why isn't he listening to me? Doesn't he care? He suddenly moves closer to me and speaks in a low, deep voice.

"You think I'll just let you go on this merry little goose chase to find him? If you try, I'll tell your mum. I'm not being mean. I'm trying to look out for you. You'll just get hurt. You can't ask me to keep this to myself."

I move away, which seems to surprise him. He tries to get close to me again, but I stop him.

"Don't. Don't you dare threaten me. I trusted you. Why are you doing this to me? If you tell my mum, I'll never forgive you. If I get hurt, then I'll deal with it, but you're not going to take this chance away from me. This is what I want. If you don't want to support me, then don't. Either way, I'm not going to give up. I'm going to find him."

I get up and make my way through Cam's house, refusing to acknowledge anyone. I find Nia and tell her I have to go. After hugging her and promising I'll take her to lunch, I leave. I get into my car and sit there focusing on my breathing. I have worked myself up, and I need to calm down. I close my eyes and try my best to ignore the constant replay of what has just happened.

This is not how it was supposed to go. I open my eyes and see Cam approaching my car. He stops by my window. He tries to open the door, but I lock it.

"Please let me in. Let me talk to you. I'm sorry I didn't react the way you wanted me to. I'm just trying to protect you. I don't want to see you get hurt."

I don't look at him. I just can't bring myself to look at him. I turn the key and start my car. Without saying a word, I pull out of the driveway and head home. As I drive home, I start thinking about what to do next. The thing is, I no longer know who I can turn to, and I certainly don't know who I can trust now. My boyfriend won't even hear me out, so how can I possibly trust anyone else? I think about calling Hayley when I suddenly remember something. Maybe there is one person I can trust. Ryan's name instantly pops into my head. I don't know why, but I feel like we could be friends. He could be someone I could trust and confide in, and since he doesn't know anything about my family or me, he might be the perfect person to talk to. There is just one small problem: I have no idea how to find him or contact him.

Chapter Four

The Waiting Game

I get home from Cam's and run up the stairs into my bedroom, closing the door behind me. I sit on my bed and pull my phone from my pocket. I have three missed calls and five messages from Cam, and one missed call from my mum. I ignore them, clearing them from my screen. I have important business to attend to, and I don't need any distractions.

I grab my laptop from my desk and sit back on my bed. I turn it on and log into my Facebook account. I search 'Ryan', hoping I can find him. After almost thirty minutes of clicking on profiles that belong to every Ryan in Perth - which, by the way, is a lot - I finally find him. I can't believe my luck. I inspect his profile, checking at least five times before confirming it is him. Part of me feels guilty. What am I doing? Am I making the right decision? Once I remind myself why I'm taking this step, I build up the courage to message him. I sit with my legs crossed, resting the laptop on my lap as I look at the blank screen. I don't know where to start, or what to say. I am about to open up to someone I don't even know. How exactly are you meant to start? I type at least ten different messages before finally settling on one. I start with something simple. That way, if he doesn't reply, I won't have given too much away. But I have to give him something, especially since I made such a big deal about Cam when we met.

Hi Ryan, I don't know if you remember me. I'm Delilah. I met you in Boom Clap a few weeks ago. I know this is totally random, but I was wondering if you were free to meet up? Hope to hear from you soon. Delilah.

I look at the finished message as the cursor hovers over the send button. I hear my mum pull up in the driveway, so I quickly hit send and close my laptop before putting it back on my desk. I grab my phone and put my headphones in, hoping it will be enough to stop my mum from talking to me. I listen as my mum stumbles around the kitchen. She boils the kettle and five minutes later my door slowly opens. I take my headphones out instantly.

"Hi, darling, can I come in? I made tea."

I can see she looks worried. To be honest, she looks dreadful.

"Sure, Mum. I'd love a cup of tea, thanks."

She smiles and closes the door behind her, then approaches me and hands me one of the cups. The smell of peppermint tea instantly begins to fill my room. She sits on the edge of my bed, looking down at her cup. I don't know what to do, or say, so I sit there, looking at my cup too.

"Cam told me you weren't feeling well so you left. Is everything okay? I don't want to pry, but I'm worried about you. You've been distant recently, and that's not like you."

I look up at her, but she still isn't looking at me. I want to ask her if Cam has told her the truth. If I do, I risk giving everything up, and that isn't a risk I'm willing to take, at least not yet anyway.

"Mum, I've always been distant. It's nothing new. You know I like spending time by myself."

She sighs.

"I know, darling, but this time seems different. It feels different."

I don't know what to say. How am I meant to sit here and talk to her when I'm going behind her back? I am doing the one thing she has tried so hard to avoid. A wave of guilt hits me again, this time knocking me harder than ever.

"I left because Cam and I had a little disagreement. Things will work themselves out, I'll call him tomorrow. I just need some time to myself. I promise you, I'm fine. Everything's fine."

She seems a little relieved, but still doesn't look completely convinced. I go to reassure her when she cuts me off.

"Delilah, I've always questioned my ability to be a good mother. I know you need a father and I know you appreciate William and your uncle, but I'm aware they don't even come close to that. I'm sorry things worked out the way they did. I hope you don't hate me. I've tried my best to protect you and give you the best life. I always wonder if I've been a good role model to my children."

I look at her, and instantly notice how sad she looks. I can't even remember the last time she looked like this. She is always happy, at least that's how she presents herself. Maybe she is hiding how she really feels too. I get up, sit next to her and grab her hand.

"Mum, don't you dare think you're not a good mother. You've always been an amazing mother, and you always will be. I know you've always done what you've needed to do, not for you, but for us, your children. We appreciate everything you've sacrificed, and you know that. I don't hate you, I never have. Am I mad that Dad left? Of course I am, but I don't blame you. You're a perfect role model. If I'm ever half the person you are, I'll be happy. I don't get where this has come from."

She squeezes my hand as a smile creeps onto her face.

"Thank you. I appreciate that. You're a good kid, Delilah. You have so much talent, and I hope you find the courage to pursue your dreams. I know your heart is telling you to chase them. Fear is scary, but regret is worse, so don't let that stop you. One day you'll be old enough to understand why I fought so hard to protect you."

Now I'm frustrated, and it's getting the better of me.

"Mum, I'm 21. Not 12! I understand now. Why won't you tell me the truth?"

She lets go of my hand and gets up, grabbing our now empty cups before heading for the door.

"One day we will have this discussion, but it's not going to be now. Promise me you won't do anything stupid. Don't break up with Cam and don't look for your father. I'm sorry he didn't want to be with us, but that's his fault, and not yours."

My phone beeps. Ryan has replied to my message. I look up from my phone.

"Okay, Mum. I'll call him in the morning. Goodnight."

She smiles and leaves my room, closing the door behind her.

I get up from my bed and grab my laptop again, this time I sit in the middle of the floor before I pull the message from Ryan up. I quickly scan it, hoping he isn't put off that I found him and messaged out of the blue.

Hey, Delilah. Of course I remember you. It's nice to hear from you, how are you? Yeah, I'd love to meet up. Is everything okay? Ryan.

I breathe a sigh of relief. Not only has he replied, but he is willing to meet up with me. Knowing I finally have someone who doesn't know me or my situation means so much. I feel as if I have the chance to open up and talk about this whole thing without being judged. I know that being able to talk about things openly with someone who won't be judgmental, means I'll be able to cope with feeling guilty. Plus, this way no one has to lie for me. I haven't told Cam about Ryan to begin with, but I know that if I tell him, he'll panic. I genuinely don't want to fight with him anymore. Things are already incredibly tense. This could potentially make everything worse. Despite knowing I should tell him, I decide it is best to keep this from him, at least for now anyway. If he doesn't want to help me, then I'll go to someone who will.

I am about to reply to Ryan when my phone starts to buzz. It's Cam. I have been avoiding him since I got home, refusing to answer his calls and text messages. I know he won't stop trying to contact me, so I answer. Before I even have a chance to talk he is pleading with me.

"Delilah, I've been trying to contact you all night. Why have you been ignoring me? Stupid question, I know. Of course you're ignoring me. Listen, I'm sorry. Let me explain. Your mum asked why you left, and I contemplated telling her the truth, but despite what you might be thinking right now, I truly do love you, so I lied. I feel so bad; I don't want to lie again."

I try to take on everything he is saying, but he is talking so quickly that I can't keep up. I go to answer him, but every time I try to he goes onto something else. I wait a few seconds, making sure he has finished explaining things, before I respond.

"I know, I'm sorry. I just needed time to process everything. Contrary to what you may think, I'm overwhelmed by all of this too. Thank you for not telling my mum. I won't make you lie again. I'm exhausted, and I want to fix things with you, but tonight just isn't the time. I need to think and clear my head. I need to figure out what I'm doing and what I'm willing to tell you. We will fix things, I promise. I just need to be by myself. I'll text you when I'm ready. Right now, I just need space. I know I sound like the biggest bitch, but I need to put some distance between us while I sort these things out."

I can hear his breathing intensifying. He thinks I am breaking up with him, and that's the last thing I would do. Although I doubt telling him that will make a difference right now.

"I understand. I'll give you some space. I guess I'll speak to you soon?"

"Yep, sounds good. Goodnight, Cam."

"Goodnight, Delilah."

I hang up the phone and place it next to me.

I return my attention to my laptop, where I have the conversation between Ryan and me on the screen. I click reply and begin to type.

Um, things are mostly OK. I need a friend, someone who doesn't know me very well, someone I can open up to. I know it might be weird, but I thought you could be that person for me? Maybe we could get coffee or something?

I hit send. Three little dots float across the screen as I wait for him to respond.

Of course, I'd be happy to help you. I'm free tomorrow if you'd like to meet up?

Knowing I have a third party to turn to instantly helps calm my anxiety, and it's beginning to take the edge off my guilt.

Tomorrow works, say 11:00 a.m., at Blueridge Cafe?

He replies almost instantly.

Sounds good. I look forward to hearing everything then.

Just like that, we are going to meet up. What I wanted to happen has happened, and I know this is the best way to keep everyone safe and out of harm's way. I have a solution to my problem. Now Cam and I can be together without him having to lie or feel uncomfortable, and I can start the search for my father.

I know at some point I'll have to tell Cam about Ryan. I know he'll ask me how I'm dealing with things, and I am lying enough as it is. Lying to my mum is hard enough, I doubt I can lie to him too. I turn my laptop off, put my phone on charge and head to the bathroom. I remove my makeup and clean my face before I head back to my room, passing Darci's room on my way.

"Delilah, can you come here?"

I hear her whisper before I poke my head into her room. She is sitting up on her bed, hugging a pillow to her chest. I walk over to her and climb in next to her. She hugs me.

"Why did you leave? I didn't mean to upset you."

I look at her and notice tears are welling up in her eyes. I pull her closer to me, suddenly feeling very protective.

"What are you talking about? I didn't leave because of you. Why do you think you upset me?"

She wipes a few tears away before she looks down and starts picking at her bed cover.

"Well, Nia and I kept following you and Cam, and we listened to your conversation outside. We couldn't hear everything, but we heard Cam say he wasn't going to lie for you. Why would he lie?"

"Darci, look at me."

She lifts her head and a tear escapes her eyes again.

"You know you shouldn't listen in on people's conversations. I don't care if you follow us - you know we love you both - but when we need to talk privately, you have to give us space. Cam and I were discussing something important, something that has to stay between us. It's nothing to do with you or Nia, it's just adult stuff. One day when you have a boyfriend, you'll understand, but for now no more listening in on my conversations, okay?"

She looks at her window before looking back at me.

"I don't want a boyfriend until I'm forty!"

She looks very serious, but I laugh.

"Good. Forty is a good age for a boyfriend. Time for bed now. Goodnight, my angel. I love you."

I tuck her in and head for the door. I look behind me and Darci is back to her happy self.

"I love you, Delilah. You're the best big sister ever."

I smile and close her door behind me, retreating to my room. I turn off my light and climb into bed. I set the alarm on my phone, put it on my bedside table and pull my blanket up to my hips before snuggling into my pillow.

Eight hours later the sound of Vance Joy's *Fire and Flood* fills my room. I rub my eyes and turn my alarm off. The time on my phone reads 9:30 a.m. I get up and head down to the kitchen. I notice I am home alone. I sit down at the kitchen table after preparing myself some berries and yoghurt. I start to eat my breakfast, while thinking about what to wear to my meeting with Ryan.

I feel nervous. Opening up about something as big as this to someone I don't know suddenly becomes real, so real that I feel scared, a feeling I am all too familiar with. I shake off my fears and finish off my breakfast. Once I'm done, I wash my bowl and spoon, dry them and put them away. I head back upstairs and start getting ready. After showering I quickly curl my hair before brushing the curls out so that they form soft waves. I do my usual lazy day makeup, which consists of a tinted moisturiser, a bit of blush and some mascara. It is a relatively warm day, so I settle on my favourite pair of three-quarter-length skinny jeans, a stripy top, and a pair of black sandals. Once I'm ready, I grab my phone and keys and head for the door, but just as I reach it, the doorbell rings.

I check the monitor. When we moved into our house five years ago my mum decided to set up a crazy security system. There were six people living here before my brothers moved out and we regularly have other family members staying over, so our house had to be quite big. My mum wanted to make sure we had plenty of room. She has always wanted to share a big house with us, so it's a dream come true for her. She has worked incredibly hard to get this house, and so she wants to protect it as much as she can.

She set up a gate that surrounds the front of the house. It has a code that not many people know. Once you get through the gate, the door is double bolted, so unless you have a key, it is virtually impossible to get inside. My mum had a wireless security system installed too. We have a monitor next to the front door and screens in all the bedrooms. That way, no matter where we are we are able to see who is at the door.

I know who is at the door the minute I look at the monitor. It's Cam. He is holding my favourite flowers and a card in his hands. I check my phone: it's twenty to eleven and it's going to take me roughly fifteen minutes to get to the café. If Cam doesn't leave now, I'm going to be late, but I'm still not ready to see him, let alone speak to him. My car is parked in the garage, so I know Cam won't be able to see if I'm home.

He rings the doorbell and knocks a few more times, but when he doesn't get a response, he places the flowers and the card down. I watch the monitor. Cam turns around and heads back to his car, closing part of the gate behind him. I wait until he pulls out of the driveway before opening the door. I grab the flowers and the card, run up the stairs and place them on my desk before I run back downstairs, lock the door and open the gate. I get in the car and begin the journey to the café, arriving just in time.

I get out of my car and head towards the front of the café. I spot Ryan almost instantly. He is waiting by the door, and when he spots me, he starts to approach me. We quickly hug before picking a table outside. It is a beautiful day. Despite the heat there is a gentle breeze passing through. We order coffee and begin to chat. Before too long, I know it's time to tell him why I wanted to meet up with him.

"I should probably tell you why I contacted you. I basically need someone who doesn't know me or my family to help me, by listening to me. Don't get me wrong, I love my boyfriend, Cam, but he can't handle all of this. Knowing about it requires him to keep it to himself, and he feels so incredibly guilty. He's close to my family, as I am to his, so not telling them the truth would ultimately take a toll on him. This is something my family can't know about – at least not yet anyway."

"So, you want me to be your confidant? Someone you can be one hundred per cent honest with. Correct?"

I nod.

"Exactly. I have two best friends, but they're in the same boat as Cam. I don't want to put that pressure on them. I know it sounds strange, but I feel like you could be that person for me, as long as you're happy to do it?"

He sips his coffee before responding.

"If that's what you need, then I'll do it. When I first met you I thought that we could be friends. I honestly didn't see it as anything more than a friendship. When you told me about Cam, I got the vibe you were trying to tell me to back off, so I didn't try to pursue anything. I just want to get that cleared up before you say anything. Just know that whatever you tell me stays between us. You don't have to worry about me telling a soul."

My lips curve upwards.

"Thank you. That means a lot. You don't have to explain. I was a bit rude, it's a bad habit. I didn't mean anything by it."

Ryan laughs.

"It's fine, don't stress. So, what's the big secret?"

Ryan and I spend the next hour and a half talking. I tell him about my dad, and I even show him the letter he left me.

"So, that's everything. I don't know where to start, but I know this is what I want to do. People leave - I understand that - but sometimes it just doesn't seem fair. I've lived long enough without my father in my life, and I have a right to find him. I have a right to see him. I'm not doing this for anyone else. This is something I'm doing for myself. We were so close and then he just left me. I don't really know why he did. My mum told me an edited version, but I'm not sure if I believe her. I want to hear it from him, it's all I can think of doing. His leaving destroyed me and I need to find peace once and for all, otherwise I'll spend the rest of my life wondering why."

The tears I've been holding back fill my eyes and I try so hard to keep them at bay, but one by one they spill onto my cheeks. Ryan hands me a napkin before comforting me.

"It's okay. I mean, it's not okay that he left you with these feelings. I think it's only natural to wonder why he left. He's your father, and you only get one father. Nothing, or no one, can replace him. If this is really what you want, then you need to do it. I'll do whatever I can to help you."

I wipe the tears from my face. I tell Ryan how much I appreciate his help for what feels like the hundredth time. We exchange numbers and agree to meet up in a few days. He walks me to my car, and we briefly hug again before I get in. I wave goodbye to him before I head home, and I feel relieved. Our meeting went exactly how I wanted it to go, and I feel better knowing that Cam doesn't have to cover for me anymore. I know the time has finally come. It is time to find my father, and I won't stop until I do.

Chapter Five

Dreams vs. Reality

The next few days are filled with never-ending thoughts and trying to avoid everyone I'm close to, except Ryan. While I can't confide in my family and friends, I find the comfort I need in him.

I continue to feel guilty. Despite not wanting to tell my family or continue to subject Cam to covering for me, I feel like I am betraying them all, and in a way I am. Turning to Ryan has been incredibly helpful, but I desperately want it to be Cam that I turn to. I know I am sparing him, but it doesn't feel right. Deception can be quite frustrating, especially when I'm struggling to fight the horrible feelings that are hitting me on a daily basis. I know I am doing this for me, but I still feel like I'm going about it in the wrong way. Maybe I am, but what am I supposed to do? Either way, I'll be hurting people. I can tell everyone and risk not being allowed to find my father, or I can keep it to myself and do what I need to do. While I manage to get a lot of thinking done, I also allow myself to be distracted by work. I've managed to pick up extra shifts and I decide to put all my energy into thinking of new songs to write. I need a distraction from everything, and music is the only thing that works.

While I focus most of my attention on my music, I completely forget all about the card Cam left me when he dropped the flowers off. It has been exactly one week since I last spoke to him. I haven't replied to his messages, which I understandably stopped receiving after the third day. I know it's wrong to ignore him, but we haven't spoken since the night I told him I'm going to find my father. After he reacted so negatively, I needed some time to process everything. I have come to terms with the fact that it is wrong to ask him to lie for me - I know it puts him in an awkward position - but I've found a way to keep him from covering for me. I do need to tell Cam about Ryan, and I will. I just don't know how.

When my final eight-hour shift for the week comes to an end, I go home, shower and grab the card from my drawer. I tear the envelope open, pull the card out, open it and read the words that Cam has carefully written.

"Delilah, I know I've said it before, but I really am sorry for how I reacted. This is something you need to do, and I understand that. You know how I feel about this; I don't think you should go ahead with searching for your father, but I know the pain is very real for you. Maybe this is what you need to find the closure you're looking for. With that being said, I need you to know that I can't be a part of your search. I will be there for you; I will listen to you and I will hold you when you're sad, but I won't lie for you. You know I'll be your support system so you don't have to go through this alone, but lying to your family and to everyone else, is just something I can't do. I hope you understand that I'm not in the best position; either way I lose. I either hurt everyone around me, or I hurt you. Regardless of everything, I hope you know that I love you, and nothing will ever change that. You mean the world to me. When you're ready to talk, please call me. Love, Cam."

Just as I finish reading the card, there is a knock at the front door. A few seconds later Cam comes barrelling into my room. He looks really, really angry. Before I can speak, he sits on my bed and looks at me with a grave expression I've never seen before.

"You've ignored me for long enough, for God's sake. I can't take it anymore. We're going to talk about this whether you like it or not. You can't avoid me forever."

He suddenly notices what I have in my hands.

"You've only just read that? Jesus, Delilah. Are you really that mad at me?"

I can't face the hurt in his eyes so I continue to stare at the card.

"I'm sorry. I meant to read it, but I've been working heaps and it slipped my mind. I shouldn't have put you in this position, I know it was wrong of me. I just wanted to tell someone, and you were the only person I trusted. It was wrong of me to assume that it was all right for you to lie for me. It's not." I raise my eyes to meet his stare. I have to make him understand. "If I pursue this, then I need to do it on my own. I'm not doing this to hurt anyone, Cam. I'm doing this because I need to understand why he left. All my life it's been this taboo subject that we've always swept under the rug, but I can't ignore it anymore. Just know that it's sorted. I need you to trust me, you don't have to lie for me anymore. I'll explain it soon, just not now. The time isn't right."

He grabs my hands.

"I believe you. Can we just go back to how we were? I know this is something you've got to do. When you're ready to tell me, you can. I'm not going to lie for you, but I will listen to you."

I hug him tightly. I'm trying to ignore the feeling of guilt that I didn't tell him the truth when I had the chance.

Cam and I spend the rest of the day together. We have dinner and watch a movie. I breathe a sigh of relief. I know I'm lucky to have him, even with the dark cloud that keeps following me around. After Cam leaves, I go back to my room, and I notice my phone is beeping. I have a message from Rosie.

Hey babe, I'm with Hadi. We miss you. It seems like forever since we saw you, even though it's only been a month ... but seriously, how have we gone a whole month without seeing each other? Not acceptable! We're thinking of getting together for lunch tomorrow. Are you free? Love and miss you!

I reply straightaway.

Hi girls. I miss you both so much. I'm sorry it's been so long. Life has been so hectic. I would love to meet up for lunch, and tomorrow is perfect! Just tell me when and where, and I'll be there. Love you, too!

A few seconds later my phone buzzes and Rosie's name flashes across the screen. After a quick conversation, we organise a time and a place to catch up. After our conversation ends, I put my phone back on charge and head downstairs. I boil the kettle, make myself a cup of tea, and sit down to watch the stars fill the night sky, thinking about how everything is slowly falling into place. Cam and I are back on track, and I'm finally going to see my friends. I feel a sense of happiness; one I haven't felt for a while. I know I have to start the search for my father while I do my best to protect those closest to me. I drink the rest of my tea and remove my makeup before snuggling into my pillows. Within seconds I am fast asleep.

Before I know it, it's 9:30 a.m. and I've been up for almost two hours already. It may be early, but I'm already exhausted. I managed to get a measly four hours of sleep before I woke up abruptly at two thirty in the morning. *2.30 a.m.!* Body, what are you doing to me? I tried to go back to sleep, but my body had other ideas. Finally, after hours of fighting with myself, I fell back into my slumber, only to be woken a few hours later. My mum was leaving for work when she dropped a cup on the floor.

"Bloody hell, I'm already late!"

I decide to get up. I know I wouldn't be able to get back to sleep, so I head downstairs to find my mum, who looks flustered. She doesn't look like her usual, happy self, so I grab the broom from her.

"I've got it, Mum."

She instantly looks relieved.

"Oh, thank you, honey. Sorry, I've got a lot of my mind."

Before I even get the chance to ask her what is wrong, she is on her way out.

"Thank you, Delilah. I'll call you later. Have a good day. I love you!"

She is gone before I even had a chance to reply.

I sweep up the ceramic cup and throw it in the bin before making some breakfast. I head outside and sit at the table. It is nearly the end of summer, and the weather will begin to change soon, so I want to enjoy as much of my favourite season as I can before it's over. I can't believe how quickly the last five weeks have gone. So much has happened in such a short time. It feels like just yesterday we were celebrating Christmas and New Year, and now it's February. Time is passing even quicker than it was last year. I'm in a world of my own, thinking about how much I long to be at the beach, when my phone beeps. It's a message from Ryan.

Hey, I've been thinking ... is there anyone on your dad's side of the family you could contact?

I reread the message before replying.

I wish there was. My mum always told us he was an only child, and both of his parents died when I was young.

I shudder at the memory.

~

I still remember the day my grandma, my dad's mum, died. His dad, my grandpa, had died a few years before I was born. My grandma wasn't very present in our lives. From what I remember, she and Dad had a falling out. I'm pretty sure it was because my mum and dad had kids so young when they couldn't afford to. Of course, they didn't deliberately try to have five kids, it just happened. If I remember correctly, my grandma stopped talking to my parents after they told her about my mum being pregnant with Darci. By then they were in a better place financially. They could afford to look after all of us comfortably, but that wasn't good enough for her. A few months after Darci was born, my dad left us. I was only seven years old.

Suddenly, it hits me. He didn't leave because he didn't love us. Lack of money and having five kids weren't the reasons he left. He left because his world had fallen apart. His mum died a few weeks before he left. It all makes sense now. Turning to drugs and alcohol wasn't his way to escape us, it was to avoid the feeling of guilt that had hit him for cutting his mum off. Despite all of her feelings towards his decisions, she still loved her son. I know she wanted to try to be in our lives more when Darci was born, but he never gave her that chance. I have moments when I don't get along with my mum, but I will always love her. I couldn't shut her out of my life. Yet that's what my dad had done to his mum, and then he did it to us too. He got the call that she had died, and he suddenly became distant. He wasn't home as much as he used to be. When he was, he always smelled of cigarettes and whisky. I hate those smells now, because they always remind me of him. I was so young, but I'll never forget those two distinct smells. They were so strong, they always filled the rooms he walked into. Removing them became almost impossible for my mum. Eventually she gave up and the smells lingered, until the breeze filtered through the room and pushed them out.

I feel my eyes getting heavy. *No, I'm not crying anymore!* I get up and head inside. My phone beeps again. I read Ryan's reply.

Is there anything your mum might have from him? Anything that you could use to find out where he could be? Any idea of how you're going to find him? Sorry for all the questions. I just know how much this means to you, and I've been thinking. I figured we could come up with a plan of attack or something.

I appreciate all of Ryan's help, and I know he is right. If I want to find my father, I need to come up with a plan. I need to find a way to take the first step in searching for him. It's one thing to say I'm going to find him, but I don't know how I'm going to do it. It's not like I can just Google him and everything would appear. Or would it? I hadn't even thought of checking the Internet. I open Google on my phone and type his name into the search bar. After sifting through pages of useless information, I give up.

I check the time. In all of my searching, I've completely forgotten about lunch with my friends. It's 11:00 a.m., which means I have an hour and a half until I meet the girls. I still have to get ready, so I head upstairs and go into my closet. It's quite warm, so I decide to wear my favourite denim shorts and a loose white top, with my favourite black sandals. I grab my shoes and my top, but I can't find my shorts. I start going through my drawers trying to find them when I remember my mum has them. I gave them to her to try to fix the hem on the left side, which came loose when I had them on the other night. I grab my phone and call her.

"Hey, Mum. Do you still have my denim shorts?"

"Yes, honey. They're in my room. I fixed the hem, they're in the chest of drawers closest to the window. While you're there, can you pick out a dress and some shoes for me to wear to a meeting tonight? I'll stop by on my way. Pick whatever you want, and just pop it on my bed. I've got to get back to work. It's flat out today. I'll see you later. Have fun at lunch. Love you."

"Sure, Mum. I'll do it now. See you later. Love you."

I hang up and head into the bathroom to do my hair and makeup first. After brushing my hair, I pull it into a loose ponytail. I put on my usual everyday makeup and head into my mum's room. I don't know why she needs a dress and a pair of shoes for her meeting, she usually goes in her work clothes. I shrug and go into her closet. After picking out a three-quarter-length black dress and cream coloured heels for her, I go to find my shorts. She said they were in the chest of drawers by the window, but now I have to dig through six drawers of clothes to find them. Why couldn't she put them on my bed? I sigh as I begin to dig through the pile of clothes.

I finally find my shorts hidden halfway through the third drawer. I pull them out and go to close the drawer. Suddenly, something catches my eye. Under one of her tops is an envelope. I know it's wrong to go through people's things, especially my mum's, but I can't pull myself away from it. I grab the envelope and sit on my mum's bed.

Running writing in thin blue ink stains my mum's name on the front. It has been opened multiple times judging by the condition it's in.

I gently take the letter out and unfold it. I scan the contents and go to the last page. It is a three-page letter from a lady called Helen. I grab my phone and take a photo of each page, making sure each picture is clear. I grab the envelope and carefully put the letter back into it. I put it back in the drawer, close it, then go back to my room and check the time. 11:45 a.m.; I have to leave soon. I quickly get changed, put my shoes on, grab my bag and head downstairs. I put my stuff by the door to the garage and go into the study. I plug my phone into the computer and find the photos of the letter. I print them out, unplug my phone, head back towards the stairs and sit down, looking at the freshly printed pages. I know this letter has something to do with my father. There's no other reason why my mum would hide it from us. She never hides anything from us, unless it has something to do with him. I focus on the words at the start of the letter as I begin to read it.

"Hello, Deidra, how are you? Well, I hope. It seems like forever since I saw you and the children. I hope they are behaving themselves for you. I know it's been a while, but I would love to see them, and you of course. I know it's a lot to ask, and I'm happy to wait until you're ready. I know you haven't spoken to Tony in a while; he stayed with me for a while too, but he's gone now. I haven't heard from him in a few weeks. That's become a regular thing, unfortunately. I don't want to bore you with the details. I'm sure you've had enough of me telling you about his problems."

I reread the first paragraph over and over again, trying to piece everything together and make sense of what this lady is saying. She knows my parents, she said my dad stayed with her recently. Maybe I can contact her and ask about him. She said she hasn't seen us in a while, so she has to be someone my dad is close to, but why is she writing to my mum? And why did my mum hide this letter from us? All I can think is that she's trying to protect us, but who is she trying to protect us from?

I check the date of the letter - it was written just after Christmas. I go to read the rest of the letter before the alarm on my phone goes off. I set it for 12:00 p.m. to make sure I have enough time to get to the café as I knew the letter would distract me. I stuff the letter into my bag, head into the garage, get into my car and start it. I blast the radio to distract myself from everything I have just read. Twenty minutes later, I pull up in the carpark of the café we always meet at.

I decide to text Ryan about the letter before I go inside to meet my friends. I have so many questions, and I need to see what he thinks about it.

Hey, so I found a letter in my mum's room. I didn't intentionally find it. I was getting my shorts out of her drawer and the letter was under them, but I feel like I was meant to find it. Now I have so many questions. I haven't finished reading the letter yet, but I will soon. Can you meet me later? Say 6:00 p.m. at Cottesloe Beach?

I hit send and within a minute, I have a reply.

I'll be there. Bring the letter with you and we can figure out who this lady is. See you then.

I put my phone in my bag and head inside. I walk in and approach the usual table. Hadi and Rosie are giggling, and when they notice me, they jump up and run over to me, hugging me tightly.

"We've missed you so much!"

I hug them back.

"I've miss you, too. It's been too long."

We sit down and order our food and drinks before we start to catch up. I look at my friends and realise I've been way too distant recently. I love these girls. They're like sisters to me, and I haven't been the same friend as I used to be. I know it's because I don't want to lie to them too. I certainly don't want to put them in the same position that I'd put Cam in. I also remind myself they made the same promise to my mum as he did. What kind of person would I be if I dragged them into this? I already feel bad, but not telling them is the only way to protect everyone. I must look miserable because Hadi grabs my hand and interrupts my thoughts.

"Hey, what's going on? Are you okay?"

My friends have the same worried look as Cam had when I last saw him. I let out a deep sigh.

"I could say I'm all right, but that would be a lie. The truth is, I miss you guys and I feel so bad for not being present over the past few weeks. Cam and I have been fighting and I've just got a lot going on, so I've distanced myself from everyone. I feel like the worst person. I wish I could tell you everything, but it's just so complicated."

They both drop their eyes to the table. They know something. Something about me. My mind begins to race. Has Cam told them the truth? I look at them, feeling my muscles tense throughout my body.

"What? What's wrong?"

They look up, but not at me.

"Please, tell me."

I am practically begging them, but they still can't meet my eyes.

Rosie finally looks up.

"We had dinner with Owen, Jacob and Cam the other night. We missed you and we wanted to invite you, but Cam said you guys weren't talking. He said he wasn't comfortable with you going, so we didn't invite you. We got talking, and he told us you were dealing with some family stuff. He wouldn't say what, but he said it was really important to you, and it was your priority right now. We thought you might have been looking for your dad. We asked Cam and he said it wasn't that. We were really worried - we still are. We're close to your family too, so we thought we'd upset you. You usually confide in us, but you've been distant recently so we assumed you just needed to be by yourself."

Hadi steps in.

"You know we love you, and we're always here for you. You can trust us with anything, and you can always come to us with any problem you're dealing with. We're sorry we didn't invite you, but Cam was pretty insistent and we didn't want you guys to be uncomfortable, so we didn't say anything to you about it, until now."

Now it's my turn to avoid looking at them. Cam covered for me. If I'm honest, he's lied for me, again. What have I done? I have put him in the worst position. This is wrong. How could I have done this to him? I've made him so uncomfortable that he didn't even want me to go to dinner with my best friends.

My friends started dating their boyfriends after we graduated, and they've all made it over the two-year mark. In that time Cam has gotten pretty close to Owen and Jacob, so we're always together. We spend almost every weekend together, but recently I've missed everything, including the fact that my boyfriend doesn't want me around. I finally look up and meet the gaze of my friends. They still look miserable.

"Girls, please don't feel bad, and don't be sorry. If anyone should apologise, it should be me. I'm sorry I've been so distant, and I'm sorry I put Cam in that position. I put all of you in that position, and that was not what I wanted to do. I did need time to process things, but everything's fine. I want to spend more time with you all, and with Cam. I'll talk to him and we'll figure everything out, I promise."

I see their bodies instantly relax. I didn't realise the toll this has taken on all those around me until now, and I begin to question if I am making the right move by wanting to find my father. If this is what it's doing to those around me, and if it's forcing me to lie to everyone I love, is it really worth it? I try to fight off these feelings. I have thought about this for so long. I can't possibly turn back now. I have to find him. If I don't, it will destroy me. I need to find him once and for all, but I need to find a way to do it so I don't hurt everyone around me in the process, including me.

We spend the next two hours sipping our coffees, eating our food and catching up. We reminisce about memories we share together, most of which make us laugh. Suddenly, Rosie's face lights up.

"We nearly forgot! This morning we were talking about possibly having a weekend trip away. Maybe four days down south is just what we need?"

I smile.

"That sounds perfect. Should we plan something now?"

We all grin before diving into planning our perfect getaway. After an hour, we call our boyfriends to make sure they are happy to go on a couples' getaway. We decide that this weekend would be the perfect time to go. We find a house in Margaret River; a secluded cottage with a huge front yard. It is on a hill, and you can sit on the grassed area at the front and see the beach in the distance. It has enough rooms, and it is big enough that we can stay there without being bored. We know it's perfect, and that we won't be able to find anything else like it, so we book.

"It was great to see you, girls. I really have missed you," I say as I hug my friends before leaving.

"We missed you, too."

After we say goodbye, I get into my car, drive straight home, park and head inside. I check my mum's room. The clothes I picked out for her are gone, so she must have been home already. I poke my head into Darci's room, but she isn't there. I grab my phone and call her.

"Hey sis, what's up?"

I have never heard Darci talk like this before. I laugh before answering.

"Hey, where are you? I just got home, but you're not here."

"Yeah, I'm at Nia's house. Mum dropped me off here. She has a date this afternoon, and she knew you were out seeing your friends, so Anna said I could stay here for dinner. Are you coming over too?"

Wait, my mum is on a date? No way! She didn't even tell me. She has started dating a bit more in the past few years, but she always tells me about it. She's like a schoolgirl when it comes to dating, she doesn't know what to do with herself. I always help her with her outfits, shoes, hair and makeup.

"Darci, are you sure she's on a date? I thought she said it was a business meeting."

Darci suddenly goes quiet before responding.

"Umm, oh, yeah I think it is a business meeting. So, are you coming over?"

She is hiding something from me, but I don't have the energy to question her. I'll do that later.

"Is Cam there?"

She doesn't even answer; she just hands the phone straight to him.

"Hey."

I must say, it is nice to hear his voice.

"Hi. Can I come over tonight?"

"Of course you can. Mum's planning on having dinner at seven, so come over at six."

I'm about to agree, but I remember that's when I'm meeting Ryan.

"I have an errand to run, but I'll be there by seven, okay?"

I wait for him to reply, and part of me is expecting him to be angry.

"What errand?"

Shit, how am I going to explain this one? I know enough is enough. Cam needs to know about Ryan. I can't take all of this lying and sneaking around anymore, but is now the right time? We have just gotten back on track, and I don't want to upset him again.

"I've got to go and see my brothers. I haven't seen them in a while, so I'm going to stop by quickly. It's on the way so I won't be late."

I feel horrible for lying about going to meet Ryan. I do actually have to see my brothers, but that isn't happening tonight. *Last time I lie,* I promise myself.

"Okay. Tell them I said hi. I'll see you later. I love you."

"Will do, Cam. I love you too. I really do."

"I know. I'll see you soon. Drive safely."

We hang up, and I go back to reading the letter that has been on my mind all afternoon.

~

At 6:25 p.m., I'm sitting on Cottesloe Beach with Ryan. We've spent the majority of the time dissecting the letter, word by word.

"Okay, well. She definitely knows your family and, more importantly, she knows your dad. What are you going to do?"

I look at the letter before looking at Ryan.

"I honestly don't know. I guess I'm going to have to try to figure out who she is."

Ryan looks at me with the same concerned look as Cam and my friends.

"Not you too!"

"What?"

I suddenly feel stupid, so I just shake my head.

"Nothing. Sorry."

"Are you okay? It seems like something is bothering you?"

I focus on the sand as I reply.

"Sorry, it's not you. I just feel like I'm sneaking around. I don't want to hurt anyone, and I know this is the only way to protect them, but I don't think Cam trusts me anymore. I'm going away with him and some of our friends on Thursday. I'm going to tell him about you. I don't know how yet, but I know it's the right thing to do."

I'm scared to see Ryan's reaction, but when I face him, he has a smile on his face.

"I think that's a good idea. I know you love him, and I don't want to stand in the way of your relationship. I'm here to help you find your father and help keep Cam out of harm's way. I totally get that, and I agree, he does deserve to know. Let me know how he takes it."

I feel relieved and I'm glad Ryan understands.

"I will. Thank you."

I check the time. "Sorry, I've got to go. I'll call you when I get back."

Ryan nods and stays seated on the sand as I run to my car.

I get to Cam's at seven o'clock on the dot. After hugging Nia and Darci, I go to find Anna. She is in the kitchen, getting dinner ready.

"Hey, Anna."

She turns from the stove to hug me.

"Hello, darling. It's good to see you, we've missed you."

"I've missed you, too."

Cam approaches us and hugs me from behind. I turn and smile before I hug him back. We sit down at the breakfast bar and talk to Anna while she serves up dinner. I look at them, ready to ask the question that has been burning away at me since I spoke to Darci.

"So, who's going to tell me about this date my mum's on?"

Anna glances quickly at Cam, then me.

"Date? What date? I don't know anything about a date! Dinner's ready, let's sit at the table."

I raise my eyebrows at Cam and he holds up his hands.

"I know nothing."

"Sure you don't. You two are acting very odd for two people who claim they know nothing about said date."

"I might tell you later, if you're lucky."

Before I have time to answer, Anna calls out, "Come on, lovebirds. The food is getting cold."

~

After dinner, we play Monopoly: the perfect way for everyone to distract me from asking about the date. After a few hours I rub my eyes.

"Okay, Darci. Get your stuff, we'd better go home."

Darci jumps up and runs towards Nia's room to get her things. I hug Anna and thank her for dinner before heading to the door to wait for my sister with Cam. I hug him tightly.

"I'm glad things are better. You know I love you, right?"

He hugs me back,

"I know. I love you, too."

I look up at him with a sooky puppy face.

"Tell me about this date."

He laughs and kisses my cheek.

"Ask your mum. She'll tell you. I've got a pretty busy schedule over the next few days, but I'll see you on Wednesday night. I'll stay over, then we can get up early and head down south."

"Okay. I'll see you then."

I kiss him and hug him again before going to my car. I'm smiling like a teenage girl who has just had her first kiss, and it feels great! Everything is perfect—well, almost everything. I know I have a lot to do to find my father, but for now I just want to get away with Cam and my friends. I need a break and I know that when I get back, I'll have a lot of questions to ask.

Chapter Six

Breaking Free

The next few days' fly by and before I know it, Cam and I are packed and ready to go. We are both excited about getting out of the city and heading to the peace and quiet of Margaret River. If only I knew my world was about to come crashing down.

Cam and I hit the road at 8:30 a.m. It's going to take us roughly three hours to get to Margaret River, and that's without traffic. As we start driving, I look over at Cam. His blonde hair is messy - bed hair really suits him - his blue eyes are sparkling and his dimples are noticeable every time he smiles. He's wearing cream coloured shorts and a black singlet, and he looks so handsome. I know there is more to Cam than his looks. Of course he is good looking, but he also has a beautiful personality and a big heart to match. I don't really care about his looks or how fit he is. Eventually looks fade and if a person isn't a good person on the inside, then no amount of looks will get you through the tough times that you inevitably face.

These days there is pressure to look a certain way, but what happens if we take appearances out of the equation? Our overall love for an individual should go beyond what they look like on the outside. What matters to me is how Cam treats others, especially his family. How someone treats their loved ones says a lot about who they are, and Cam certainly treats his family - and mine for that matter - with the utmost respect. He is courteous, kind, caring and compassionate. He always goes out of his way to help those in need, and he puts others before himself. I smile as I think about all the things I love about him. I realise how truly lucky I am to have him in my life. I am lucky to say he is my boyfriend. I must have caught his eye because he looks over at me and flashes his perfect smile.

"What?"

"Nothing. I'm just thinking about how lucky I am to have you."

He grabs my hand and squeezes it tightly.

"No, it's me who's lucky to have you."

I smirk before I poke my tounge out at him. He laughs and we got back to listening to the radio. We spend most of the drive talking and singing along to the songs we love. I find myself wanting to tell him about Ryan, but I can't bring myself to say the words. I know it has to be the right time, but I don't know when that will be, or how I will know. I guess it's going to be when my gut tells me it's the right time, or when I build up the courage to tell him. Either way, I try my best to forget about it, even if it is just for a moment, but it is haunting me. I keep thinking about how Cam is going to react. I already hate myself for lying to him, I don't think I can handle him hating me too. I decide to try and distract myself again.

I look out of the window and watch a single cloud float through the blue sky, before it disappears behind the car. I rest my head on my hand as I focus on the other people driving down the long stretch of never-ending gravel. I start to wonder what each individual in each car is going through. Are they chasing their dreams? Are they trying to mend a broken heart after the end of a relationship? Are they grieving the loss of a loved one? Are they happy? Are they hiding a part of themselves so the world can't take it away? Question after question keeps popping into my head. I am amazed at how much a person can be going through without telling a single soul. Every person we encounter, whether we know them or not, is going through something we don't know about. I know I am, and I'm hiding it from everyone. I question how many people are doing the same.

I must have allowed my thoughts to take me away because before I know it I'm fast asleep, although I'm awake in my dreams. *Oh no, please, not another dream!* I can see my parents. My dad is watching *The Grinch* with me and Dakota. We are giggling at him. He is repeating lines from the movie, except he is doing it in different accents with different faces. We think it is hilarious, and we keep asking him to do it again. He just laughs and does it without hesitation. My mum walks into the room, and I notice she looks sad. She smiles at us when we all look at her standing by the television.

"Girls, why don't you go find your brothers? We're going over to Uncle Derek's house for a swim. Go and get your bathers, then wait with your brothers until we're ready."

I look at my dad and he isn't smiling anymore. He looks really scared.

"Daddy?"

"It's okay, Delilah. Listen to your mother. Go and get your stuff, then we can go for a swim."

I get up from the couch and hug him before grabbing Dakota's hand. We walk towards our bedroom and I tell Dakota to go and get her stuff. She asks me where I'm going, but I tell her to be quiet. I quietly go into the hallway and creep towards my parents.

"No, she can't be gone!"

My dad throws a glass across the room and it shatters everywhere. He gets up and begins pacing around the room before suddenly leaving. He grabs his keys and a bottle of whisky and leaves through the front door, slamming it behind him.

~

I wake from my dream, desperately trying to find air to fill my lungs. Cam pulls over while I struggle to get my breathing under control. He unbuckles our seat belts and grabs my hands.

"It's okay. It was just a bad dream. You're okay."

His face is creased with concern. "Another dad dream?"

I nod, unable to find any words. He looks at me sympathetically.

"Let's get out of the car and get some fresh air. We can sit down and wait until you're feeling better. It's okay, I'm here."

We get out of the car and sit down on a grassy patch next to the road. I close my eyes and focus on the darkness, working on calming my heart rate down. I take slow, deep breaths before I feel strong enough to open my eyes. The sun is too bright so I put my hands up to protect my delicate eyes. Cam is watching me closely. I shake my head and look at the ground.

"Sorry. These dreams are becoming a recurring thing. I'm remembering things, things I didn't think I'd be able to remember. It's scaring me. Why won't they just stop? I can't handle them."

Cam pulls me towards him and hugs me protectively.

"You don't have to apologise. I think you're having these dreams because you're thinking about your dad more. It's only natural to be scared. I don't know if you've considered it, but maybe you should see a therapist? You can talk to a professional about everything, especially about wanting to find your father. They can help you."

I suddenly pull away from Cam. Now is the perfect time to tell him about Ryan, but I fear his reaction so much that I just can't find the strength. No, we can't have this conversation here, not now.

"I'll think about it. Let's get back on the road."

Cam looks confused, but he doesn't say anything. We get back in the car and head off into the blue horizon.

An hour later, we finally arrive. Our friends are already here, and when we get out of the car we can hear the girls laughing. We get our stuff from the car and head inside. Marc is sitting at the table with his girlfriend, Alyssa. I am yet to meet the famous Alyssa, although Cam has told me all about her. She is the one Marc started seeing a few months ago, but with everything going on, Cam and I didn't get around to setting up a time to have dinner with them. I'm glad to finally be meeting her. She is stunning. She has long brown hair, brown eyes and a warm smile. She seems quiet, but once she warms up to me, she allows her personality to shine. She is hilarious, bubbly and friendly, and I know she is going to fit into our group perfectly.

After talking to Alyssa for a while, the rest of our friends come into the kitchen. After hugging everyone, Cam and I get a tour of the house, and it is stunning. After getting the tour, Cam and I put our stuff in our room. We have our own ensuite and the most beautiful view of the hills and the ocean. Cam is beaming. He picks me up and spins me around the room, before gently placing me back on the floor.

"This is exactly what we need. It's going to be an amazing trip, I can feel it."

We hug and as Cam holds me another wave of guilt hits. I try my best to ignore it, I try to fight it, but the more I ignore it, the more it hits me. I can't go on like this for much longer, and I know that for the sanity of my boyfriend and myself, I need to come clean.

Rosie knocks on the door before opening it. "Hey guys. We're going to have some wine and plan some things to do. Care to join us?"

We spend the rest of the day planning our trip, although it is almost impossible for me to focus on anything other than the secret I am desperate to tell Cam. It has started to become impossible to ignore, and I don't know how much longer I can hold it in.

~

The first few days are incredible. We relax, travel around, spend quality time together, and re-establish our amazing bond. We know this is the only group of people we can share this experience with. We even talk about going on an international trip, which the girls excitedly start discussing. Everything feels perfect, and I've completely forgotten all about Ryan and what I have to tell Cam. But everything I've been avoiding finally catches up to me, and the time has finally arrived. It is time for Cam to find out the truth.

It is a sunny Saturday and we are due to head back to the city on Monday morning, so we want to make the most of our last few days in Margaret River. After a day of being on the beach, the girls and I decide to head out and get dinner. We get home and I leave the five shopping bags in the kitchen while everyone else unpacks and prepares dinner. I go into the room to find Cam.

"So, we got way too much food ..."

I stop talking. His eyes are narrow, and his jaw is tense. I can feel the heat radiating off of his body when I notice he has my phone in his hand. I'd left it to charge.

"Who the hell is Ryan? And why is he texting you about your dad?"

I grab my phone from Cam and quickly read the message.

Hey I've been thinking; is there a way you can contact that Helen lady? Surely she's a member of his family? Especially if she knows so much about your family.

"Delilah, don't ignore me!"

I have to tell him the truth, I can't avoid this secret anymore.

"I can explain. Although I can't believe you read my message. Have you read them all?"

"Don't try to change the subject! Of course I've read the messages! What was I supposed to do? Wait, this is why you pushed me away, isn't it? This is why you didn't want my help? You turned to him, some guy you don't even know. How can you trust him? He doesn't know anything about you or your family. Surely you know you can't trust him? You're not stupid, Delilah!"

"That's the point, Cam. He doesn't have any previous knowledge. He knows nothing, so he doesn't have to lie to anyone. This saves me from asking you to lie. It's bad enough that I'm sneaking around, but this is the only thing I can do to protect you. Please try to understand things from my side."

He looks angrier than he did when I walked into the room. I've never seen him like this before. I try to approach him, hoping he won't push me away.

"Don't. Don't come near me. I don't want you talking to this guy. You pick: him or me. If you can't pick, I'll pick for you, and you won't like my choice."

I'm stunned. Is he serious? Have I just cost myself the chance to be with the love of my life for good?

"Are you threatening to break up with me?"

My question goes unanswered as he grabs his jacket and pushes past me. When he reaches the door, he turns around and glares at me.

"You do the math. I'm going to get some fresh air."

My phone suddenly goes off. I know it's Ryan, and so does Cam. I see the rage take over his whole body.

"You'd better answer. He's obviously desperate to talk to you."

I feel horrible. This is not what I wanted to happen. I wanted to protect Cam, not hurt him.

"No, it's not like that."

He doesn't give me time to explain. He opens the door and slams it behind him leaving me to feel the force of what I've done. Within seconds, I'm crying.

A few seconds later the door flies open again and Cam looks directly into my eyes.

"At least my father wants me!"

He yells the words at me with such force that all I can do is stand there in silence. His breathing has intensified, the heat has risen to his cheeks, and the furry in his eyes has gotten stronger. For the first time since knowing him, I feel afraid to be in his presence. The minute he says those six words I know he's said them to hurt me, and they have cut through me like a knife. I feel like he has ripped my heart out of my chest and is now holding it in his hands. I'm waiting for him to put me out of my misery, to say something, *anything*, but he doesn't say a word. I look up at him, praying he won't leave me. As much as I feel afraid, I also feel the need to fix things, and all I want is for him to stay.

"Don't go, please."

"I'm sor- ... actually no, I'm not sorry. That's not the actions from someone who is supposed to love you."

He is quoting me: that's exactly what I'd said to him when we had our first fight. I'm trying to stop the tears that are now drowning my face. I know I've messed up, but I did it to protect him. Now I've done the very thing I tried so hard to avoid. I've hurt the person I love more than anything, and I know I may well have just cost myself the best relationship I've ever known.

I don't know what to say, so I stand there in silence. Cam finally opens the door and walks through it, slamming the door with more force than before. I sink to the floor as I listen to him walk into the kitchen. There are muffled voices and then I hear footsteps approaching from the hallway. The door slowly opens and the girls walk in. They sit on the floor with me in silence, while I cry. When I can't cry anymore I try to explain everything to them, but I can't find the words.

After a while, my friends give me some time to myself. My mind is racing, so I curl myself up on the bed and wait for Cam to come back. After what feels like hours, he finally returns to the room. He walks in, kicks off his shoes and gets into the bed. I sit up, desperately wanting to hug him and tell him how much I love him. I go to speak but he won't let me.

"Don't. I don't want to talk to you."

I roll away from him and try to keep the tears at bay, but I can't. I lie in the dark crying all the pain from my body, knowing the only person who can make me feel better is right next to me, and he doesn't want anything to do with me.

The next morning, I wake up and turn over to face Cam, hoping to talk to him, but he is gone. I get up and head into the bathroom. I stop and look at my reflection in the mirror. My eyes are red and puffy, my hair is a mess, and my face has lost all its colour. I shake my head, knowing I've done this to myself. I turn the taps on and splash the warm water over my face, hoping it will help, but it doesn't. I give up and head to the door. When I open it I hear Cam talking to our friends.

"She lied to me about something and I just don't know how to come back from it. She's broken my heart. She didn't trust me, or love me, enough to turn to me in her time of need, and that's damn near destroyed me."

Rosie starts to reply.

"Oh Cam, we're so sorry. She was devastated last night. Trust us, you mean more to her than life itself. She loves you so much. We don't know what's going on, but we know she only wants the best for you."

"I don't think she does love me though, Rosie. She wouldn't put me in this position if she did."

Everyone but Cam notices me standing in front of the entrance to the hallway, and Rosie quickly jumps in.

"Delilah! Good morning. We're going out for breakfast soon. You should get ready."

I don't bother to reply; I just look straight at Cam.

"Do you really think I don't love you? Of course I love you. That's why I did it!"

Hadi gets up from her chair. "Delilah, let's go and get ready."

"No! Don't you get it? I know I've messed up and I want to fix things, how can he question if I love him? Of course I love him. That's the whole damn point. I love him more than I love myself. Why can't you just see that?"

Cam turns to look at me and I can feel the awkwardness fill the room. This is not the time, nor the place, to be having this discussion.

"You guys go to breakfast. I'm going to stay here. I'm sorry I've ruined the trip."

I turn around, hurry back to the room and close the door behind me. I sit on the balcony and listen as Cam comes in to get dressed before he leaves for breakfast. Neither of us says a word. After I hear the group leave, I decide to have a shower. I turn the taps on and wait until the water is warm. I stand under the water and cry. I can't stop the tears, and I can't get rid of the pain. Crying is all I can do to feel something, although it is the worst feeling I've ever felt. I wash my face again before turning the taps off.

As I get changed I question whether finding my father is worth everything I'm sacrificing. If he rejects me, then all of this will be for nothing. I'll lose everything, and I don't know if I could come back from that. I'm not sure if it is worth it anymore. If I lose Cam, then I'll lose the most valuable relationship I've ever had. I can't imagine my life without him, and now I am facing that reality, it scares me more than anything.

After my shower I decide to get some fresh air. I grab a bottle of juice from the fridge and head outside. I find a spot on the hill, sit down, find Dakota's number and hit the call button. A few seconds later I hear her voice and I can't even get a word out before my chin begins to tremble. Within seconds I'm crying again.

"Delilah. Oh my gosh, what's wrong? Talk to me."

I continue to sob as I tell her what's happened. I don't tell her why it's happened. I want to, but I want to tell her in person. I just hope she doesn't react the way Cam did.

"So, that's pretty much everything. I've well and truly stuffed it up, Dakota. I really don't think we can come back from this. He's so angry."

I wait for my sister to reply and I know she is trying to make sense of everything.

"Delilah, what did you do to make him so angry? He wouldn't just snap like that. What's going on?"

I want to tell her everything. I want to get it off my chest, but I can't.

"I can't tell you on the phone..."

"Come to Sydney. Don't even think about it. Book a ticket right now. Go home and pack. I'll pick you up and we can talk about everything. I'll help you get through this, I promise."

I don't really process her idea before agreeing.

"Okay. I'll book a ticket now. I'll text you with the details once I've done it. I'll see what's available."

"Perfect! Text me when it's organised. You'll be fine Delilah, I promise. Call me if you need me. I love you."

"Thank you. I love you."

Despite still having a day left before we are due to go back home, I decide to leave that day. Cam needs his space, and so do I. I text Rosie asking her if I can drive her car back. I explain the need to go and see my sister, and she agrees, saying that she and Jacob can get a lift back with Cam. After thanking her, I head to the room to pack my stuff. I want to get out of here as quickly as I can, and I want to leave before Cam gets back. I don't want to fight with him. I know it will just be easier to leave as soon as I can.

I have most of my stuff packed when I hear the front door open. Shit! They're back, and I'm still here. Now I know I'll have to explain to Cam why I am leaving. I hear footsteps approaching the room, and I brace myself to see Cam walk through and see my packed bags. I hope with everything in me that we don't fight. I'm not strong enough to go back and forth. I just want to go home, get clean clothes, hop on a plane and go to my sister.

The door slowly opens and Cam walks in. He starts walking towards me and notices my stuff.

"You're leaving?"

He looks as horrible as I feel. His face is pale and his eyes are puffy too.

"Yeah. I think it's for the best. You should enjoy the rest of the trip without me here. It's too awkward. I'm going home, then I'm going to see Dakota in Sydney. I need to get away, and you need time to yourself. I never meant to hurt you. I'm so sorry. I hope one day you can forgive me. This is not what I wanted to happen. I hope you know how much I love you. You're the best thing that has ever happened to me, and I was stupid to think this was the right thing to do. I was trying to protect you, to keep you from lying, but now I see that I've made a terrible mistake. I hope I don't lose you, but if you don't want to be with me anymore, then I'll understand."

He takes a step towards me and grabs my hands.

"Let's go and sit outside. We need to talk."

This is it. He is going to break up with me. My heart feels heavy and I brace myself for the worst.

We sit outside, in the same spot I'd sat thirty minutes earlier. I look at Cam, waiting for him to end things. Time seems to be moving so slowly, and he just keeps looking at the grass, avoiding me altogether. He finally looks up and starts to talk.

"I didn't tell our friends the truth. I mean, I've already lied for you, so I may as well just keep going."

I want to respond but he won't let me.

"No, it's my turn to talk. Please, just listen. Firstly, I'm sorry for what I said about your dad not wanting you, it was wrong to say that, and I was just trying to hurt you. I didn't mean it. I'm hurt that you went to someone else, to another guy, someone you don't even know, to get help, especially with something as big as this. I always thought that if you were going to open up to anyone about this whole thing, it would be a therapist, not another guy. I guess I just don't understand why you made that decision."

I try to explain it to him, it's the least I can do.

"I've never thought about a therapist. I guess I should have considered it. Maybe it's something I should look into. Cam, believe me when I say this, I wanted it to be you. I tried, but you didn't want to be a part of it. I needed someone to confide in, and he was there. He didn't know anything about us, or my family history, so he couldn't get hurt by anything. That's why I picked him. I did it so you would be spared. I was trying to protect you and make sure you didn't get hurt. But I can see now that I've hurt you, and I am so sorry for that."

We spend the next hour talking, and when everything is out in the open, I feel a sense of relief. He now knows the truth and I won't have to lie to him anymore.

"That's everything. That's the whole truth. I know it's a lot to take in, but please understand that this is something I have to do. I have to find him. I will tell you everything from now on, if you want to know. But if you don't, I'll keep you out of it. It's up to you. I know you need to process everything, we both do. I need to go to my sister. And you need time to yourself. Time will heal things, I know it will, but if you don't want that, then I'll respect your decision."

Now it's his turn to try and stop me from leaving.

"Please don't go. Stay with me. Let's fix things. I don't want to lose you."

"Cameron Collins, look at me. You're not going to lose me; I promise you that. We need time. You need to be by yourself for a bit, and I need to be honest with my family. When I get back, we'll talk. Heck, we can even talk when I'm in Sydney if you want. But I think we both need this."

"Okay, I understand. You're right, we need time."

He stands up, offers me his hands and helps me up. We hug and after saying goodbye to my friends, I head to Rosie's car. I get in and wave at Cam who stands in the driveway with his arms across his chest. It takes all my strength to drive away. As much as I want to stay, I know leaving is the right thing to do. I head for my house, knowing that I can escape to Sydney and try to find a way to fix the mess I have made.

Chapter Seven

Sydney Shelter

(Part One)

I pull into my driveway three hours and fifteen minutes later. I grab my bags out of the car and head for the door. After letting myself in, I hear a familiar voice coming from the kitchen.

"Darci? Is that you? I thought you were staying at Nia's tonight?"

"No, Mum. It's me."

She pokes her head around the corner with a confused look on her face.

"Delilah? What on earth are you doing here? I thought you were coming back on Monday afternoon?"

I put my bags by the stairs and head into the kitchen. The minute I am within a few feet of my mum, my throat burns, and I start to cry.

"Oh Delilah, honey. What's wrong?"

I sit on one of the kitchen chairs and put my head in my hands, trying desperately to stop the tears. My mum sits on the chair next to me and pulls me towards her.

"You may be twenty-one, but you'll always need your mum. Talk to me."

I hug her and she sits there, patiently holding me until I find the strength to look up at her and tell her some of what's happened. There's no way I can tell her the whole truth without revealing my secret, so I sugar coat it.

"Cam and I had a fight and I needed to leave. I needed to give him some space. I don't know if we're going to get over this. I really love him, Mum. I don't want to lose him. I know I shouldn't rely on someone else to make me happy, but he does, and I can't imagine my life without him."

She gently wipes the tears from my face.

"Honey, sometimes you fight with those you're closest to. Sometimes you go through rough patches, but when you're in love you work through it. It sounds like you two do need time, and you've both taken that step. I haven't seen love between two people like you and Cam in a long time. These days it's so rare. But, my love, you two are meant to be. You have been destined to be together long before you were even born. I know it's not ideal, but he needs time to think, and so do you."

"I know, Mum. That's why I left. I spoke to Dakota and I'm going to Sydney tomorrow morning. I need to get out of Perth, and I need my sister."

"If that's what you need to do, then do it. Did you get time off work? I know you had a few shifts next week."

"Yeah, I called Hayley and she's given me the week off. I come back from Sydney on Friday, so she said I can go back the following Monday."

I yawn and rub my eyes as my mum gets up from her chair.

"It's only five o'clock, but I think you need to get some sleep, honey. You can get up early tomorrow to pack, and I'll drop you off at the airport."

I get up and hug her.

"Thanks, Mum."

I grab my bags and head up the stairs. I'm halfway up before I turn around. My mum is standing at the bottom, watching me as I head towards my room.

"I forgot to ask, who were you on a date with the other day?"

She becomes nervous and starts to fidget: something all of us Walkers do when we want to avoid answering a question. I instantly know she isn't telling me something. Oh, the irony!

"Oh, it was just a man I met at work. Male yoga is becoming quite popular, you know! But it's nothing serious. It was just dinner. We talked, and then I came home. I don't think anything will happen, but if it does, I'll tell you all about it."

She winks and I laugh.

"Okay, Mum. I only want the best for you. You deserve to be happy."

A warm smile appears on her face.

"Thank you, Delilah. Now go and get some rest. I'll see you in the morning."

I go into my room and close the door behind me. I put my bags next to my desk, and grab my phone and headphones out of my handbag. I plug my headphones in and go to launch my Spotify playlist when I notice I have two messages. One of the messages is from Cam and the other one is from Ryan. I have a feeling Ryan thinks I am ignoring him, and I guess in a way I am. I haven't replied to his last two messages. I meant to, but it slipped my mind. I decide to read the one from Cam first.

Just wanted to make sure you got home safely. I know we need space. Let me know when you're home and when you make it to Sydney. After that, I don't think we should talk until you get back. Cam x

I reply straightaway.

I'm home. I know it's going to suck, but you're right. I need to tell Dakota and figure out what my next move will be. I know I've said it repeatedly, but I am sorry for hurting you and I do love you. I'll let you know when I get to Sydney. D x

I stare at the screen, waiting for a reply, but after ten minutes there is nothing, so I read the message from Ryan.

Hope everything is OK? Haven't heard anything back so I assume something is up? Here if you need me.

I suddenly feel uncomfortable. I need to tell him that Cam knows about everything, but I can't be bothered explaining it. I don't have enough energy to go through things again, at least not yet anyway. I know I should reply, and I don't want him thinking he has done anything wrong. In the end this is my fault; he is just trying to help me.

Hey, sorry. It's been a hectic forty-eight hours. I'm going to Sydney for a few days. I'll text you when I'm back and we can talk about things. Delilah.

He replies almost instantly.

No worries, I hope everything's OK. Sometimes having a break is just what you need. Have fun in Sydney. Speak to you when you get back.

I take a deep breath and then let it out. *Have fun?* I wish! I head over to my chest of drawers and open it. I pick out my favourite grey pyjama shorts and an oversized t-shirt, which happens to be Cam's. It is one of his favourite shirts; he gave it to me the day before we went down south. He knows I love sleeping in his shirts when he's not with me. I find comfort in them. They smell like him and it makes me feel safe. I laughed when he gave it to me, but I also appreciated the gesture. I bring it to my chest and hug it, breathing in the scent of his cologne.

I get changed and snuggle into my bed. It feels so good to be back in my bed, back in the comfort of my room, where I feel safe, and where I can hide from all the pain I've caused all while hiding from all the pain I'm in. I put my phone on silent and hit play on my Spotify playlist. I put my head on my pillow and let the music do what it does best: take me away to a happier place.

A few hours later, I wake up. My music is still playing. I'd set it on repeat, which it has now done three times. I take my headphones out and turn the music off. I check the time on the clock that hangs above my door, it's 12:10 a.m. I've been asleep for about seven hours, and I feel a thousand times better.

I am excited to get out of Perth, and I am beyond excited to see my sister. This is the perfect time to visit her, and I know it's exactly what I need right now. I know I have to make some changes, and I know I've been running away from things, so it is time to face everything. But, for now, I only have one thing on my mind: unpacking and packing again.

I turn my bedroom light on and rub my eyes. I pick up my bags from the floor and place them on my bed. I unzip them and go through the pile of clothes. I grab my washing basket and throw my dirty clothes into it. After an hour I've finally sorted through what I am going to take and what I need to wash. I pack my clothes and a few pairs of shoes, then pack my handbag, putting my phone charger, my headphones, my lip balm and my purse in it. I put my bags by my door and climb back into my bed.

I grab my phone and stare at my locked screen for as long as I can. There's a photo of Cam and me, we both look so happy, and so in love. I find myself wanting to talk to him. I know he won't be awake, but I decide to text him anyway. My head is telling me no, but my fingers can't stop typing.

It's 2:00 a.m. and I'm wide awake. I know it's for the best but I don't know how I'm meant to not talk to you, when that's all I want to do. I know going to Sydney will be good for me, and us, but I don't want to leave. I'm scared, and I don't like being scared.

My finger hovers over the send button, cautious about the consequences of sending the message. I hit send and put my phone back onto my bedside table before focusing my attention on the night sky that is visible through my bedroom window. The sky is crystal clear, the moon shines bright and is surrounded by the glowing stars. It looks breathtakingly beautiful. I look at the sky, concentrating solely on my breathing, carefully taking a deep breath in before letting it out.

~

At 7:30 a.m., my mum comes into my room to wake me up.

"Delilah, it's time to get up. You've got to have breakfast and get ready to go to the airport. We're leaving in an hour. I've made some porridge, so come downstairs and eat."

She opens my curtains before heading back downstairs. I open my eyes. The sunlight has now flooded into my room. I blink, giving my eyes time to adjust to the morning light before I quickly check my phone. Cam hasn't replied to my message, and I feel a sense of disappointment. I don't want to focus on this feeling anymore, so I climb out of bed and head downstairs. My mum is making tea when I enter the kitchen. I yawn before sitting down, placing my elbows on the table and putting my forehead in the middle of my hands. I close my eyes while I listen to my mum pouring the milk into cups of tea.

"Here, honey. I made porridge with berries and this is fresh, organic breakfast tea. Eat up, you've got a long day ahead of you."

The smells fill the room, and make me realise how hungry I am. My mum is now sitting across from me. She has her reading glasses on and she's reading the paper while she eats her breakfast.

"Thanks, Mum. For making me breakfast and tea, and for being an amazing mother. I'm really lucky to have you."

She looks up at me and smiles.

"That's what I'm here for, my love. Eat up before your breakfast gets cold."

I pick up my spoon, eat my breakfast and drink my tea. Once I've finished, I head upstairs and check my phone, hoping Cam has replied. Still nothing.

I head into the bathroom and jump into the shower. I stand under the warm water, hoping it will wash all my problems away. I look at the wall, staring blankly at the cream coloured tiles, desperate to feel something other than these shitty feelings that have taken over my mind. I shake my head. This is exactly why I need to get out of Perth, why I need to see my sister. I need to come clean and discuss everything with someone I trust. I know I can talk to Ryan, but my sister knows Cam, and she is about to know everything that Ryan knows. So, given the circumstances, it makes more sense to talk to my sister.

I am lost in my thoughts when my mum knocks on the door.

"Delilah, it's eight o'clock. Get a move on or we'll be late. You don't want to miss your flight, and I still have to pick your sister up from Anna's."

I turn the stream of water off before I grab my towel. Once it is secured, I get out of the shower and go into the hallway. I walk over to my mum's room and sit down on her bed while she is looking for something to wear.

"Mum, can you get Darci after you've dropped me off? I don't want her to ask me a million questions about why I'm back, and why I'm leaving so quickly, and I don't particularly want to see Anna, or Nia either."

My mum steps out of her closet with her hands on her hips.

"Honey, at some point you're going to have to face ..."

She stops mid-sentence and looks over at me. I must look really miserable. She approaches me and sits down before she grabs my hands and looks into my eyes.

"Baby girl, I don't know what has happened, but I haven't seen you look this sad since, well, since your father left."

I pull my hands away and stand up.

"Mum, please don't bring him into this."

I turn towards the door, desperate to get away from this conversation, but my mum continues to talk.

"Sorry, I just want to be honest with you. I'll get Darci after I've dropped you off. Everything's going to work out, I promise."

I sigh and walk back to my room. I go into my own closet to pick something to wear. I know I want to wear something comfy, but I don't know what the weather is like in Sydney. I grab my phone and call my sister.

"Hey! I can't wait to see you!"

"I can't wait to see you too, but I've got a quick question: what's the weather like?"

As I wait for my sister to reply, I can hear something in the background, but I can't quite make out what it is.

"Sorry. Just had to open the blinds to see what the weather's doing. It's been pretty cold this week and they've predicted rain and storms over the next few days. One minute it's cold, and then it's warm again. You can never really tell until the day starts."

I laugh.

"That's a great description, thanks Dakota."

My mum walks into my room.

"Is that your sister? Tell her she needs to call me soon!"

I start delivering my mum's message, but Dakota cuts me off.

"Put me on speaker."

I do as she says and call our mum back into my room.

"Mum, I'm sorry. Work has been kicking my ass!"

My mum's face turns red. She hates it when we swear.

"Oh for goodness sake, Dakota. You talk just like your sister!"

"Sorry. I'll call you this afternoon. I'll be back home in the next week and a half or so. Just waiting to get the final date for this campaign. Speaking of which, I've got a meeting, so I've got to run. I'll talk to you soon, Mum. I love you. See you soon, Delilah!"

My mum answers for both of us.

"We love you too. Bye, sweetheart."

I hang up the phone and watch as my mum heads downstairs. I go back to my closet and decide to wear a pair of long leggings, a white singlet and an oversized jumper with my black and white Converse. I throw my clothes on and go to the bathroom. I stand in front of the mirror, pull my hair into a high ponytail, brush my teeth, pack my toiletries, grab my phone and my bags and head downstairs.

At 9:00 a.m. my mum pulls into the drop-off zone at the airport. She helps me get my suitcase out of the car before we share a hug.

"Take care, Delilah. Spend some quality time with your sister and clear your head. It's okay to seek refuge when life's hard, but don't run from your problems. It will only make things worse. You know I'm here for you and I love you very, very, much. I'll see you on Friday. Half past five, correct?"

I hug my mum just a little bit tighter.

"Yep, that's right. Thanks, Mum. I'm not running, just trying to take a breather so I can figure everything out. I love you. I'll see you on Friday afternoon."

I grab the handle of my suitcase, throw my handbag strap over my shoulder and wave as my mum pulls out of the drop-off zone. I head into the airport, check in and make my way to the waiting area. I get myself a coffee and sit by gate seven. I pull my headphones out of my bag and plug them into my phone before hitting play. I spend the next hour listening to my favourite songs and sipping my hazelnut latte, and before I know it, it is time to board.

The plane ride to Sydney is peaceful. There isn't anyone sitting next to me, so I have plenty of room. I spend most of the flight looking out of the window, watching the clouds float by, thinking about anything and everything. We soon land in Sydney, and I collect my suitcase before heading out to the waiting area. I start scanning the room, trying to locate my sister. Before I have the chance to find her, I hear her calling me. I turn and see her running at me. She reaches me within seconds and throws her arms around me.

"Delilah! I've missed you so much. I can't believe you're here! I'm so excited!"

I hug her back, trying to fight the unhappy feeling that has suddenly hit me. I know I'm about to cry, but I try to hold it in.

"I've missed you too. Can we go? I hate airports."

Dakota nods before she grabs my suitcase and I follow her to the visitors' carpark. I trail behind her as I try to spot her car; which is difficult since I don't know what she's driving. Suddenly we stop, and I look at a black Jeep Wrangler before looking at my sister, who is putting my bag in the back.

"Uh, Dakota, how did you get this car? It's a Jeep! How did you afford it?"

She giggles as we hop into the two front seats.

"Perks of the job. It's a rental car. Because I've stayed longer than expected, the company loaned it to me. It makes it easier for me to get around, and they don't have to provide me with a driver every day. They just give me a card to pay for fuel, and then I can drive myself everywhere, which is great. Now I'm not trapped in the apartment all the time."

The car is incredibly nice. It's mostly leather on the inside, the seats are ridiculously comfortable and it's got the latest speaker system, according to Dakota.

"So, I thought maybe we could stop at the shops and get some stuff for dinner? We can make our famous Walker nachos."

My sister looks so happy: she has the brightest smile and the happiest vibe. I guess that's one of the perks of chasing a dream and capturing it.

"That sounds perfect. Quiet night in? We can catch up and maybe watch a movie?"

"Perfect!"

We start catching up on our way to the shops when I remember I have to message Cam. He still hasn't replied to the last message I sent, but I message him anyway.

Just letting you know I got to Sydney safely. Hope you're okay.

I hit send and look at all the unanswered messages. They just sit there, staring at me, taunting me. Sadness instantly takes over my body. *You said you wanted space, well that's what you've got,* my mind screams. I shake my head and after texting my mum to let her know I've arrived safely, I turn my phone off and put it back into my bag. I stare out of the window, and a few minutes later we pull into the carpark of an organic shop.

We spend the next thirty minutes getting all of the ingredients for our nachos. We pick out the salsa, corn chips, a capsicum, tomatoes, mushrooms, olives, and an avocado. After we've paid for everything, we head to Dakota's apartment. The company she's working for has rented it for her; talk about taking care of your clients! She parks the Jeep, I grab my handbag and my suitcase, and we head up the lift to her apartment. She unlocks the door and I follow her in. Her place is stunning. It only has two bedrooms, but it looks a lot bigger. It's also close to the Sydney Harbour, which means she is close to all the places she needs to go to shoot her campaigns.

"Jeez, they don't spare any expense, do they?"

Dakota puts my stuff in the guest room, walks back out and heads into the kitchen.

"Yeah, they take good care of me when I'm here."

Something isn't right, my sister is acting weird. She's not making eye contact and she's finding things to do to distract herself, so she doesn't have to talk to me.

"Let's make dinner. I'm starving."

I check the time on her clock.

"Uh, Dakota, it's only 4:30 p.m. Isn't it a bit too early for dinner?"

She follows my gaze to the clock.

"Oh, sorry. It is too early. Want a coffee? We could go and sit on the balcony?"

I nod and let myself through the balcony door while Dakota makes the coffee. A few minutes later she hands me a steaming mug.

"I know mocha is one of your favourites. I've got this awesome machine that makes any coffee for you. Twenty-first century must-have. I mean, who has time to make coffee anymore?"

She giggles nervously as she sits next to me. I give her a curious look. Enough is enough. It is time to find out what she is hiding. Then I have a few truths of my own to tell.

"We haven't had a sisterly deep and meaningful conversation for a while …"

Before I can even finish my sentence, Dakota starts laughing hysterically.

"Delilah no one calls them 'deep and meaningful conversations' anymore. They're just 'D&Ms'. No need to say the whole thing. I would know what you mean."

Now it is time for me to let out a nervous giggle.

"My bad. Anyway, let's have a D&M. What's going on? And don't say 'nothing' because I can see right through you."

My sister begins to fidget. When she is ready, she puts her coffee mug down and begins to talk.

"Don't freak out, but things have changed for me. I love Perth, I love you guys and I'm proud to be from WA, but my life is mainly based in Sydney now. It just makes sense to move here, permanently. All the opportunities for me are here. It's easier to get to Melbourne from here and my agent is talking about sending me to America to get my name out there as that's where the majority of the work is. It just seems like the next step in my career, and I feel ready to take it. Justin knows about it, and he's thinking about moving with me. We love each other, and I may only be nineteen, but this is my life now. He knows that and he just wants me to be happy. We're ready to start our life together, so it just makes sense. I've been getting used to this place. My agency owns a few of the apartments in this building, and they use them for new talents they have signed up. If any of us decide to permanently relocate here, we're able to rent them straight from the agency, and sometimes they discount them for us too. I've already spoken to Mum and Declan about it, and they think it's a good idea. I mean, Mum's not particularly happy about it, but she knows this is my passion, so she's happy to support me. I'm making enough money to support myself and I can rent the Jeep too. Everything is worked out, which I think eases things with Mum. She's not so worried now that she knows I can actually survive here on my own. I know it's a lot to take in, but I hope you can support me too. I hate the thought of living away from you and our family, but it's a sacrifice I have to make."

I can see Dakota getting teary, which she never does. She isn't one of those people who wears her emotions on her sleeve. Come to think of it, she doesn't show her emotions at all, regardless of what she is feeling, so to see her like this shows me just how much this move means to her. As much as it's going to suck seeing my sister move to the other side of the country, I know I have to support her. She deserves the chance to follow her heart. I put my mug down, move closer to her and grab her hands.

"I just want you to be happy, Dakota. That's all I've ever wanted for you. If you feel like it's time to move on and relocate here, then that's what you've got to do. It will suck not having you in Perth, but we're your family and we're always going to be here for you. We're always going to support you. And it's not like you're moving to Mars! You're only a plane ride away. You've got to do what's best for you. I know how much you love modelling and if you're ready to make this change, then I say go for it. You're my best friend. I'm so proud of everything you've achieved, and everything you're going to achieve. I'm happy you're moving with Justin too. You're both madly in love and I think he's the one for you. I know you don't like to be emotional, like me, but it's okay to let your walls down sometimes. We all just want the best for you."

My sister immediately leans over to hug me.

"Thank you for understanding and supporting me. I really couldn't do this without you. I'm always going to be your best friend, nothing will change that. But now you've got an excuse to travel more!"

We both giggle and get comfortable in our chairs. I know this would have been a difficult decision for her to make, and I appreciate her honesty.

My mind starts to wander, until I remind myself that I have something to confess to my sister too. I know now is the time, and if I don't do it now, I won't do it at all. I drink the rest of my mocha before attempting to tell my sister the truth about finding our father.

"I ... ummm ... I've got something I have to tell you too. You can't tell anyone, not even Declan. I know you two share everything with each other, but please promise me you won't tell him? I mean it Dakota, you cannot tell a soul."

My sister looks at me and tilts her head. She finally nods and, after she promises not to tell anyone, I begin to tell her the truth. This time, I keep nothing from her.

"Growing up I was always closer to Dad than I was to Mum, and when he left I didn't deal with it very well. I've always thought about trying to find him, but I didn't know how to approach it, especially since Mum told us not to bother. She even made our own friends promise not to let us try to find him. I don't know if our siblings have ever thought about finding him, but it's gotten to the point where I *need* to find him. Dakota, I need my father. This pain is unbearable. I want to know why he left, I want him to explain it to me. We deserve an explanation. He just left us. How could he just leave us?"

The pain suddenly becomes unbearable. I feel the tears escape from my eyes but, for once, I don't care. In a way it feels painful to be this honest, but telling my sister the truth suddenly sets me free. I feel like I don't have to lie anymore. My sister pulls me into her arms and hugs me as I cry.

"I know you've struggled with it. You two were like best friends and it's only natural for you to wonder why he left. I've certainly thought about it, and Declan and I have had countless conversations when we've discussed it. We obviously don't want to say anything around mum. We know how sensitive she is about the whole thing, and we don't want to upset her, we all love her too much to want to hurt her. But none of us ever talk about it. I think we need to talk about it. How can we just pretend it didn't happen? It did happen, and it's affected all of us. Mum can't just sweep it under the rug and expect us to ignore the fact that he walked out on us. I've been thinking about it for a while too. I miss him. And I certainly wish I could just talk to him again. I promise I won't tell anyone, but when you find him, will you let me come with you? Or at least tell me when you're going?"

I wipe the last few tears from my eyes and sit up. My sister is right. We need to discuss what happened.

"I'll definitely let you know. I know you're busy, but maybe once a week we can discuss it? I need someone to talk to about it, and Cam doesn't like me talking to Ryan. Which reminds me, I need to tell you about him ..."

I spend the next hour and half talking to my sister, telling her everything that has happened, telling her about Ryan, and about how Cam reacted.

"I get where Cam's coming from, but I know you're only doing what you need to protect him. I think he just needs time, but he'll come around. He knows how much Dad means to you. I'm sure he just doesn't know how to approach it."

I know my sister is right, and I feel so relieved that I have someone to talk to and be honest with. She even offers to take Ryan's place, and while I appreciate that, I know that her schedule is incredibly demanding. I also need someone I can physically talk to, someone who can be there for me when I find our father. If that person isn't Cam, then it's going to be Ryan, which I explain to Dakota. Thankfully, she understands and she supports my decision.

After our conversation we make our nachos, which are delicious, as usual, watch *Bridesmaids* and then head to bed. After saying goodnight to my sister, I retreat to the guest room. I grab my phone and turn it on. As soon as it starts up, I receive a message from Cam. He has finally replied and I excitedly open the message.

I'm glad you got there safely. I ended up leaving Margaret River this morning. Wasn't having fun. My girlfriend, the love of my life, has been confiding in another guy, so I wasn't really in the mood to have fun. Have a good night.

I feel my heart break. He is still angry, which he has a right to be, and I totally understand that, but I thought he might have had time to calm down. I just want things to be okay again. I know I should just leave it, I know I should just turn my phone off again, but I can't.

I don't know how many times I have to apologise. If it helps, I told Dakota and she thinks I should find our dad. I've talked to her about everything else too, so no more secrets, I promise. I'm sorry you left early. I love you.

I hit send and within seconds he replies.

You said you wanted space. You're the one who left me, so go and have your space.

My heart sinks. No matter how many fights we've had in the past, whenever one of us says 'I love you' the other one always says it back. That's how it's always been, but this time it's different. Cam doesn't say it back. What have I done? I don't reply, as I know it won't do any good, it will only make him angrier. I throw on the same top I wore to bed last night and curl myself up into a ball on the bed. I hug one of the pillows to my chest and hope with everything in me that this pain will disappear. No matter how hard I try, it won't leave and I can't fall asleep, which makes me feel on edge. I see the door slowly open, and Dakota pokes her head into the room.

"Delilah?"

The minute I hear her voice my breathing becomes erratic and my mood intensify. My sister comes over to the bed and hops in.

"Oh Delilah, it's okay."

She pulls me into her arms and hugs me, trying her best to comfort me and calm me down. Although nothing seems to help.

"If Cam could see you now, I think he'd truly see how apologetic you are. Do you want me to call him? I can explain things to him?"

"No! He doesn't want to see me, or speak to me. He hates me, Dakota. He's never going to trust me again, and I doubt he will ever love me the way he used to. I've really stuffed things up this time. I never meant to hurt him. I want to spend the rest of my life with him. You know I didn't believe in finding a soulmate, or even getting married and having kids, but I see all of that with him. I want to marry him. I want to build a home with him. I want to be the mother of his children. I want to grow old with him. I want to be the person he wants to love for the rest of his life, and now I don't think we will ever have that."

My sister hugs me protectively.

"I don't have the right words to help you, and even if I did I don't think they'd help. I'll do my best to keep your mind off it this week. You just need to give yourself some time to think. It'll all work out. I've got an idea, let's share my bed, like we used to when we were little. Remember you'd always put cushions next to me so I wouldn't fall?"

I laugh and smile as I remember our childhood sleepovers.

"That would be perfect. Thank you."

We head into Dakota's room and snuggle into her bed. We spend some time talking about favourite memories of our childhood before we go quiet. I suddenly feel exhausted, but before I close my eyes I thank my sister again.

"Thank you, Dakota. You're the best."

~

I wake up the next morning to the sound of birds chirping on the balcony. I open my eyes, expecting the sun to blind me, but it doesn't. In fact, there is no sign of the sun at all. I assume Dakota has left the curtains closed, but when I look across the room, I notice the curtains are open. Dark grey clouds fill the sky. The pavement outside the balcony is dark, showing signs of the heavy rain that has soaked the concrete. I walk out of the room and head into the kitchen, assuming I'll find my sister there, but the apartment is empty. I go to the fridge to see if Dakota has any juice when I notice there is a note stuck to the refrigerator door.

"Hey sis, I got called into work for a promo shoot. I won't be home until 5.30 p.m., sorry! Go and explore today, don't stay cooped up. Go walk around the harbour: it's stunning! I've left some money for you on the bench. Please go and treat yourself to lunch; there are a few good cafés and restaurants around. Get some fresh air, take a book with you, order some food and coffee, and relax. Call me if you need me. If not, I'll see you later. Love you xx"

I think about staying in the apartment all day. I could snuggle up on the couch and watch TV, or a movie, and drink copious amounts of tea. That sounds like the perfect plan to me, but my sister is right. I need to get out. The weather may be dull, but that doesn't mean I need to wallow in my self-pity all day. I go into the guest room and, after a quick shower, I open my suitcase and pull out some of my clothes. I settle on a pair of workout leggings, which go perfectly with my black and white Nikes. I throw on a loose grey top and my thick Nike zip-up jacket. Once I'm ready I head back into the room.

I grab my phone and turn it on, not allowing myself the chance to see if I have any messages. I don't necessarily want to take my phone with me, but if I somehow manage to get lost I need something to help me find my way back. I shove my phone in my pocket, grab a bottle of water from the fridge, and put the money Dakota left me into my purse. I grab the set of spare keys she's left me and head for the door. After making sure it is locked, I head down in the lift and out into the fresh Sydney air. The rain has cleared up, but the sky is still dark. I pull the hood on my jacket closer to the back of my neck and start to walk.

I head towards the harbour, walking along the path, before stopping by the famous Sydney Harbour Bridge. I sit on the wall in front of the water. I look around me and watch all the people in the area. There are tourists, proud Sydney-siders, families, and couples kissing, holding hands and smiling. Seeing all of these people doesn't help the feeling of loneliness that is consuming me. It's crazy how lonely you can feel when there are so many people surrounding you.

As I observe my surroundings I realise how hungry I am, so I decide to take my sister's advice and get some food. I go for a walk, passing a number of cafés and restaurants before I find a bookshop with a café in it. It looks interesting, so I walk inside. Hidden Star is a popular place, by the looks of it. There are people everywhere and the staff are running around trying to serve people. I decide to go into the bookshop first, and I spend almost thirty minutes wandering around, trying to find a book. I'm standing in the Fiction section when a girl, who looks like she is about my age, leans over and hands me a book.

"If you're looking for something new to read, try this. I just finished it, and it's amazing!"

I smile as I take the book from her.

"Thank you, I'll have a look at it."

I stand there and read the title: *Drive Away* by Bethany-Anne Murray. I flip the book over and read the blurb,

"Lilly Andrews wasn't trying to find her knight in shining armour, but a chance encounter with bad boy Grayson Kennedy soon changed her life."

I stop reading right then and there. There is absolutely no way I can read a book about two people falling in love. The girl who handed me the book is still standing in the same aisle as me, so I politely give the book back to her.

"Thanks, but I don't think reading about a couple is the best thing for me right now."

I want to hit my forehead. Why did I just tell a stranger that? And why am I still holding the book? I try to hand it back, but she has other ideas.

"I know what you mean. I felt the same way too. I'd just broken up with my boyfriend when I read it, but there's more to it. Trust me, it's worth the read."

I finish reading the blurb.

"Lilly is thrown into an unknown world, and just when she thinks everything is perfect, the impossible hits, and she must learn to cope with one of life's toughest lessons."

Okay, so I wasn't expecting that. I look back at the girl.

"I will take your advice and give it a go. Thank you. Have a nice day."

She smiles at me.

"Enjoy!"

She waves at me as I head to the counter. After paying for the book, I order a hot mocha and a chicken salad. I find a free seat by the window that overlooks the harbour and I open the first page of the book. For the next three hours I sit in the café, reading the novel. I manage to read most of it. It's not very long, but it's addictive and I can't put it down. I get lost in time and in the novel. It isn't until my phone starts to ring that I put the book down. I check the caller ID. It's Dakota.

"Hey, what's up?"

"Hey. I took your advice, and I'm in a café, reading."

"Good. I'm glad you're not sitting at home. Speaking of which, I thought we could go out tonight. There's a pub I want to take you to, and then I was thinking tomorrow we could go to the aquarium and on Wednesday we could go to the zoo. The weather is supposed to be nice then."

I wait for my sister to take a breath, but she doesn't.

"And on Thursday and Friday we can hang out at home. Maybe go to Bondi Beach? I've got a shoot on Thursday morning, but you can come with me! It'll be fun."

Once I know she is done, I answer her.

"Uh Dakota, it's Monday. Who goes to a pub on a Monday? I like the other ideas though."

My sister gets defensive.

"Actually, Mondays are a pretty popular Sydney pub night, plus booze and meals are usually cheaper."

I laugh.

"Okay, fine. We can go to the pub."

I hear my sister's tone of voice change as she gets even more excited.

"Yes!"

"Okay, calm down. I'm going to head home now. I'll see you in a few hours?"

"Yep, I'll see you then."

I hang up the phone, pick up my new book and make my way back to the apartment.

I am surfing through the channels on the television when Dakota walks in. She looks exhausted.

"Long day? Are you sure you want to go out?"

"Heck, yes! I just need a shower and a quick nap. I'm going to do that right now. Wake me at 6:30 p.m.? We can get ready together."

Before I have time to answer, Dakota is heading for her room. I sit there, looking at the television. I know my sister is trying to help me, but I really don't think going out to a pub on a Monday night is a good idea. It's the last thing I feel like doing. But I know that trying to argue with my sister is a stupid idea, and I don't have the energy to argue with her right now. Maybe a night out will do me good.

Chapter Eight

Sydney Shelter

(Part two)

After waking my sister up, I have a quick shower before I go into her room, where we begin to get ready together.

"What do you even wear to a pub?"

My sister looks at me, putting her head to one side, the way a puppy does when you talk to it.

"Pub's aren't like clubs or bars. There isn't a dress code, just wear shorts and a top."

I don't know if she is serious or not, but I decide to tell her anyway.

"Um, Dakota, I'm not sure if you're aware of this, but it's freezing outside. It's raining and it looks like there's a storm on the way."

She walks towards the window and looks out at the sky.

"So it is. Wear jeans and a jacket then. It really doesn't matter."

After doing my makeup, I go to the guest bedroom and search through my suitcase, trying to find something to wear. I settle on a pair of black skinny leg jeans, black ballet flats, a soft pink shirt and my favourite leather jacket. Once I'm dressed, I head into the living room. Dakota is already there, waiting for me. She is wearing black faux leather leggings with black ankle boots and a white singlet under an oversized red and white checked long sleeve top.

"I've poured us a shot of tequila. It's not an option. I've ordered an Uber too. It'll be here soon."

She picks up one of the shot glasses and hands it to me.

"Cheers!"

She hits her glass against mine and I quickly drink the tequila. I'm not usually a fan of tequila, but this one is nice, really nice. A few minutes later Dakota gets a call from the Uber driver; we grab our things and head down to the ground floor. We find the Uber, hop in, and within fifteen minutes we arrive at The Blue Runaway pub.

"What's with the name?" I ask as I look at the sign.

"I actually have no idea. I've never really thought about it before. Not the greatest name, but the setup, atmosphere and prices are good."

I shrug, and follow my sister inside where we find a table close to the bar and sit down.

An hour later we've eaten and we're now drinking like it is going out of fashion.

"Dakota, I don't think we should be getting drunk, especially on a Monday."

I notice I'm slurring my words as I talk, but I start giggling, letting the alcohol take full effect. My sister gives me a stern look.

"Sis, you need to relax. Have some fun! It's not about getting drunk, just chill."

I nod and we both start laughing. I try to take her advice, but it doesn't pay off. A few hours later we are very drunk, playing pool with a few people we've met. At 12:15 a.m. the pub manager tells us it is time to go as they're closing for the night.

Dakota and I grab our things and stumble out into the rainy street. We stand outside the pub looking for a taxi, trying to shelter ourselves from the rain with our bags. We finally spot a taxi, hop in and head home. Once we get back to the apartment, I thank Dakota for a fun night and we stumble off to our rooms. I don't even bother getting out of my clothes, despite them being soaked. I sit on the end of the bed and throw the contents of my bag on the floor. I fish through my things until I find my phone. I unlock it, go through my contacts and find Cam's name. I know we still need space, but I am so drunk that I feel confident enough to call him without thinking. I just want to hear his voice, and despite my brain screaming at me to put the phone down I hit the call button. *Too late now*, I say as I wait for Cam to answer.

"Hello?"

That's not Cam, that's a female. I hear Cam yell something in the background, then I hear his voice in my ear.

"What is it, Delilah?"

I instantly feel defensive.

"Excu-excuse me, Cameron. Why the hell is another girl answering your phone?" I stumble over almost every word, but I don't care.

"Are you drunk? Jesus, Delilah. It's Monday! Why are you drunk?"

I go from being defensive to being angry.

"I don't know. I thought it would help. You're mad at me, so I just wanted … actually no, I just did, okay? Don't turn this around on me, mister. Why are you with another girl?"

I hear whispering before the line goes dead. What the hell? A few seconds later my phone starts to buzz. It's Cam. I accept the call, but he doesn't give me a chance to talk.

"Why are you calling me? You said you wanted space, yet since you left, you haven't stuck to your word."

I listen to his words, and I don't know if it is the alcohol or the fact that I am sick of apologising, but everything finally bubbles to the surface. And I am ready to lose my temper.

"Why did you hang up on me? Geez, I said sorry. I'm not saying it again. I know we need space, but I miss you and not talking to you sucks! Who are you with? And don't say 'no one'. Some idiot answered your phone. Who was it?"

I can hear noise in the background, and I feel my anger building to an explosive level.

"Cam, answer me!"

"It's no one. It's just a friend."

The girl's voice starts yelling in the background.

"Hello, Delilah. It's Heather."

Heather? Oh my God, no! This can't be happening. I start to panic. Is he trying to get back at me? He really doesn't love me anymore. I feel the heat rise to my cheeks, my throat begins to burn, and I feel the need to throw up.

"Wh-why is she there with you? And why is she answering your phone? My boyfriend's phone!"

I shout 'boyfriend' loudly, and defensively, just in case Heather has forgotten I'm still with Cam.

"It's nothing, don't worry. Sorry, I've got to go."

The line goes dead. I feel numb as I quickly log into my Snapchat account. Sure enough, there are photos all over Cam's Snapchat story. Marc has updated his too. He's with Alyssa, and they're with Cam and Heather. It looks like a double date. They are at Cam's house, in his room, smiling and laughing. Heather seems pretty comfortable with her arms around Cam. I drop my phone on the floor and kick it as hard as I can. It flies across the floor before stopping on the other side of the room. *Well, I guess this is the end of the relationship then,* I think before I pass out on the bed.

The next morning arrives all too quickly, and I'm pulled from my sleep as Dakota bursts into the room to wake me up.

"Get up! We're going to meet one of my friends. She's nice, you'll love her."

I lean up on my elbows and look at her. Is she serious? I'm hungover. My head is pounding, and I drunk dialled my boyfriend. He was with another girl, one who has always had one thing on her mind: making Cam hers. The last thing I feel like doing is going out, again.

"No, Dakota. I want to stay in bed. Why did I ever listen to you? Drinking on a Monday night is not what I needed and this hangover is making things worse. God, my head is pounding."

Dakota disappears then returns with a cup of water and some Panadol.

"Drink this, take two tablets, have a shower and get dressed. Wear nice clothes and put on a bit more makeup than you usually do during the day. We're leaving in an hour."

I try to protest, but Dakota leaves the room so quickly that I don't get the chance. I sit up in bed and take some Panadol. I drink the cold water before putting the glass on the bedside table. I sink back into the bed and look up at the ceiling. I start to sulk when my phone starts to vibrate. I get out of bed and find it on the other side of the room. I raise my eyebrow before reminding myself that I'd kicked it there after finding out about Heather. I look at the screen and see Cam's name, but I don't want to talk to him. After the phone stops ringing, I get an alert that he has left a voice message. I go to my voicemail system and hit play.

"I can explain everything. It's not what you think, I promise. Nothing happened. Please call me."

He sounds desperate and sad. I want to call him and tell him everything is fine, but I can't. We both need space, and regardless of what has happened, I need to keep my distance until I get back to Perth. *I should have done that to begin with,* I tell myself as I put my phone down on the bedside table. I walk into the bathroom and notice I still have my makeup on from last night. I reek of vodka and tequila, and the thought of alcohol makes my stomach churn. I jump into the shower and wash the makeup off my face before I scrub my body in a desperate attempt to get rid of the smell of alcohol. After showering, I put my hair into a loose ballerina bun. I do my makeup, putting on more than I usually do, as per the request of my sister. Once I'm finished, I walk back into the room and try to find something to wear. I search through my bag and find a black turtleneck crop top, which I pair with my leggings, but I don't have a jacket to wear. After throwing my top and leggings on, I slip into another pair of black flats. I search my bag again, trying desperately to find a jacket to wear, but I can't find one.

I go into Dakota's room and sit on her bed.

"Um, I don't want to be the bearer of bad news, but I literally don't have anything to throw over this. The only jacket I have is my one from last night, and it smells of alcohol. I have my Nike one, but that would look ridiculous with what I'm wearing."

Dakota looks at me and smiles.

"I like what you've got on, the all black look is nice."

"Oh I'm glad you approve," I say sarcastically.

She disappears into her closest and comes back out holding a black leather jacket that has a red plaid shirt sewn into it.

"Here, wear this."

She throws the jacket at me.

"Are you serious? There's no way I'll be able to fit into your jacket. We're not the same size."

"Just try it! It's one of those ones that stretches, so it'll fit."

I know Dakota means well, but it isn't going fit. I look at my sister, who is waiting for me to put it on. I throw it over my back and pull it on and to my surprise, it fits perfectly.

"Told you."

I laugh and roll my eyes as I wait for her to finish getting ready. Twenty minutes later we jump into the Jeep.

"Are you okay to drive?"

I look at my sister as she starts the car.

"Yep. The agency gave me some breathalyser kits that I keep at home. I used one this morning, and I'm fine to drive. Plus, I didn't drink as much as you did."

I shrug as we pull out into the Sydney sunshine. It makes a change from all the rain we've had since I got here.

Ten minutes later we pull into a coffee shop car park. I turn to my sister.

"Why did you make me get out of bed, put on makeup and wear nice clothes just to get coffee?"

I slump into the chair, annoyed at my sister. This feels pointless. I don't want to be around people, I just want to stay in bed all day.

"Get out of the car, Delilah. I want to introduce you to someone."

Introduce me to someone? Wait, what? I get out of the car and follow my sister into the coffee shop, suddenly intrigued by who we are going to see. My sister starts waving at someone and walking towards her. I follow, trying to look over her shoulder to see who it is. A young woman gets up from her table and hugs Dakota. She looks like she is in her mid-twenties. She has shoulder length blonde hair that complements her brown eyes. She's wearing red lipstick, which also looks good with her pale complexion. She is dressed in black jeans with a white top, a black blazer, and black ankle boots.

"It's so good to see you again, Dakota! I've missed seeing you around the office."

My sister pulls away from the woman before answering.

"I know. It's been too long."

Dakota then turns to me and introduces me.

"Melody, this is my sister, Delilah. Delilah, this is Melody Cooper."

Melody extends her hand for me to shake.

"Hello, nice to meet you."

I shake her perfectly manicured hand and she smiles.

"You too. I've heard so much about you. It's nice to finally put a face to the name."

I smile nervously and sit down. I look at my sister, hoping she will fill me in, but she doesn't. I am beyond confused. We order coffee and Melody and my sister begin to catch up. I awkwardly sit at the table, wondering who this lady is, and wondering why I have to be here when all I'm doing is sipping coffee. I turn to my sister, hoping she'll look at me. Suddenly my sister claps her hands together, scaring me.

"Delilah, I should probably tell you why I wanted you to meet Melody."

Finally!

"I used to be a part of Melody's talent agency, but then I got signed up to the current one, and I left. Melody and I kept in contact though. Over the last few months she's been scouting unknown talent, mainly focusing on singer-songwriters. I had lunch with her a few weeks ago, and she told me about it. So, I told her about you and, well, she wanted to meet you."

I look at my sister. I'm shocked and flattered, but she could have at least warned me. I can't believe she's sprung this on me, especially when I'm incredibly hungover! Melody looks over at me and adds to my sister's statement.

"Your sister has been telling me all about you. I can only go from what she has been telling me, but if you're interested I would love it if you would record a demo in our studio to see what you can do. I'm a manager and a talent scout. My mum owns the agency, Brooke House Entertainment, but I'm in charge of a lot more now that she's not working so much. If you've got potential, I'd love to sign you. I'll give you some time to think about it. I've got to go to the bathroom. When I get back we can discuss it more."

Melody smiles at us before excusing herself from the table. I look at my coffee, trying to process everything that has just happened. Dakota grabs my hands and lifts my head up so I am looking at her.

"I remember when we were in primary school, and every class in the school was asked to write a paragraph about what we wanted to be when we were older. We had to take them home and show them to our families and explain why we picked what we did. I remember we sat at the table and Mum asked us to go through ours, so we did. Dylan wanted to be a pilot, Declan wanted to be a policeman, I wanted to be a vet, and you wanted to be a singer-songwriter. You're the only one who has stuck to what you wanted to do ever since we were little, but you're not doing anything about it. Why?"

I shrug.

"I don't know, Dakota. I guess I've always been too scared to do it. I always question if I'm good enough. You get told 'no' a million times, you get rejected a million times, but you never give up. You just keep going. I don't know if I have the strength to do that."

"Delilah, that's the point. If you quit every time someone says 'no' or 'you can't do it', you'll never succeed. It's about taking a risk. It's time for you to take a chance. You can do it."

Melody soon returns to the table, and we spend the next few hours discussing the logistics. I agree to record a demo, but I have two conditions: I want to record the songs in my uncle's studio, and if I do get signed up to Melody's agency, I want my uncle to be my co-manager. When Melody agrees, I tell myself it is the right time to take a risk. With everything else going on in my life right now, maybe this is the best thing for me.

~

The rest of the week flies by. Dakota and I spend most of the time wandering around, exploring Sydney and talking about what songs I could record for my demo CD. We do as much as we can together and before we know it, it is time for me to head home. After packing my things, Dakota and I hop into the Jeep and head to the airport. When we arrive, I hug Dakota before getting out of the car.

"Thank you for this week. It's been amazing, and it's helped me a lot."

"Of course. You know I'm always here for you. Let me know when you get home, and don't forget to keep me in the loop about the whole dad thing. I love you, Delilah."

We embrace again.

"I will, I promise. I love you, too. Bye sis."

I get out of the car, grab my bags and head into the terminal. After checking in, I wait to board the plane, knowing that when I get back I'll have to face everything, and that it will soon be time to tell my mum the truth. But first, I have to confront my boyfriend: not something I am entirely looking forward to.

Chapter Nine

Back to Reality

The trip back to Perth goes by quickly, probably because I sleep the whole way home. After the plane lands, I grab my suitcase and start looking for my mum. As much as I loved being with my sister, it's nice to be home. Although it's now time to face the truth, no more running.

As I look for my mum, part of me wishes Cam was here, waiting to give me a big hug. I want to fix things with him, but I know that we are a long way off being back to how we were. At this point we're not even on speaking terms. It is beyond frustrating. We just keep going around in circles. One minute we're back to normal, and the next we can't stand being around each other. While I went to Sydney to give us some space, I also know myself well enough to know I was trying my best to avoid all the problems I have caused. I know deep down I'll have to tell my mum. Sneaking around has become too hard, it is costing me too much. In the end, I'm an adult. Mum's just going to have to accept the decision I've made.

After walking through the terminal, I spot my mum, who is frantically looking for me. I approach her and see the relief in her eyes when our eyes meet.

"Hi, honey. How was Sydney? How is your sister? Have you had time to think about everything? Darci has been missing you. Your brothers are at our house, looking after her. Declan can't wait to see you. He said Dakota told you about her move. I think he's a bit scared that she's leaving. I must admit I am too. Do you think she is making the right decision? Anyway, shall we go home?"

"Mum, one question at a time. Let's go to the car, I'll tell you all about it on the way home."

She laughs and takes my suitcase.

"Good idea."

I follow her out to the car, and when my bags are in the boot, I hug her.

"It's good to see you. I've really missed you, Mum."

She hugs me back.

"I've missed you, too."

We spend the thirty-minute drive home talking about my trip, although I leave out the part about finding my dad. I'm going to tell her, but I need to get things sorted with Cam first.

We pull into the driveway and I jump out of the car. Before I even have a chance to get my bag, Darci is running towards me.

"Delilah! You're finally home. I missed you!"

I giggle as she squeezes my stomach.

"I missed you, too. Let's go inside."

I follow her inside as my mum gets my suitcase from the car. When we get through the door, Darci lets go of my hand and runs into the kitchen.

"Dylan and Declan got a puppy. Look!"

I walk into the kitchen where Darci is sitting on the floor with a tiny puppy in her arms.

"It's a Pomeranian and his name is Max."

I look at my brothers, and Declan puts his hands in front of his chest.

"We picked him up today. We hadn't settled on a name, so Darci decided Max suited him."

I laugh and hug my brothers. I stand next to Declan and lean towards him.

"I imagine you've spoken to Dakota by now. Want to go outside and talk?"

He nods and we head outside to sit on the chairs that our mum set up years ago.

"So, what did she tell you?"

My brother looks nervous.

"Oh God, she told you about Dad, didn't she?"

Declan looks at me sympathetically.

"Yeah. She feels bad. She said she promised not to tell me, or anyone for that matter. It's my fault. I sensed she was hiding something from me. It's a twin thing."

"Do you seriously get away with the 'twin thing' excuse?"

Declan chuckles.

"Sometimes. But it's true. So, what are you going to do? Are you really looking for him? And why isn't Cam helping you? Dakota mentioned some Ryan guy? Don't be mad at Dakota. You know I won't tell anyone."

I sigh. Wow, she really didn't keep anything to herself.

"Okay, our family asks way too many questions at once. But to answer your questions: yes, I am looking for him. Well, I'm trying to look for him. I'm not having much luck. I don't really know what to do anymore. I don't know how to find him. I tried to confide in Cam, but he felt bad for lying to Mum, so I went to Ryan, who I met when I was working one day. He's become a pretty good friend. He's been helping me, but I didn't tell Cam about him. When Cam found out, he wasn't very happy. That's why I went to Sydney, I needed some time to think about what I was going to do, and Cam needed time too. He was pretty pissed."

Declan and I stare out over the pool.

"Yeah, I can imagine he was pissed. I get why you did it though. You were just trying to protect him. I'd probably do the same. Have you thought about going back to our old house? I mean I know we haven't lived there for a while, but maybe the owners have some of our old mail or something?"

I hadn't even thought about our old house.

"Actually, that sounds like a good idea. I doubt they have any of our mail, but maybe they can tell me something about Dad. I don't know, maybe they know something. Would you come with me? I don't want to go by myself and, until things are sorted with Cam, I don't really want to go with Ryan. I don't want to put him in another awkward situation."

"Yeah, I'll go with you. I know it's soon, but I've got the afternoon off tomorrow. I could pick you up and we could swing past and see if anyone's home?"

"Tomorrow would be perfect. Don't tell mum though. I assume you'll tell Dakota, but make sure she doesn't tell mum either."

He laughs again.

"Don't worry. I'll make sure she doesn't tell a soul."

After dinner, we sit down and watch a movie. It's nice to see my brothers and spend time with my family, even if it's just for a few hours. After saying goodnight to everyone, I head to bed. I'm exhausted and looking forward to getting a good night's sleep in my own bed. I put my suitcase on the bed and go through my clothes, putting most of them into my washing basket. While I was gone my mum washed all the clothes I'd put in the basket when I got home from Margaret River. She ironed everything and put it on my freshly made bed, ready for me to put away. I sort out my clothes, put my toiletries away, take off what little makeup I have on, brush my teeth, moisturise my skin and throw on my pj's. I get into bed and lean on the pillows that sit neatly along my faux white leather headboard. I open my text message inbox and message Cam. Despite not answering his previous call or voicemail, I know he'll want to know I am home safely.

Just letting you know I'm home. Tell Heather I said hi.

I know I sound immature. I don't really need to say something stupid like that, especially after the whole Ryan thing, but I can't help it. I hit send and then send Ryan a message.

Hey, sorry for being so MIA lately. I'm home from Sydney. I've got a full on day tomorrow, but if you're free on Sunday I'd love to meet up?

My phone starts to buzz. It's Cam. I answer almost immediately.

"Yes?"

I hear Cam sigh.

"This is stupid. One minute I'm mad, then you're mad. I don't want to be mad. Let's fix things."

"I don't either, but right now I'm not ready to deal with everything. I just want a day or two to myself."

"Um, wasn't that the reason you went to Sydney? Come on, Delilah, enough is enough. Let's just get this shit sorted before it destroys us."

It makes me feel better that Cam doesn't want us to break up either, but I still can't get the thought of Heather hugging him out of my mind.

"Goodnight, Cam."

I hang up, feeling horrible. Why did I just do that? I could have fixed everything, but my stubbornness got the better of me. I sigh before reading Ryan's reply.

Hey, that's okay. I've got some stuff to do in the morning on Sunday, but we could meet at the beach again? Say 1.30 p.m.?

Perfect. I'll see you then.

My phone continues to buzz for the next twenty minutes. Cam is desperately trying to get through to me, and I know there is a chance he will turn up at my house. I jump out of bed and lock my bedroom door so that no one can get in. I turn my phone off and after turning my light off, I go straight to sleep.

~

The next morning, I wake to a quiet house. My brothers have gone home, and my mum is at work. I poke my head into Darci's room and she is fast asleep. I head back into my room and throw on some workout clothes. I grab the letter that Helen wrote and I head out the back to get Jessie. After securing her lead, we head to the park.

After thirty minutes of walking, we sit down under an oversized tree. One of my neighbours, Leah, is playing with her Labrador, Talia. After I say hello to Leah, I let Jessie off the lead to run around with Talia. I know I can trust Jessie around Leah and Talia, and I keep a watchful eye on her while looking at the letter. I analyse every single word, reading paragraphs over and over again, trying to make sense of everything. I have to work out a way to find her, but I know it's going to be difficult. There isn't a return address anywhere on the letter, and I didn't see one on the envelope when I first found it. This lady could have vital information that I need to find my father, but I have to figure out how I'm going to track her down.

After another fifteen minutes, I grab Jessie and say goodbye to Leah. We head home, and I know I have some searching to do.

When I get home, I let Jessie off her lead and fill her water bowl up. I go inside and start walking up the stairs towards my room. I want to get out of my gym clothes and go for a swim. Thankfully we have a heated pool, so even though the weather is changing we can still enjoy swimming. I decide to make myself some fresh orange juice as well. Just what I need! Some vitamin

D, a swim, and a fresh juice sound like the perfect combination. As I reach the top of the stairs, I can hear someone going through my drawers. Who the hell is in my room? I open the door to find Darci frantically rummaging through my clothes.

"Darci! What the hell are you doing?"

She is startled by my sudden interruption. She stops dead in her tracks before she turns to face me. That's when I see she's been though my makeup too. She has mascara on her eyelids, along with eye shadow and eyeliner, and she has stained her lips with red lipstick. I look at her hands and see she is holding a pair of my favourite bathers.

"I didn't realise you were home. I was just looking for something. Sorry."

She pushes past me, drops my bathers on the floor and runs into her bedroom, slamming the door behind her. I know something is wrong, and I know I have to find out what it is. I know at Darci's age she is going through a lot of transitional things - good old puberty - and I know she is trying to figure out who she is, and who she wants to be. But this is so unlike her. If she ever wants to borrow anything of mine, she usually asks, and I usually say yes, but this time is different.

I approach her door and gently open it.

"Darci?"

I walk in and see my little sister sitting on her bed with her head in her hands. The sound of her crying fills the room.

"Darci, what's wrong?"

She looks up at me and I instantly notice the mascara has run down her face.

"Piss off, Delilah! I don't want a lecture from you. Sorry I took your things, but just leave me alone!"

I stop three feet away from her bed, stunned. Darci never swears, let alone raises her voice. I slowly approach her and sit down on the edge of the bed. She looks up at me and then, without saying a word, she puts her head back into her hands and starts to cry again. I lower my voice and try to sound as calm as possible.

"Darci, I'm not mad at you. It's okay. Tell me what's wrong. Talk to me. I'm here for you. You can trust me with anything."

Without lifting her head, she interrupts me.

"No, I can't. I can't explain this to you. I just can't!"

Her crying becomes more intense, so I move next to her. I don't say a word to her, just pull her into my chest and hug her while she cries. After ten minutes, she lifts her head and begins to confide in me.

"I'm not good enough. Everyone at school is pretty and all the girls have nice hair and I don't. I'm not beautiful like all the others at school and none of the boys like me. I see all these perfect girls on Instagram, and it makes me feel like I'm the ugliest person on this planet. You and Dakota are stunning and I don't look like either of you. It's not fair!"

Her tears stop while she explains everything to me, but before too long she is crying again. I feel horrible. Darci may not see it, but she is incredibly beautiful, and she needs to know that.

"Darci, there's more to a person than what they look like. And, baby girl, even in saying that: you're beautiful. You have clear skin and beautiful green eyes. You have amazing hair, which I'm jealous of, and you look stunning in everything you wear. You don't have to look like Dakota, or even me. We're sisters, but we don't have to look the same. That's what's beautiful about us, we all look different."

She smiles briefly before wiping her eyes.

"But the girls on Instagram are perfect. They have perfect bodies and they look perfect with their hair and makeup. Why can't I look like that?"

I sigh before trying my best to answer her question.

"You know you don't have to look like that? People edit photos to make themselves look a certain way; it's an edited version of someone's life. I know there's that pressure from the photos you see, but Darci you're beautiful in your own way. Your body is beautiful, and you'll learn how to do hair and makeup, once you leave school. You don't have to worry about that yet.

Don't you let anyone tell you you're not beautiful, because you are. You're funny, confident, and so full of life. I admire that about you. I'm proud of you and the person you are."

She smiles again and wipes the tears from her face.

"Really?"

"Really, really!"

She hugs me

"Thank you. I love you."

I hug her back.

"I love you, too. Now come on, little lady, let's get this makeup off your face."

We head to the bathroom, I take my makeup remover off the counter and remove the makeup from her face. Once we are done, she hugs me again.

"Thank you, Delilah. You're the best sister ever."

"Kiddo, you're the best sister too. Want to go hang out by the pool? I'll make some orange juice."

She smiles and nods. After helping her pick out her bathers we get changed and head downstairs. We jump in the pool and swim around. We have swimming races and pretend we are mermaids. We sip our orange juice and spend time relaxing. Darci suddenly jumps out of the pool and runs inside. I shrug before lying on my back, allowing the water to carry me around the area of the pool. I look up into the blue sky as I float through the water.

I love the way floating through the water feels. I am weightless and calm, and all my worries drift away. I close my eyes and imagine that I am floating in the ocean. I can smell the salt water and I can faintly hear the sound of the waves as they crash against the shore. My whole body goes limp. I am in the most beautiful transitional state when a shadow suddenly appears. I open my eyes, blinking as the sun blinds me. I stand up in the shallow end of the pool and look up. Darci is standing by the pool fence and Cam is next to her.

I get out of the pool and suddenly feel uncomfortable. I'm proud of how I look, and I'm certainly not embarrassed by my body, but this situation feels nothing more than awkward. I cross my arms over my body as I look at Cam.

"What are you doing here? Come over for round two?"

The question comes out a lot ruder than it sounded in my head. I feel bad so I drop my head and look at the floor.

"I just want to talk to you. We can't do this anymore, we need to fix things. I know you don't want to lose me, and despite how I've been feeling, I don't want to lose you either. Please just talk to me. Are you feeling better?"

I look at Darci, who is watching us closely. I ask her to go inside, but she protests.

"But I want to swim."

I walk over to her and put my hands on her shoulders.

"Darci, listen to me. Go inside! You can swim in a minute."

She pushes my hands off her shoulders and backs away from me. I can tell she's going to yell at me.

"Why don't you go inside? I didn't stuff up your relationship, so why should I have to suffer?"

I can't be bothered arguing with her.

"Fine, have it your way. We'll go inside. Stay in the shade."

She sticks her tongue out at me as we walk past her.

I wrap a towel around my waist and we sit in the lounge room that overlooks the backyard. I keep my eye on Darci, as a way to distract myself from the conversation I am about to have. We sit there waiting for each other to talk while the awkwardness fills the room. This feeling has become all too familiar. Finally, when we can't stand the silence any longer, Cam asks me a question I'm not expecting.

"Do you remember the first time I told you I loved you?"

"Of course I do. I'll never forget that day. It was one of the happiest days of my life."

He takes my hands and moves closer to me.

"That's exactly how I feel too. I was nervous telling you that for first time, but I knew from a young age that I loved you. I always have, nothing will ever change that. I know we've been through a lot recently, but I just want to fix things once and for all so we can move on."

I know he is right. It is time to sit down and sort through everything. Otherwise we will stay in the same cycle, and eventually it will tear us apart for good. I certainly don't want that. I have to ask about Heather though. I need to find out the truth, and he is the only one who can tell me. I look down at the floorboards, too scared to look at him.

"Did you sleep with her?"

"No. We stayed in the same bed, but I wouldn't do anything. She tried to kiss me and she wanted more, but I wouldn't go there, ever. I ended up letting her stay in my bed and I went into Gavin's old room. Even when we fight, I'd never consider cheating on you. I don't ever think about kissing someone else. You're the only one I want to be with."

I feel some sense of relief knowing nothing happened, but I still find myself questioning if it is true. Is this my karma? This is exactly how Cam would have felt when I told him about Ryan. Heck, he probably still feels the same now.

"I didn't understand it before. I mean, I didn't know how it felt, but now I do. I was so stupid to do this. I never want to lose you. I know it's hard to understand, but I really did do all of this to protect you. Ryan was just there when you couldn't be, but I can see why you couldn't be. I know it would have been easier if he was female, but there is nothing there other than a friendship. I promise."

"I know. If I'm honest I definitely don't like it, but I also know you're protecting me from lying. As long as it's nothing more than a friendship, you can confide in him. One condition though: I want to meet him."

I hug him and feel a weight lift off my shoulders.

"Okay. You can meet him tomorrow, if you want. I'll tell you everything, but I'll tell you in a way that doesn't require you to lie. Soon no one will have to lie anyway. I'm going to tell my mum. I can't take the sneaking around anymore."

"That's a good idea. Once you've told her, do you think you'll need Ryan? Once everyone knows, no one's going to have to lie, right?"

I bite my lip and look out towards Darci.

"I guess. But I can't just tell him to piss off, can I? He's been there for me, and as much as you're going to hate it, I'd still like him to help me."

I look through my eyelashes, hoping to see Cam's reaction. After he lets out a deep breath, he lets me know where he stands.

"Yeah, I guess you're right. I'm sure I'll feel better when I meet him. Anyway, Dakota called me. She didn't want you to know. She said she's never seen you as broken as you were on Monday when you got to Sydney. I'm sorry I pushed you away. I was just angry. We've both apologised now, so I think we should move on. If that's what you want?"

Geez, is there anyone my sister hasn't spoken to?

"It's been a rough week, but I accept your apology if you accept mine? I just want to move on too. Life has been miserable without you in it."

"I accept your apology, and I love you. Let's never fight again."

I giggle.

"Deal!"

After we clear the air, we join Darci by the pool. I hear my phone go off, so I get up and leave Cam with Darci while I read the message. It is from Declan.

Hey, I finished work early. If you're home, I can come and get you?

I look over at Cam, who is watching me closely. I approach him and kneel down next to him.

"You're going to hate me, but is there any way you can stay here with Darci for an hour or two? Declan's going to take me back to our old house."

He looks at me as he raises his eyebrows.

"Long story. I'll explain when I get back, but I really need to go."

Cam kisses my forehead and nods.

"Go and do whatever you've got to do. I'll stay here, and when you get back, we can get dinner or something."

I smile and kiss him.

"Thank you. I'll see you soon."

I run up the stairs and go into my room as I quickly reply to Declan.

I'm home. I'll just get ready. Beep when you get here.

I send the message and frantically run around, trying to get changed. I throw my wet hair into a bun before pulling denim shorts and a black singlet over my bathers. I throw on my Converse and a minute later I hear Declan beep. I run down the stairs, almost bumping into Darci.

"Is that Declan? Where are you going? Can I come?"

This family really does ask too many questions at once!

"Yes, somewhere and no, you can't come. Cam's staying here with you. Go swim or play Wii or something. We will be back soon."

I run through the door as Darci tries to protest. I jump into Declan's car as quickly as I can.

"Go! Darci will be out here in a second and you know how quickly she moves. If she gets into the car we're going to have to take her with us."

Just as Declan begins reversing I see the front door fly open. Darci runs out with Cam chasing after her. We pull out of the driveway just in time. Declan and I burst out laughing as we see Darci yelling at us in the middle of the street. As we drive to our old house, I tell Declan about the letter I found. We discuss it, going over every detail, trying to dissect everything. We soon pull into our old street and memories begin flooding back. I turn to my brother.

"I don't know if I can do this. What if we find something? What if the owners don't let us in?"

Declan pulls into the familiar driveway.

"It's okay. I called our old number earlier today, it's still connected to this house. I spoke to the owners. They've lived here since we left, they're the same people who bought the house all those years ago. They're expecting us, so let's go."

I take a deep breath and unbuckle the seatbelt. I get out of the car and follow Declan who knocks on the front door. A lady opens it.

"Hello, you must be Declan and Delilah. I'm Katherine. My husband had to pop out, so it's just me. Please, come in."

We walk through the front door, go into the dining room, and see that the house is still set out just the same as it was when we lived there.

I can't even describe the feelings that hit me as I walk inside. It almost doesn't feel the same, yet it feels overwhelmingly comfortable. It feels like home. Memory after memory hits me, each one becoming more visible, and my emotions are running high. Katherine is an older lady who looks at least sixty. Her shoulder-length hair is grey, and she wears glasses. She is short and thin, and she's wearing a long flowing skirt and a white top. She gives us a moment to go through the house.

"Feel free to walk around. My grandkids are out with my husband, so you can go into any of the rooms. Just don't touch anything."

We thank her before walking through the hallway. I reach a door, knowing that behind it is the room Dakota and I used to share. I open the door and walk in. It looks different, yet it feels the same. The walls, which used to be a lilac colour, are now painted light pink and there is only one bed by the window. The floor has colouring books and toys scattered everywhere. I suddenly see Dakota and me hiding under my bed: my dad is in one of his bad moods and he is fighting with my mum. They are screaming at each other. Dakota is crying and I have her in my arms, singing to her so it distracts her. I try to get rid of the memory as I walk through the rest of the house. Declan and I sit at the dining table with Katherine, and she hands us a cup of tea. We talk to her about why we came back. Well, Declan does most of the talking. I am lost for words, so I just sit there in silence. I suddenly remember the letter I found from Helen. I interrupt my brother as he is in the middle of a sentence.

"Sorry, I have to ask: did you ever receive any mail for anyone who used to live here?"

Katherine looks over at me and smiles.

"Yes, dear. I got quite a lot of mail for your parents. I did try to forward it to them, but I didn't have an address. There were a lot of cards. I made sure they weren't important before I threw them out."

I look down at my tea, which is now cold.

There goes any hope of finding Helen, I think to myself. Suddenly, Katherine interrupts my thoughts.

"Actually, that reminds me: I was meant to tell you earlier, I actually knew your mother. She went to school with my daughter. I used to call her when I got mail for her, but she would never answer my calls. She did pick something up one day, but after that I never heard from her again. I got another letter the other day. It was addressed to your mum, I was going to send it back, but since you're here I'll give it to you and you can pass it along to your mother."

Katherine gets up from her chair and walks into the kitchen. She opens a drawer and pulls a white envelope out.

"Here you go. It's all yours."

I turn the envelope over, and notice it's from Helen. I can't believe it. It actually has her address on it.

"Oh my God, Declan. This is her."

I look over at my brother, who looks as shocked as I do. Katherine has no idea what is going on.

"Thank you for allowing us to come back to our old home. You have no idea how much it has helped."

"You're welcome, my darling. I'm glad it helped."

After thanking Katherine again, we get back into the car and head home.

Declan turns to me.

"What are you going to do?"

I look at the letter in my hand.

"I know exactly what I've got to do, I've got to go and see her. This is what I've been waiting for, this is the answer I've been looking for. This lady knows where Dad is, and by the end of this, I hope I will too."

As we head home, my mind begins to race. I have to try to process everything before I tell Cam. Oh shit, that reminds me, Cam and Ryan are meeting tomorrow. This is either going to be a good or a bad thing and, for once, I hope it's a good thing. I look down at the unopened letter in my hands. Maybe now I'll be able to take the first step in finding the location of my father.

CHAPTER TEN

RIPTIDE

Declan and I pull into my mum's driveway after our meeting with Katherine. Thankfully her car isn't there, which means we have time to come up with a backstory. Darci, like Dakota, has difficulty keeping a secret, and we know we can't tell her the truth.

The minute we step inside the house, Cam approaches us.

"Oh, thank God you're back. Your sister's been a handful. She's been quizzing me the whole time you've been gone. She wouldn't relax, and she even tried to push me into the pool."

Declan laughs, thanks Cam for helping out, and goes to find Darci, while Cam and I go to my room. I leave the door open in case Darci tries to find us. If she comes anywhere near the stairs, I'll know. I need to be alert since I'm about to tell Cam everything I've just discovered. Before I even get a chance to fill Cam in, he tells me to close my eyes.

"Why?"

"Just do it. I've got a surprise for you."

I pretend to close my eyes, but I'm peeking through them.

"It's not a puppy, is it? You know my mum wouldn't approve of another dog."

Cam puts something into my hands.

"It's not a dog. Open your eyes."

My curiosity peaks. I open my eyes, look into my hands, and grab the tickets that are sitting there. I read the thick bold text in the middle of each ticket. They are tickets to see Vance Joy, tomorrow night.

"Oh my God."

Cam has the biggest smile on his face.

"I know he's your favourite singer, and I know you missed out on getting tickets when they went on sale. I wanted to surprise you earlier, but then all that other stuff happened, and I didn't know when I could give them to you. I planned to give them to you when we were down south, but obviously, the timing wasn't right. How do you feel? Are you excited?"

I jump up and give him the biggest hug.

"I'm beyond excited! Thank you."

I sit back down next to Cam and realise I have to tell him about where Declan and I have just been.

"What's up?"

I take a quick breath.

"Declan and I did it. We went back to our old house today."

"As in the one you lived in with your dad?"

I nod.

"Declan suggested that we go there because of the letter I found. I won't bore you with all the details, but I found a letter from a lady who knows my parents, mainly my dad. She's been trying to see us, but I can only assume my mum hasn't replied, or isn't keen on her seeing us."

I get up and take the letter out of the pocket of my dressing gown. I knew no one would find it there, it was the only safe place I could think of to hide it. I hand it to Cam who reads through it as I walk back and forth in my room.

"We went to the house today and we asked the owner, Katherine, if she had kept any mail. I honestly didn't expect her to. She said she used to get some letters and cards. She told us she knew our mum. She tried to get her to get the mail, but she refused. She picked that letter up though, which is bizarre. The letter Katherine gave me today is from the same lady who wrote the one you're reading now. It's got her address on it. I think she might be related to my dad. Which makes sense, my mum would avoid these people at all costs since she knew they'd lead straight to my dad."

Cam looks up from the letter.

"This is insane. In a good way, I think. I get why your mum avoids those people. She cut your dad off for a reason, but maybe this lady knows where your dad is. What are you going to do?"

I sit back down next to him.

"I've got to think about it, I guess. I mean, this is what I've been looking for: a clue to the whereabouts of my dad. Now I've got it, I can take the first step in actually finding him, but I'm scared."

"Why? What's scaring you?"

"Everything. What if I find him? Then what? Do I go and see him? He told me not to find him. Pretty much all of me wants to, but there's a tiny part that's warning me not to do this. I get that this is risky, and I know what I'm putting on the line to find him. I'm not sure how my mum will react to all of this. Even if she asks me not to do it, I'm going to do it, but what if he pushes me away again? I don't know if I could handle that."

Cam puts his arm around my shoulder and pulls me towards him. I rest my head on his shoulder as he tries to comfort me.

"It'll be okay. You've got to do what's best for you. I've known you long enough to know that this has always been something you've wanted to do. You have a right to see your father, so if you find him, then take the risk. If it fails, I'll be here for you, all of us will be, you know that."

"Yeah, you're right. I can't keep wondering 'what if?' I just hope my mum understands. I'm not trying to go behind her back, or upset her, I just want to see him. I want to make sure he's okay"

That night Cam stays over. We have dinner with my mum, Declan and Darci, and we even go for a night swim. After Declan goes home, I quickly shower, making sure I wash the chlorinated smell out of my hair. After drying my hair, I throw on my pj's and snuggle into bed with Cam. I instantly feel the same sense of safety, comfort, and love I always feel when he stays with me. We're finally back on track, and it feels amazing, but now my mind keeps thinking about how Cam will react when he meets Ryan tomorrow.

~

The morning of the day that we're meeting Ryan drags on. Cam sleeps in until 11:00 a.m., but I've been up since eight. I tossed and turned all night, and the same thing happened this morning, so I gave up on the idea of sleeping and got up instead. I've spent the last three hours aimlessly walking around the house, trying to find something to do to distract myself. I've spent an hour helping my mum plan Darci's surprise sweet sixteen birthday party and another hour putting our DVDs in alphabetical order. When I have finished with the DVDs, I go back to my room to find Cam waking up.

We now have two hours and thirty minutes to kill before we have to meet Ryan. We make brunch and watch an episode of *Entourage* and, before we know it, we are on our way to the beach. My nerves have all but taken over my body.

I've informed Ryan that Cam will be coming with me. When Cam and I get to the beach, we head towards Ryan, who is sitting in the same spot where I usually meet him. Cam is holding my hand and, as we get closer to Ryan, he squeezes it. I squeeze it back and offer him a comforting smile, although I doubt it'll help.

When I look at Ryan, I notice he's cracking his knuckles while starring off towards the horizon. When we get closer he turns and spots us. He jumps to his feet and smiles as we approach him. I look at Cam, who is closely watching Ryan. We stop, and the awkwardness fills the space between the three of us. I try to clear the knot in my throat, but I can't. After clearing my throat again, I introduce the boys to each other.

"Cam, this is Ryan. Ryan, this is Cam."

I look back and forth between the boys, waiting for one of them to react. Then Ryan extends his hand to Cam.

"Despite the circumstances, it's nice to meet you."

I know Ryan is being sincere, I just hope Cam sees that too. Cam finally takes Ryan's hand and shakes it.

"Nice to meet you, too."

We sit down on the sand, and I fill Ryan in about everything that has happened over the last few days. I feel awkward and uncomfortable, but when I see Cam relax, I'm able do the same. After explaining everything, Cam finally speaks, which he hasn't done since we sat down.

"Babe, do you mind giving us a few minutes? I think we should talk to each other, one on one."

I look over at Ryan, who nods.

"Sure, I'll go for a walk. Let me know when you're ready for me to come back."

I get up and make my way down to a quiet spot on the beach. I stop about thirty feet away from where the boys are sitting. I can't see them clearly, but I can see they are talking, which I hope is a good sign. I sit down on the sand and pull out the letter Katherine passed on to me. I tear the envelope open and begin to read it.

"Hello Deidra. I don't know how many of my letters you've received. I know you got my last one, of course, because you were there when I gave it to you."

Wait. Helen gave the letter I found in my mum's room to her personally? That doesn't make sense. Why was she sending them to our old address? Unless my mum told her we still lived in the old house? Or maybe my dad thought we still lived there. This is hurting my head: question after question keeps arising, but where are the answers? I continue reading, hoping something good will come from this letter.

"I know it's hard to hear about Tony, but I know you two still love each other. You've done what is best for yourself and your children, and I respect that. Please know that I'm not contacting you to upset you. I'm doing it because I want to be a part of your children's lives. I believe they should be allowed to get to know someone who's related to their father. After all, I'm all Tony has left, and I'm sure they have many unanswered questions. If I can help to answer them, I'd be happy to do so. I hope you understand, and please remember: I'll always be here for you. I always have been, and that won't ever change. All my love, Helen."

Well, there it is. She is related to my father somehow. I know that she will be able to help me, and now I have a way to contact her. I look over at Cam and Ryan; they are still chatting, so I pull my phone out of my pocket and dial the number on the back of the envelope. After five rings, a woman answers.

"Hello? Helen speaking."

It's really her! My mind starts racing. I haven't even thought about what I should say. I hear her voice again.

"Hello?"

Without thinking, I answer.

"Hi, sorry, this is totally random, but I think you know my father."

I wait for the woman to answer, but when she doesn't I decide to continue.

"Um, sorry. My father's name is ..."

"Tony. Your father's name is Tony. Is that Delilah?"

How does she know it's me?

"Yes. It's Delilah. How did you know?"

"Oh, sweetheart. I've been expecting this phone call for a long time. Both your parents told me if any of you were going to contact me, it would be you."

I don't know how to answer her, but I try my best.

"Really? I'm sorry. No one's ever told me about you. I don't have much time, but I'd really like to meet you. Would it be all right to meet for coffee or something?"

I hold my breath and hope for the best.

"Yes, that would be lovely. I am home all day next Sunday. If you're free, please stop by. I assume you have my address now you've got my number?"

I look over at the boys. Cam is waving at me, indicating it is clear to go back. I hold up my hand, signalling I'll be over in a minute.

"Sunday is perfect, and yes, I've got your address. Thank you. I'll see you then."

I put my phone and the letter back into the pocket of my leggings and make my way back over to the boys, hoping everything is fine between them.

When I reach them, they are laughing. This is not what I was expecting, although it is a good sign, and a relief.

I sit next to Cam.

"Hi. How did your chat go? Do you want to hit each other?"

They laugh and Cam answers.

"No, we don't. We talked, and we're all good. We might even hang out one day."

I laugh, assuming they are joking, but when I look at them I see they aren't.

"Oh, you're serious?"

I look between them.

"Yep. We feel like we can be friends. I mean, Cam seems like a cool guy, so we will definitely go out for a beer one night."

I look at Ryan, force an awkward smile and try to make sense of everything.

"Well, that sounds good. I didn't expect you guys to hate each other, although I kind of thought you might. If you can see a friendship between the two of you, then that's good. That's better than good, that's great!"

We all go quiet and after a few minutes of silence, I tell the boys about my phone call with Helen. Before too long, Cam and I have to head home. We still have to get ready for the Vance Joy concert, and we have reservations for dinner at 6:00 p.m. The boys exchange numbers and, after I hug Ryan, we head home. I breathe a sigh of relief. That went better than I expected, and it feels good knowing I don't have to lie anymore. Well, I'm still lying to my mum, but it won't be for much longer. Soon everyone will know the truth.

When we get to my place, Cam walks me to the door.

"Hey, I'm going to go home to get ready. I'll be back to pick you up at 5:30 p.m. I'll see you then, okay? Thanks for today. I'm glad I met Ryan. He seems like a nice guy. I'll see you soon."

He plants a kiss on my lips before running out the gate to his car. I wonder why he is in such a hurry to get home. My mind starts racing. Maybe he isn't so happy about today. Maybe he is just pretending so I don't feel bad. I have to stop analysing things like this. I head inside and check the time; it is just after 3:00 p.m. Perfect! I head upstairs and take my jacket, shoes and socks off. I put the new letter in with the other one and climb into bed. I set my alarm for 4:30 p.m. That way I can have a much-needed nap and still get ready in time. I put my head on my pillow and within seconds I am asleep again.

I've never feared going to sleep, but the closer I get to finding my father, the more dreams I have. The only problem is, they aren't necessarily dreams, they are memories from when he was still around. I don't understand why I keep having them. Sometimes they come out of nowhere, and other times they hit me when I think about him.

Today is one of those days when it hits me after visiting my old home. This time we're back in our old house. My brothers, Dakota and I are playing hide and seek. It is Declan's turn to count and I am hiding behind the curtain in my parents' room when I hear him yell.

"Daddy's home!"

I throw the curtain in the air and run towards the door. He really is home. I run straight into his arms, and he picks me up off the ground.

"Hey, kiddo. I've missed you."

I wrap my arms around his neck, squeezing him as tightly as I can. I don't want to let him go. I know if I do, he will leave again. I can smell the whisky and cigarettes on his breath, and on his clothes. I don't really know what those smells are when I'm younger, but they are distinct and they smell disgusting. He's home though, so I don't care. He puts me back on the floor and looks into my eyes.

"Delilah, I've got to go on a holiday. Everything's going to be okay, but I'll be gone for a while. When I get back, I'll be able to be the father you deserve. You're my buddy, aren't you?"

"I'm your best friend, Daddy!"

He smiles before continuing.

"I know, and you're mine too. I need you to promise me that you'll look out for everyone, especially your sisters. Always be there for them, don't ever turn your back on them. They are all you have in this world, so don't make the same mistakes as me. I love you, Delilah. I'll see you real soon, okay?"

I start to cry.

"Please don't go, Daddy. I don't want you to leave. I can come with you."

He hugs me again, and I notice he has tears in his eyes. Why is he crying?

"No, honey. Not this time. You have to stay here. Look, I got some toys for you. There are a few colouring books too. Go and show your brothers and your sisters, and make sure you share with them. I love you. I always will, don't you ever forget that."

He hands me a bag and hugs me like he's never hugged me before. I run over to my siblings to show them what he got for us.

I hear the door close, and he is gone. I run to the window and see him get in the car. I start screaming.

"No, please don't go. Daddy, please come back!"

~

I wake up, gasping for air. I sit up and grab my water bottle, quickly drinking the contents. When it's empty, I get up from my bed and go over to the window in my room, focusing on my breathing. Once I have calmed myself down, I look up to the sky. I start talking out loud.

"Liar! Everything he said was a lie. He was never coming back."

I hear a voice that's not my own.

"Delilah, what are you talking about?"

I turn around to see my mum standing in my doorway.

"Oh Mum, you scared me. Nothing. I was having a nap and I just had a bad dream. I'm fine. What's the time?"

I have to ask her something to distract her from asking more questions, I know she will continue to question me until I tell her the truth. Usually I can avoid her, but this time, I can't. She has blocked off my only exit.

"It's quarter past four and you've been asleep for a while. Are you sure you're okay?"

I notice my mum looks tired.

"Yeah, Mum. I promise. I'm fine. Do you want to help me pick out something to wear to the concert? I have no idea what to wear."

I know this is my only chance to distract her, and hopefully it is enough. I see the fatigued look fade away, replaced by a smile and a look of excitement.

"Of course. I'd love to."

We spend the next fifteen minutes going through my clothes before settling on my black Converse, one of my many pairs of black ripped skinny leg jeans, a plain grey high-low top and my black faux leather jacket in case I get cold. I quickly shower before doing my makeup. I curl my hair, go back to my room, put my clothes on and spray some perfume on my wrist and neck.

Once I'm ready, I grab my bag and my phone and head downstairs. I am hoping Cam will be waiting for me, but he isn't. At precisely half past five I hear him pull up in the driveway.

"Is that Cam? Why on earth isn't he coming inside? Are you two fighting again?"

I unlock the front door.

"No, Mum, we're not fighting. We're on a bit of a time crunch. We've still got to have dinner and get to the concert. It starts at eight and you know parking when a concert is on is ridiculous. I'll be home later. Love you!"

She comes towards the door, poking her head out so she can wave at Cam.

"Have fun. You look beautiful. Love you."

She kisses my cheek. I close the door behind me and head to Cam's car. After dinner, Cam and I head to Challenge Stadium, where we manage to get one of the last parking spots available. After paying for our parking, we head towards the entrance gate. We wait in line for twenty minutes, then finally reach the front. Our tickets get scanned, and we head in to find our seats. We aren't too far away from the stage, so we can see everything. We sit and talk as the audience piles in and the seats quickly fill up. At eight, when Vance hits the stage, I look at Cam and smile.

"Thank you. He really is my favourite singer, and it means a lot that you got us tickets."

"I knew you'd love it, and you're welcome."

A minute later the lights go out and Vance begins to sing.

The concert is amazing. I get to hear all my favourite songs, and I get to see my favourite singer live. Nothing can top this night! Or at least that's what I think. When we get back to the car, Cam looks at me.

"So, there's a reason I ran off this afternoon. I have another surprise for you. I need you to put this sleep mask on. I know it sounds weird, but please trust me."

I giggle.

"Of course I trust you. Pass it here."

I take the sleep mask out of his hands and put it over my eyes. Once it's secured, I hear Cam start the car. We speak the whole time we are driving, but Cam won't give anything away, no matter how hard I try to get it out of him. After what feels like an eternity, we finally stop.

"I'm going to get out of the car and come and get you. Hold on."

I sit in the passenger seat, patiently waiting for Cam to open the door. He opens the door and grabs my hand as I step out of the car. I listen to him as he directs me to a spot before telling me to stop.

"Take the sleep mask off when you're ready."

I gently pull the mask off of my eyes, open them and stand there in shock. Oh my God. We are standing in the middle of my uncle's paddock: the same paddock where we had our first date. He has literally recreated our first date.

"You know we celebrate our five-year anniversary soon? We will do something else for that but, after the last few months, I thought we needed something special now. So, I planned this whole night, the concert included. I went to your uncle and asked him for his help, and he suggested recreating our first date."

"Thank you. This is perfect."

We get into the back of the ute and snuggle up under the blanket. When we're comfortable, we lie down and rest our heads against the pillows. As we lie there, I start to think about my future, which has constantly been on my mind since I got back from Sydney, and I feel like getting some advice from Cam.

"You know, tonight made me realise something. I looked around when Vance was singing *Georgia*, and I saw thousands of people who were all different connected by one thing: music. It makes me want to fight for my dream even more. I love writing and singing, but I've always let my fears stop me. I feel like I have nothing to lose now, and maybe I am good enough to succeed. It would be the most amazing feeling to step on stage and see so many people there to hear me sing."

I proceed to tell Cam about Melody and the opportunity she has offered me.

"Babe that's amazing! You have to do it. You don't have anything to lose, and you really do have an incredible talent. Don't let anyone stop you. Go for it! You know we're going to be here to support you."

I rest my head on Cam's chest as I look into his eyes.

"That really means a lot to me. I'll go and talk to my uncle in the morning. We should get some sleep, though."

Cam agrees and we snuggle up again and fall asleep.

The sun begins to rise just after 6:30 a.m. When I open my eyes, I notice Cam is already awake. He is leaning against the back of the ute, so I move towards him, wrap my arms around his midsection and rest my chin on his shoulder.

"Good morning, beautiful. I must say that was the most magical night. I'm glad I got to spend it with you."

I kiss his cheek before I answer him.

"Me too. Thanks for planning everything."

"Of course. Anything for you. I didn't pack anything for breakfast, but we could go somewhere?"

I yawn before answering him.

"If you don't mind I think I'll drive the ute back to the house and go and speak to my uncle. I want to see what he says about the contract Melody sent me, and I might try to set up a time to record some songs. Plus, I've got to go home and get ready for work. I go back today."

Cam turns around to face me, then helps me down from the ute.

"Oh yeah. I keep forgetting it's Monday. I've got some stuff to do anyway, so I'll call you later. You can tell me how things go with your uncle."

"Yep. I'll talk to you then."

I watch Cam head to his car; he waves goodbye before driving off. I secure the back of the ute and head towards the house. After parking the car, I go through the back door of the house and head into the kitchen, where I find my aunt and uncle sitting at the table, sipping coffee.

"Morning."

I pour some coffee for myself.

"Good morning, superstar. How are you today?"

I sit down next to my aunt and quickly hug her before looking at my uncle.

"I'm good, thank you. Cam says you helped him plan our secret date."

My uncle takes a sip of coffee and continues reading the paper.

"I might have had something to do with it."

He peeks up at me through his glasses and I smile at him.

"Thank you."

He winks at me before looking back down at the paper.

"Anything for you, superstar."

Ever since I was little, he has called me his little superstar and every year on my birthday he gives me a card that he draws a star on.

"Another star for you, my little superstar. One day you will be the world's superstar, and they will see what I've always seen."

The corners of my mouth turn up as I think about that memory, which reminds me I have to tell him about Melody.

"Uncle Derek, do you think we could go into your office? I've got something I want to talk to you about."

He puts his paper down and takes his glasses off.

"Sounds serious. Everything okay, love?"

"Yeah, everything's fine. It's just that, well, while I was in Sydney seeing Dakota, I met up with one of her friends who works for a talent agency. She's been scouting new musicians and, well, she wants me to send her a demo and if she likes it she'll offer me a contract."

My aunty lets out a little squeal.

"Delilah, that's incredible! Congratulations! Oh, we always knew you'd make it!"

She leans over and hugs me as I laugh at my uncle's expression. He looks over at me and laughs with me before he focuses his attention on her.

"Calm down, love. She hasn't signed any contracts yet! Have you?"

"No, I haven't. I want you to look over it with me."

He gets up from his chair and signals me to follow him to his study. I quickly hug my aunty again before heading down the hallway. Once we're inside his office he signals me to sit down in one of his comfy swivel chairs. I move from side to side as I wait for him to print out the contract. I haven't had time to print it, or more to the point I just don't want to tell my mum or sister about it until I know what I am doing. He goes through everything with me.

"Alright love, it's a legit contract, and it's a legit business. From what I can see this is just a proposal for now. It's still a contract, but it's an outline of what they want. Essentially, it's asking you to record a six song demo track, they want a mix of original songs and cover songs of your choice. If they feel you'll fit in with their business, they want to sign you up to a one-year deal. You'd record an album and film music videos. If you sell enough albums, you can even go on tour."

Tour! I haven't really thought about being good enough to go on a tour. I love the idea of touring, and I thought about it last night after the concert, but am I even good enough to put on a concert? I look at my uncle, who is closely watching me.

"What is it, love?"

I start to fidget with my fingers.

"This is so exciting. I can't see myself doing anything else with my life, but I don't want someone I don't know managing me. I know it's her job, but I've always told myself that if I ever got to the stage where someone could represent me, well, I'd always hoped it would be you."

My uncle puts the pieces of paper down.

"I'd love nothing more than to be a part of your journey if that is what you want. Do you have Melody's number? I'll call her and see what we can do."

I hand him her business card, which I've kept in my purse since Melody gave it to me in Sydney. He dials the number and spends the next twenty minutes talking to her.

"Done. Melody and I have agreed to co-manage you. If you're ready, we can record your demo CD in the studio here, then we'll send it to her. The rest is up to the company. But we'll do what we need to help you succeed. You need to commit to this, there's no backing out. Are you ready?"

I take a deep breath. Is this really happening? I always said I'd only do it if my uncle helped me and now he is willing to be my co-manager. Nothing is standing in my way now. When I was in Sydney, I sang a cover of one of my favourite songs, *Nothing* by The Script, and Dakota recorded me. That's about as far as my music career has gone, and I was nervous enough just performing for my sister. I have a feeling my life is going to change, and I know that maybe it is time to take the risk of a lifetime.

Chapter Eleven

Perfection Perception

I head to work a few hours after talking to my uncle. I've agreed to sign the proposal, and we have set up a time for me to go into the studio to record my demo tracks. My uncle has given me a week to sit down and think about what songs I want to use. I have to choose three songs that show my range and three songs I've written myself, to show my creativity. Despite feeling nervous, I also feel on top of the world, and I can't wait to get started.

I'm in the middle of my shift at Boom Clap. Hayley and I spent the first half of my shift catching up, she keeps looking at me with a funny look on her face, but I just figure she's excited for her upcoming holiday. It's a relatively quiet day, so we don't have much to do. Hayley is serving a customer, so I stock some of the shelves; I am minding my own business when two girls, who look like they are the same age as Darci, approach me.

"Oh my God, are you Delilah Walker?"

"Um, yes, do I know you?"

They start jumping up and down.

"We love your video! You're incredible! When will you be putting up a new one?"

I am so confused, but they are looking at me with such excitement that I just make something up.

"Uh, soon?"

They start giggling and jumping up and down again.

"We can't wait! Can we get a photo with you?"

Hayley suddenly approaches us and takes one of the girls iPhones off of her.

"Uh, sure."

I stand in the middle of them, smiling, while Hayley takes the photo. They thank me and hug me before leaving the shop. Hayley is now laughing.

"Okay, have I missed something?"

She stops laughing and looks at me with a confused look.

"Fame suits you. But do you really don't know why they recognised you?"

I shake my head, so she continues.

"The video you posted on MusicNow is getting a ton of views. You've become pretty popular. I know you probably wanted it to be a surprise, but you could have warned me."

She notices I still look confused.

"You did post that video, didn't you?"

"Hayley, I genuinely don't know what you're talking about. What video?"

She pulls her phone out and brings up the MusicNow home page. Hayley types my name in the search bar and a video pops up.

"What the hell? This is so embarrassing! I didn't post this."

"Really? Who posted it then? You shouldn't be embarrassed. You've got such an amazing voice. You should be proud; I know I am. We all are."

I look at her, worried.

"We?"

Hayley looks at the ground.

"Um, yeah well before you started this morning I kind of showed a few people in the staff room. They were blown away by your voice. I shared it on Facebook too, to show everyone how talented you are. I'm so sorry, I thought you'd posted it yourself, so I assumed you were confident enough for it to be shared with the world."

Hayley looks like she is about to cry, her cheeks are flushed with red.

"It's fine, honestly. Don't feel bad. Someone obviously thought I needed a kick-start, so they took the first step for me. Do you mind if I finish early, I know I've only just gotten back, but …"

She instantly looks relieved.

"Of course. But are you sure it's fine? I can remove the post if you want?"

I smile.

"Honestly, Haylz. It's fine. Thank you for supporting me. You're a great friend."

"Of course. I always knew you were going to be a star. You're about to start such an amazing journey. Don't forget me when you're a famous pop star!"

I laugh.

"I could never forget you, but one step at a time. I don't even want to think about being a pop star, yet!"

I go into the staff room and clock off, grab my stuff and head for the door, waving to Hayley on my way out. I pull my Ray Ban aviators out of my bag and put them over my eyes. As I am walking to my car, another girl recognises me. After signing an autograph and taking a photo with her, I get into my car. I pull out my phone and find Dakota's number. It rings twice before she answers.

"Hey sis, what's going …"

"Why did you do it?"

I'm trying my best to stay calm, but my anger is starting to rise.

"Why did I do what?"

"Dakota, don't act like you don't know what I'm talking about! Why did you post that video of me singing? That's not your decision to make. You took that chance away from me! Why would you do that? I would have taken that first step in my own time, but you've practically opened the door and pushed me through it before I'm ready!"

I wait a few seconds for her reply, but she is silent.

"Dakota, don't ignore me! Answer me!"

"Seriously, Delilah. Do you want to have this fight? I could apologise for doing it, but I'm not sorry. I'm not sorry at all. I'm sick of hearing you go on about how you want to sing, but you won't do anything about it. I get that you're scared, but if you don't try, if you don't put your music, your voice, out there, then no one will ever see or hear how talented you are. Do you not get that? You have such an amazing voice, but you won't let anyone hear it. It took you nineteen years before you felt comfortable enough to sing in front of me, and I'm one of your best friends. Heck, I'm more than that: I'm your sister! I didn't take the decision away from you. I made it happen. If I didn't open the door and push you through it, you'd be sitting on your hands, not doing a damn thing about it. You can hate me all you want, but now your voice is out there, and I'm not taking the video down. I asked Melody before I did it and she thought it was a good idea. She watched the video and was blown away by your voice! This is a good thing. Stop being a bitch for two seconds and realise I didn't do it to hurt you. I did it because I know what you're capable of, and I freaking love you. Jesus, I did it to help you."

I sigh. I know she's right, but I'm terrified of putting myself out there like this. Writing songs and singing is the only thing I can see myself doing with my life. It is what I want to do, but my own self-doubt has always stopped me from committing to it. I've only ever sung in front of my uncle, and it took me so long to even do that. I mean I have sung multiple karaoke songs, but I only ever did it with other people, like Nia and Darci. I had finally found the courage to sing in front of my sister in Sydney, but she'd posted the video online, for the world to see, without even asking me. My fears of not being good enough haunt me. But my sister is right. She didn't do it to hurt me, she did it because it's time to take the first step.

"I'm sorry. I know you didn't mean to hurt me. The truth is I just don't think I'm good enough, so putting myself out there scares the hell out of me. This is what I love, this is my passion, but what if I'm not good enough?"

"Delilah, if you don't make it, it doesn't matter. As long as you try, and as long as you continue to do what you love, then you're going to win. You think you don't have what it takes to be a professional musician? Haven't you heard your own voice? It's incredible, and the rest of the world thinks that too! Haven't you seen the reaction to your video? People are getting behind you, they want you to succeed. It would be a mistake if you don't at least try to see where this may take you. We're only given one life, so don't regret anything. Look how many people told me I couldn't model, yet here I am. I'm in Sydney, in the middle of a shoot for a company who want to offer me a regular contract. How can you say that dreams don't come true?"

She is right. I'll regret it if I don't try.

"I know you're right. This is a huge opportunity for me. I just don't want to stuff it up. I just want to take it one day at a time, and I don't want to get too far ahead of myself. I appreciate all your love and support. Why was Melody so keen on posting my video anyway? Doesn't that defeat the purpose of me recording a demo track?"

"Nope. She wants to get your name out there, so you already have a following, so people will get behind you and support you. That's what people are doing. She already knows she's going to sign you. As soon as she saw the video, she saw first-hand what I'd been talking about. There's a panel of people who make the final decision with Melody, so go and record your demo track, give it everything you've got, and blow them away."

I smile, but I feel the butterflies in my stomach when my sister mentions a panel of people. I decide not to think about it. I just need to focus on what songs to sing.

~

I have spent the past three days going through what feels like thousands of songs, before finally settling on three of my favourites. It's been almost impossible to pick just three, since I have so many songs I would love to sing. I sit down with my uncle and he agrees to my choices. I have settled on *Superheroes* by The Script, *Team* by Lorde and I couldn't go past a Vance Joy song, so I picked the first song I ever heard by him, which was *Fire and the Flood*.

After I have my three cover songs ready to go, I focus on picking three songs I've written myself. Thankfully, I've written a lot of songs over the past few years, so I have plenty of options. I choose *Wildfire*, which is the first song I ever wrote, although I have since edited it multiple times. I also pick *Grassroots*, which my uncle and I wrote together after my twenty-first birthday last July. My final song is *Somewhere Out There*, which I wrote about my father.

My uncle and I are happy with my choices. I have enough range to show the panel that I can sing different varieties of music. I've never wanted to be stuck with one genre, as I love lots of types of music. When we have the songs ready to go, I print out the lyrics to each one, and my uncle and I go over to the recording studio, ready to begin the recording process.

After warming up, I go into the booth where I'll be singing. I'm looking at my uncle through the glass that separates us when Cam walks in. He sits next to my uncle, smiles and pushes the button to communicate with me.

"I know this is a big deal for you. I've hardly heard you sing, and I want to be here to support you. Don't focus on me being here. Sing with all of your heart. I'm so proud of you."

I suddenly beam with happiness. I appreciate him being here, although it does make me even more nervous than I was before. I want to thank him, but I need to sing, otherwise I'll get too scared and bail. *It's now or never Delilah, you can do this.* I give my uncle the thumbs up, indicating that I am ready to record the first song. I take a deep breath, and as the music hits, I begin to sing.

Chapter Twelve

Sweet Sixteen

For the next few days, my uncle, Cam and I spend almost all of our time in the studio, working tirelessly to get my demo tracks recorded. After four long days, we are finally done and, despite feeling exhausted, I'm feeling better than ever. I'm excited to see where this journey takes me. Although I can't help but feel a weight on my shoulders: one I hope will disappear when I meet Helen.

It is now Saturday, and Darci's surprise party starts in a few hours. My mum and I have spent the majority of the morning running around our backyard preparing for the party, while Dylan and Declan have been keeping Darci busy at their house. When everything is set up, I grab my present for her and head to my brothers' house. Darci thinks we're just having dinner for her birthday. Little does she know our mum has planned the most amazing sweet sixteenth for her.

I pull into my brothers' driveway, head inside and find Darci playing with Max. Declan comes over to me as soon as I walk in. He hugs me and pulls me aside.

"So, I've got a surprise for everyone. Come into my room."

I try to figure out what he is up to as I follow him down the hallway. He opens the door and sitting on his bed is Dakota.

"Oh my God! What are you doing here? I thought you couldn't make it! That's what Mum said anyway. Does she know you're here?"

Dakota gets up and hugs me.

"Nope. Darci doesn't even know I'm here. Surprise!"

"Wait. How does she not know you're here? She's literally fifteen feet away from you."

My brother and sister laugh.

"I flew in last night. Declan picked me up, and I've been hiding here since I got back. There's a lock on the door so Declan told Darci he had to keep the door locked so Max couldn't get in."

Now it is my turn to laugh.

"So, you're telling me that our now-sixteen-year-old sister believes you have to lock a door so a two kilo Pomeranian can't get in? Does he have a habit of jumping up and opening doors now?"

"Actually, he's only a puppy, so he's not even two kilos yet. But yes, she did believe it. I'm a convincing actor."

We all laugh as I turn to face my sister again.

"So, when are you going to tell everyone you're here? Darci's going to lose it. She was devastated when you told her you weren't coming."

"We don't know, to be honest. Declan and I have been discussing it. Do I surprise her now, or do I wait and turn up at the house?"

I look between my sister and brother as we try to figure out what to do.

"We all know Darci isn't the best at keeping secrets, so maybe go over with Declan and surprise Mum at the same time?"

After we discuss how to get Dakota into the house to surprise my mum and sister, I head out to find Darci so I can give her the gift basket I have spent the past week filling for her.

"Hey Darci, come here. I want to give you your present."

I sit on the couch in the living room and Darci comes over. Declan joins us, and Dylan makes everyone a cup of tea.

"Now, I got this especially for you. I went all over Perth to get these things for you because I want you to feel good about yourself, but half of this stuff is only to be used on special occasions."

I hand her the basket, which I have wrapped in pink cellophane and an oversized purple ribbon. Darci peeks into the basket.

"Delilah, this is incredible!"

Without even opening it, she hugs me. As she starts opening each present in the basket, I explain what I've gotten her.

"I got you this playsuit to wear tonight. You should wear something extra special for your sweet sixteenth, and I know you've wanted a playsuit for a while. When I saw this one, I thought it was perfect for you."

I have picked a floral playsuit that has a white top. The pinks, blues and purples that flow through the shorts are stunning, and they are colours that suit Darci. I know she'll look beautiful in it.

"Thank you, it's beautiful. I love it. I know what shoes I can wear with it."

I look at the basket.

"Well, I got you shoes too. I wanted to get you a whole new outfit, shoes included, so I picked some out for you. They're at the bottom."

Darci pulls them out and looks at them. They are white and have little diamantes over the strap.

"These shoes are so much nicer than the ones I had in mind. Seriously, Delilah, you didn't have to do this."

I notice the sad expression take over her face.

"Hey, don't you dare be sad today. I wanted to do this for you, you deserve this, Darci. I got you one more thing. I don't want you to think you need makeup, because you don't, and trust me you will have plenty of time to learn about makeup as you get older. You know you're always welcome to use my stuff, but sometimes you need your own stuff, so I got you a few things to start you off. It's not much, but it's good to begin with. I'll do your hair and makeup tonight, okay?"

Darci sits there with the basket in her lap; she is looking at the ground. I thought this would make her happy. Have I done the complete opposite? She looks up and she has tears in her eyes. She throws her arms around my neck.

"Thank you. I really appreciate everything. I would love for you to do my hair and makeup."

"Come on, then. Let's go and get you ready, beautiful girl."

We go into the guest room. I put foundation on her face, followed by a bronze eye shadow, which makes her eyes pop. I put a bit of eyeliner over the eye shadow, which I follow up with some mascara. I put some blush and highlighter on, then a soft pink lipstick on her lips. It's more makeup that she's ever worn, but since it is a special occasion, I go all out. Finally, I curl her hair.

I join Declan and Dylan in the lounge room, and we wait for Darci. She comes out of the room and stands in front of us. She's looking between the three of us, waiting for any kind of reaction. She looks beautiful, and she has the most amazing glow surrounding her. Her energy is so positive and happy that you can feel it the minute she walks into the room.

"Well?" she nervously asks.

Dylan answers for the three of us. "Darci, you look stunning."

A confident smile spreads across her face, and we can tell she feels as beautiful as she looks. We take a few photos, and then it's time to reveal the surprise of her party before everyone starts arriving. Our brothers tell us they'll see us soon, we hug them and leave. It is now 5:30 p.m., and Darci's friends are due to arrive at 7:00 p.m. As we pull into the driveway, Darci notices our uncle's car parked in the driveway.

"I thought Uncle Derek was meeting us at the restaurant later."

She unbuckles her seatbelt and climbs out of the car.

"You know what he's like. He probably just wants to see you before dinner."

We walk through the house and make our way out the back. The backyard has been transformed into a fairy wonderland, with pink ribbons, balloons, tinsel, fairy lights and two giant, blow-up swans floating in the pool. Before Darci has a chance to catch a glimpse of the yard, I stop her.

"Close your eyes. I've got one more surprise for you. I'm going to guide you outside. Only open them when I say so."

Darci does as I say, and I carefully help her outside before stopping her by the door. I smile at my mum and our family - my aunties, uncles and cousins - who are standing by the pool with a 'Happy Birthday Darci' banner in their hands. After getting the nod from Mum, I tell Darci to open her eyes.

"Surprise!"

She looks at me, instantly confused.

"What's going on?"

I chuckle to myself before filling her in.

"We're not going to dinner. Mum's been planning a surprise Sweet Sixteenth for you for months now. Your friends will be here at seven. This is your night, it's all about you. Happy birthday, kiddo!"

She looks at our mum.

"Is this true? Is this really all for me?"

"Yes, baby girl. I want you to have the most amazing birthday."

I leave Darci to explore the backyard while I go sit with my uncle.

"I've sent the demo track to Melody, love. It's gone over by express post. It's out of our hands now, it's all up to them. But I don't think you have anything to be worried about. I know this took a lot of strength for you to do this. I'm proud of you, Delilah."

"Thank you, for everything. You've always been here for me. You're like a dad to me, and I can't imagine what I'd do if I ever lost you."

"I'm not going anywhere, superstar. I'm always going to be here for you."

Once Darci has finished looking at the setup she joins us.

"Delilah. I know this is a lot to ask, but would you sing a song tonight? I know you don't usually perform in front of people, but it would mean a lot to me. Please?"

I look at my uncle, who nods his head.

"Don't be scared. This is a perfect opportunity for you."

I look back at Darci, and I know I can't say no to her, especially on her birthday. I just don't know if I am strong enough to get up and sing in front of everyone.

"What do you want me to sing?"

"Well, I've heard you sing *Beauty and a Beat*, and that's one of my favourite songs, so I'd love it if you could sing that?"

I know my uncle is right. It is the perfect opportunity for me. If I get signed, I'll have to sing in front of even more people, so I need to start building up my confidence.

"All right, I'll do it. I need to get ready anyway so I'll run through the song while I'm upstairs. I'll be back down at 6:45 p.m."

I head to my room, close the door and lock it. I check the time. I have forty-five minutes to get ready and prepare to sing in front of everyone. With my nerves running rampant, I need all the time I can get to try to calm myself down. I sit on my bed and close my eyes. *It's okay, you can do this.* I keep repeating this mantra out loud to myself, over and over again. I slowly open my eyes and allow them to readjust to the light that is now beginning to disappear from the sky. I get up from my bed, head over to my closest, and start going through my clothes, trying to decide what to wear. After trying on a few things, I settle on a white top under my favourite pair of short denim overalls, which I pair with my white Converse. I fix my hair and makeup, then pull my guitar out of its case and sit on my bed.

I take a few deep breaths before warming up my voice. I begin playing the song, firstly without the lyrics, and then, when my nerves are under control, I add the words. I keep stumbling and I keep questioning if I really can do this. I finally play the song in its entirety, and I feel a wave of relief. I play it once more before there is a knock on my door.

"Delilah? People are starting to arrive. Cam just got here, so it's time to come downstairs."

I unlock my door to see my mum standing on the other side, waiting for me.

"Okay, Mum. I'll be down in a second."

As she reaches the stairs, she turns around to face me.

"I'm proud of you. I know how much it's taken for you to agree to sing in front of everyone and, for what it's worth, you sound better than ever."

"Thanks, Mum. That means a lot to me."

I grab my guitar, follow her down the stairs and head out the back to find Cam. I pull him to the side and explain how Darci has asked me to sing for her, and how I am silently cursing myself for saying yes. I explain that I know it is good for my self-confidence, and it is good for me as a singer, but I don't know if I can get through this without my nerves taking over my body. Cam smiles and puts his hands on the side of my face.

"When you get up there, take a deep breath, and turn around if you have to. We love you, and we're going to cheer for you, regardless of what happens. This is exciting. Allow yourself to be excited and enjoy it, otherwise your nerves will consume you. You can do this."

"Thank you."

My phone vibrates in my pocket, so I pull it out and read the message.

Hey, we're about to leave home, see you soon!

"Who is it?"

"It's Declan, he's on his way."

I stand with Cam as all of Darci's friends begin to arrive. When everyone has arrived I quickly message Declan, and a few minutes later I see him walk in with Dylan. They call our mum and sister over before getting everyone's attention. Declan stands in front of everyone as he makes a quick announcement.

"Hi everyone. Sorry to interrupt your night, but we have another surprise."

My mum looks over at me.

"Delilah, what's going on? Oh God, please don't tell me it's your father!"

I raise my eyebrows.

"Yeah, like we'd ever bring him here." I say under my breath as I point to the door as Dakota struts in.

"Dakota! Oh my gosh, I can't believe you're here!"

Darci runs towards her at full speed. My siblings and my mum spend time with Dakota, while I socialise with everyone else. My best friends are here, and that makes me happy, it's nice to see them again. We haven't been able to catch up since I've been back from Sydney. I am in the middle of chatting to them when my phone interrupts our conversation. I pull it out of my pocket and read the message.

Hello Delilah, I hope all is well. I just wanted to confirm our meeting at my house tomorrow at 11:30 a.m. Helen.

I have almost forgotten about that, which is surprising since it had consumed my thoughts all week, well, at least when I wasn't recording my songs anyway. I quickly send a reply.

Hi Helen. I'm fine, thank you. I hope you're well. Yes, 11:30 a.m. tomorrow is correct. My friend Ryan will be joining me; I hope that's alright. I can't wait to meet you. See you then.

I hit send as Dakota comes over.

"Sorry, girls. I'm just going to borrow my sister for a moment."

I wave to my friends as Dakota and I head over to a quiet spot by the pool.

"Firstly, I want to apologise for the whole MusicNow fiasco. I really didn't do it to hurt you, I hope you know that. Secondly, what's been going on with the whole dad thing? Any news?"

Dakota leans back against the fence that runs against the pool.

"Firstly, it's fine. I understand why you did it, and I'm not angry. It's over now, so let's move on. And secondly, yes, there is some news. It's a long story but remember that Helen lady?"

My sister nods before I continue.

"Well, Declan and I went to our old house, and the owner had a letter from her. It had a return address and a contact number on it, so I called her. I'm going over to meet her tomorrow. I'm scared, but I think she knows where Dad is. This could be just what I need to find him, Dakota."

"Shit, you might have actually found him. I wish I could go with you, but I promised Declan I'd spend the day with him, and then we have our family dinner."

"Don't stress. Ryan's going with me. I'll tell you all about it once I've seen her. Just don't tell Mum. I'm going to tell her tomorrow night, but I have to be the one to tell her."

Dakota bites her lip.

"Want me to sit with you when you tell her? The moral support could help, huh?"

"That's not even a question. I need you there. I just hope she doesn't feel overwhelmed. Do you think you and I should talk to her? Well, I'll do the talking, you can just jump in if she reacts badly, which I'm sure she will."

Our uncle suddenly appears at our sides.

"Sorry to interrupt, ladies. Delilah, it's time for you to sing. You ready?"

I stand frozen to the spot as my nerves take over my body, again.

"Um, yeah, I'm ready."

I take another deep breath, hug Dakota, and follow him over to my guitar. As I pick it up and put the strap over my body, he clears his throat loud enough for everyone to look at him.

"Hello, everyone. I'm Darci's uncle. I just want to get everyone's attention quickly. We have a special performance for you tonight from our very own superstar.

Please welcome my talented niece, Delilah Walker."

Everyone claps and gathers in front of me. I look out into the sea of people, and I see my family, along with Cam's family, standing together. My best friends and their boyfriends are standing with Cam, and Darci's friends are standing with her. They are all smiling and beaming with pride. They look so positive, and I know they will be proud of me, regardless of how my performance goes. I feel my nerves explode, so I take Cam's advice. I turn my back to everyone, take a deep breath and whisper to myself.

"For my dad. I wish you were here."

I turn around and introduce myself. It's not really necessary because everyone knows who I am, but for some reason, I feel the need to tell them anyway. I clear my throat before speaking.

"Hi, I'm Delilah. Firstly, I'd just like to thank everyone for coming out to celebrate Darci's birthday. This is my first ever live performance, and I hope you enjoy it. For you, Darci. Happy birthday!"

She gives me the thumbs up followed by a grin. I take another deep breath and begin to play the chords on my guitar. A few minutes later, as I sing the final note and play the final chord, the crowd erupts into applause and whistles. Everywhere I look I am greeted by smiles. When I put my guitar back and head into the group of people, everyone comes to hug me. I can't stop smiling. This has been such a defining moment, and I know then and there that I have made the right decision in pursuing my dreams. This is all I want, and I have finally proved to myself that I can do it. I know this is the first step in the most unbelievable journey, and I am now more determined than ever to give this everything I have.

I walk over to Darci and hug her. Everyone goes back to talking and dancing, and I join my friends and Cam, who are now sitting with my uncle Derek. As I approach them, they stand up and cheer and clap for me. I feel slightly embarrassed, but I am so grateful to share this moment with them. I sit next to my uncle.

"I'm so proud of you. I knew you could do it, superstar."

I thank him and look around the backyard. There is so much love and happiness surrounding us. Everyone is smiling and laughing, and it is surreal. As I sit there, observing everything, I can't help but think about my dad. These are the times he should be here. How many birthdays has he missed? How many significant events has he missed? He hasn't ever spent a birthday with Darci, so I guess it makes it easier for her. She was only a newborn when our father left, so she doesn't have any memories to constantly remind her of what she is missing out on. The more I think about it, the more difficult it becomes to enjoy myself and relax, especially knowing that in less than twenty-four hours I will be meeting someone from my father's side of the family. This is a huge step, and a part of me questions if I am really ready for it.

Darci's party ends at midnight; I have managed to enjoy the rest of the night and tried to put the thoughts about my father to the back of my mind. I danced with my sisters and my friends, ate cake, and helped Darci celebrate her birthday in the most magical way. After helping Mum tidy up, Cam and I join Dakota, Justin, Dylan, Declan, and Darci in our front room, where pillows and blankets cover the mattresses that are scattered on the floor. We have decided to have a slumber party, and while everyone else falls asleep almost instantly, I struggle to even close my eyes. I try my best, but it's not good enough. I can't stop thinking about how the next twenty-four hours are going to go.

I had Darci's birthday to distract me, but now it's over. The time has come. It is now or never, and I could be just one person away from finding the whereabouts of my father.

Chapter Thirteen

New Beginnings

I am awake long before the sun begins to rise. I have tossed and turned all night. My mind is racing and my heart is pounding. The day has arrived, and I know that in a matter of hours I will be meeting someone who can potentially answer all the questions that have consumed my life for the past fourteen years. This could be the first step in a new chapter of my life, one I have been desperate to uncover for as long as I can remember.

After everyone wakes up, my mum makes pancakes for breakfast. We sit around the table talking about Darci's party and our plans for the day. I try to stay quiet. Everyone but Dylan, Darci and Mum knows where I am going today. I'm planning on telling her the truth today, so my brother, sister and Cam do their best to keep her from questioning me, which I appreciate. Just when I think she is going to ask me about my plans, she gets up from the table, clears the plates, and turns to face us.

"I've got some errands to run and some business things to take care of, so I won't be home today. Can one or two of you stay with Darci? You know she hates being alone."

Everyone looks at each other before Dakota answers.

"Declan and I are meant to be spending the day together, but we can stay here."

Dylan suddenly speaks up.

"I don't mind staying. I haven't been around much lately, so I can do it. You guys all have plans, so don't cancel them. I'm honestly happy to stay here."

We thank him before our mum interrupts us.

"Well, that's settled. Thank you, Dylan. Don't forget about dinner tonight, it's it uncle Derek's. I'll meet you all there. Have a good day."

Before anyone can reply, she is heading towards the garage. We sit there discussing the obvious: she is clearly hiding something from us, but we know she will tell us when she is ready. Although I know from first-hand experience that sometimes that is easier said than done.

Soon after, Cam leaves, and I walk him to his car.

"Good luck today. I'm sure this meeting will shed some light on everything. Ryan's still going with you, isn't he?"

I wrap my arms around his waist and look into his eyes.

"I hope it does. He should be. I haven't heard otherwise. I'll call you when we're leaving."

"Please do. I've got to get ready for work, but I'll talk to you later. I love you."

"I love you, too."

I stand on the grass, watch him pull out of the driveway, wave as he drives off, then head back inside to get ready. I quickly get dressed before I head into the bathroom. Once my hair and makeup is done, I grab my bag and head outside.

It is just after 11:00 a.m., and Ryan is waiting in the driveway for me. He has offered to drive so I don't have to stress about finding my way to Helen's, which I appreciate. I climb into the car and secure my seatbelt.

"So, how are you feeling?"

"I honestly don't know how to explain it. I'm nervous and excited. I just want to find out who this lady is. I want to know if she knows where my dad is."

Ryan and I spend the next fifteen minutes talking about some of my favourite memories of my dad. We pull into a driveway, he turns off the ignition and faces me.

"We're here. Are you ready?"

I take a sip of water.

"As ready as I'll ever be."

We approach the door and I gently knock on the wooden frame. I notice my hands are trembling and my legs feel like jelly as the door slowly opens. A man appears. He's wearing a white singlet and black shorts. He opens the door and steps out.

"You must be Delilah. I can't believe you're here, I haven't seen you since you were seven. You've grown so much."

I take a step back. I don't know this man, but he clearly knows me.

"I'm sorry. I don't want to be rude, but do I know you?"

He senses my hesitation, and steps back too.

"Sorry, I should have introduced myself. I'm Adrian. I'm your father's best friend. I have been for the past forty years."

I look closer at Adrian.

"You know my father?"

I know it's a stupid question to ask since he has just told me the answer, but this is the first person I've actually met outside of my family who knows my father. He actually knows him.

"Sure do. Saw him yesterday actually. Please, come in. Helen's expecting you."

We enter the house and Ryan introduces himself to Adrian. I stop in the hallway and wait for Adrian. He brushes past us before he takes us outside to a table, where a lady is sitting. She looks up from her book and smiles. She stands up and hugs me tightly. I sense she has been waiting for this moment for a while, and I find something comforting in her hug. It's like I've known her all my life.

"It's so nice to see you again, Delilah. Let me look at you."

She takes a step back, keeping her hands on my shoulders. She has medium length, honey blonde hair and she is wearing a long skirt with a white top sticking out the bottom of her white jumper. She doesn't look very old. I assume she's in her late fifties.

"You look just like him. Your father, I mean. You have the same eyes and the same smile."

I suddenly feel awkward, and I don't know where to look.

"Oh sweetheart, please don't be afraid. I know how much this has taken you to get here and I want to help you as much as I can. Please, sit down."

Ryan and I sit down as Helen pours us a cup of tea from her floral tea set. She hands us our cups, and I smile before asking her how she knows my father.

"I'm his aunt. I'm the only family he has left - other than you, of course. After his mum, my sister, passed away he moved in with me. He's been living in and out of my home for a while now. Adrian lives down the street, so he's always in contact with your father."

I realise I am looking at Helen more closely than I meant to, but I recognise her and suddenly it hits me.

"Oh my God. I know you. Not personally or anything, but I've seen you before. I've served you at least three times at Boom Clap."

She looks down at the ground and sighs.

"Yes, that is correct. I wanted to tell you who I was, but I didn't want to scare you. I didn't know if your mum had told you about me and I didn't want to upset her, or you, by telling you who I was. I guess I just wanted to make sure you were happy, but when you served me the first time, I could tell something wasn't right. It's a look I've seen before, it's the same look your mother had when she came over to see me."

I look at her, unable to find any words, so she continues to explain.

"Just after your parents broke up, your mum came over to talk to me. I was all your father had left from his side of the family. I suppose there are others, but he doesn't talk to them, so I'm it really. Anyway, she came over to see how he was, to see if he was ready to speak to her and sign the divorce papers. She wanted a clean break, a fresh start, for you and all of her children, but she loved him so very much. I saw the part of her that wanted to fight to keep the marriage alive. She wanted to fight for the man she had once loved, but his dark side had pushed her away. I don't think anything could have saved them. She had the exact same look on her face that you had that day, the same look you have on your face right now."

I avoid looking at her.

"I don't know what look you're talking about."

In reality, I know exactly what she's talking about. I have tried to hide that look from the world ever since my father left. It is a look of pain and suffering, of knowing the truth, but not wanting to accept it. It is almost impossible to tell people I'm fine when they ask about it, but I can't tell them the truth. Helen suddenly interrupts my thoughts.

"Delilah, I know you're scared. I know you miss your father. I'm here to help. You can ask me anything and I will be honest with you."

I look at Ryan for comfort.

"It's okay, I'm here. You have so many questions. Now is the time to get some answers."

Ryan is right. I have to take this opportunity to ask her all of the questions that have been floating through my mind since he left.

The four of us sit around the table talking for almost three hours. Helen and Adrian try to answer every question I ask, and the answers they give me are comforting. It is like I am learning all about my father for the first time, and I guess in a way I am.

"Is he still funny?"

Helen smiles as Adrian answers.

"He used to be. I'm sure you remember that. But he hasn't had the same sense of humour since he left."

I feel a sense of sadness. My father was always so funny, and he could always make us kids laugh. I can't imagine him not having that same sense of humour. Helen interrupts my thoughts again.

"I hope you don't mind, but I saw the video of you singing online. I saw such pain in your eyes and it showed through in your singing. Don't get me wrong, your voice is incredible, but I felt like you were singing that song for your father. Were you?"

"When that video was filmed, I was going through a lot. It was partly from the sadness I felt from fighting with my boyfriend, but the majority of it was the pain and sadness I've felt year after year since my father left. That's why I sang a song called *Nothing*. That's what I've struggled to face without him in my life. I feel like I'm nothing to him anymore."

I can feel the tears gathering in my eyes and I try so hard to fight them.

"I sent the video to Adrian and he showed your dad."

"He saw it?"

The tears are now falling from my eyes.

"Yes, he did. He was blown away by your voice. I don't want to upset you, but he wasn't very happy with me for showing it to him. I guess it was a reminder of what he'd left behind. Delilah, are you willing to go see him? I can give you his address. He has a place he goes to when he wants to escape from everyone. It's his refuge. I know I'm risking our relationship by doing this, as he won't be expecting you, but we won't tell him. It's time for him to face you and forgive himself. He's been tearing himself apart for years, and I honestly believe you're the only one who can help him heal."

I bite my lip. I know I can't back out now. I've come too far, and Adrian is willing to give me everything I have been searching for. Regardless of how scared I am, I know it is time for my father to face his past. I know it is time to get the closure I've been searching for ever since he left.

"If you're willing to give me his address, then I'll go and see him. I agree with you: it is time he faced his past. I need to hear his side of the story, and if I can help him find the strength he needs to forgive himself, then that's what I'm willing to do."

I wipe my tears away as Adrian writes the address down. I look at it and recognise it straight away.

"This is the same street we used to live on. Why does he have a place so close to our old house?"

Helen looks at Adrian before explaining.

"We don't know, honey. He's never actually told us. I guess he finds comfort being there. I think he feels a sense of family there. I assume it's his way of being close to you without actually being with you. I don't think he's ever been able to face the past, so he runs from it, but for some reason he runs right back into that street. We've never asked him why. I used to write letters to your mum, too. I got one to her, when I saw her at her old house, but after that she refused to talk to me, or answer my letters. She changed all of her numbers and she obviously moved away. I knew she wasn't at your old house, but I know Katherine knew your mum, so I had hoped she would get the rest of the letters to her. I see Katherine here and there, so I got updates on the letters. I figured you found the latest letter I sent since you called me."

That explains the letters, but it still didn't explain why my mum had kept Helen a secret. I'm going to have to ask her about that.

I pull my chair closer to Helen and look at her.

"Helen, can I ask you something?"

She nods.

"Of course. You can ask me anything you want."

"Why didn't he come back? Why did he leave me? I needed him."

She pulls me closer and hugs me.

"Oh Delilah, I'm so sorry. It was never your fault, he loved you more than anything, but he couldn't be the father you needed. He was dealing with his demons and he just ran away so he didn't hurt you. I guess he didn't do a good job at protecting you. All I can see is hurt. But it's going to be okay, I promise. Seeing you is what he needs, and I know it's going to help you, too."

I sit there, hugging Helen for as long as I can. Then she shows me photos of my father when he was young and tells me everything she knows.

At 4:30 p.m. - five hours after we arrived - Ryan and I thank Helen and Adrian, then get into Ryan's car to head home. Before we leave, I roll down my window and ask one more question.

"Is he happy? I mean, has he been happy since he left?"

Helen leans down to face me and lets out a deep breath.

"I wish I could say he is, but he is far from it. He has days when he seems to be fine, but he certainly isn't happy. I'm sure once he sees you he will find his happiness again."

I smile and thank them again. Ryan slowly pulls out of the driveway, and we wave as we drive off. We're leaving with everything I've been searching for, and I feel something I haven't felt in a long time, *hope*.

"So, now I have the information I need, do I just get in the car and go to see him? I don't even know what to say. I didn't think it would happen this quickly, I thought it was going to be difficult to find him, but everything I need to find him has practically been handed to me. What am I supposed to do now?"

Ryan concentrates on driving, but he tries his best to help me.

"Maybe everything's happened so quickly and easily for a reason. Maybe you're meant to find him now. Everything you wanted has happened. I know you're scared and you don't know what to say, but you heard Adrian: your dad doesn't stay in one place for too long, so you need to act quickly."

We spend most of the drive home discussing everything and trying to figure out what to do. But for now, I have to focus on telling Mum.

"Hey, can you drop me off at my uncle's? I'll direct you there."

Ryan agrees, and twenty minutes later I am sitting in one of my safe places. My uncle has a pretty big backyard. Most of the paddocks have animals in them, but his backyard only had a pool when he first moved in. Since then, as he had extra space, he decided to build a pond. He put it in the corner where the fence separates the house from the paddocks, he also put a wall along the front end of the pond. There is a waterfall on the right hand side and there are big rocks, plants and trees everywhere. It almost has a forest-like feel to it. The pond is quite big too, and there are fish and frogs in the water. He put solar lights along the edge so you can see everything at night too, it always looks stunning.

He also put a coffee table and some chairs near the wall so we can sit there and relax. It's built specifically to be a relaxing place, and we used to come here all the time when we were little. As we got older, most of my cousins and siblings stopped coming, but it is a place I always come to, especially as I get older. I never get sick of the view, which is beautiful. My uncle recently put up a fancy gazebo, so no matter what the weather is doing, we can sit out here without having to worry. It is quiet and relaxing. No matter what is going on in my life, I can sit by the pond and do nothing but think. It really has become a place of refuge.

I sit there, looking at the address written neatly on a small piece of paper. I listen to the water flowing from the waterfall into the pond as the fish swim around. I continue to think, not noticing Cam approaching me.

"I can always find you here. Whenever something's bothering you or you just need space, you always come here."

He sits down next to me and kisses my cheek.

"So, how did the meeting go? Who is this Helen lady? And what did she say?"

I hand him the piece of paper as I answer his questions.

"She's his aunt. I got his address. Cam, I can go and see him. What am I talking about? I *am* going to see him."

"Wow, this is huge. When are you going?"

"I don't know. I have to tell Mum first, then I guess I'll go from there."

As Cam and I start discussing how I'm going to tell my mum, my aunt appears at the back door and calls out to us.

"Dinner's early tonight."

I get up, grab Cam's hand, walk inside and sit down with my family for our usual Sunday night dinner. I try to enjoy myself, but the thought of telling Mum makes me feel sick, and the last thing I feel like doing is eating.

We arrive home at 9:30 p.m., and I sit on the stairs waiting for my mother to come inside. When she walks in, I stop her.

"Hey, Mum. I know it's late, but I really need to talk to you. Can we go and sit in the kitchen?"

"Sure. I'll make some tea."

I smile, thank her and go to get Dakota. Cam and Declan go into the front room. They aren't too close, but they're close enough to intervene if I need backup. I'm pretty sure I'll require it if she reacts the way I am expecting.

Dakota and I sit down, and our mum sits across from us. Here we go. It is time to be honest. I take a sip of tea before I begin to explain.

"Please don't be mad. I'm choosing to be honest, because I hate the fact that I feel like I'm sneaking around, and I want you to know the truth."

I look at Dakota for support. She is closely watching our mum, but she smiles and nods her head, signalling that I need to continue.

"You've always been an amazing mum to us, and we appreciate everything you've done. We know how much you've had to sacrifice for us, but Mum …"

She puts her head in her hands and starts crying.

"This is about your father, isn't it? God, you're going to try to find him, aren't you? Delilah, why are you doing this? He doesn't want to be with us. You need to let this go."

She looks up at me, tears running down her face, and I feel pain running all through my body.

"Mum. I know you did what was best for us, but you need to understand things from my side. I know about Helen. I know about the letters. I know everything. Except for why you kept her a secret."

My mother stops crying and I can tell she is about to explode.

"Delilah, you listen to me very carefully. You are not to talk to Helen. I don't want anything to do with her, that's why I kept her a secret. I cut all ties with your father, and his aunt. I don't care what you think you want. Your father is gone, and he isn't coming back. Not now, not ever. Stop pursuing him."

I feel the anger rising in me too.

"Well, it's too late. I've already seen Helen and I know where Dad is. Why would you try to keep his family away from us? Don't we deserve to know them?"

Everything has been building up to this moment, and my mum has just about taken all she is willing to take.

"Delilah. Enough! I told you I don't want anything to do with him, I don't want any conversations about him, I don't want to see photos of him or read old letters. I moved on from that part of my life. I'm not discussing this anymore. If you want to pursue this, then fine, but you will not do it under my roof."

I am shocked. I didn't expect things to go well, but I didn't think it would turn out like this.

"Are you seriously going to kick me out? What are you so afraid of, Mum?"

Now I'm yelling at her.

She gets up from her chair, walks towards the door, and turns around.

"I'm scared of you getting hurt. You don't know him the way I do. You remember all the good times, you don't know half of what he put us through."

I chase after her as she tries to walk away.

"Mum, stop. Please. Listen to me. I remember more than you think, and I know he put you through hell - he did it to us all - but he needs us. If we can't do this as a family, then I need to do it by myself. I'll leave if you really want me to, but I'm going to see him. I'm sorry if that upsets you, but I'm an adult and you can't stop me. I need to know why he left me, why he left us. Please respect that."

In that moment, everything I've been feeling for the past few months hits me at full force. I sink to the floor and cry my heart out. My mother slowly approaches me.

"I didn't know you felt this strongly about it. I always said if any one of you was going to find him, it would be you. I just didn't ever believe you would do it. I'm not comfortable with you doing this, but if you really must do it then I can't stop you. Until it's over, I don't want you here though. I won't have him finding me again."

She leaves and heads to her room. I hear the slam of the door behind her and her television going on. I sit there, with my sister, brother and boyfriend trying to comfort me, but nothing can take this pain away. What am I supposed to do? I am in the worst position. I've finally been honest with my mum, and now she wants me to leave. Plus, I have a growing fear of not knowing if my father will even talk to me.

Cam helps me up, and then helps me pack a week's worth of clothes. He tells me I can stay with him while I get everything sorted, and I appreciate him being there for me, especially on nights like this. Dakota and Declan leave at the same time as Cam and I do. I thank them for being there for me, and they both hug me.

"Please keep us updated, I know Mum's not happy, but she will come around. We're here, don't ever forget that."

Dakota gets into the car.

"Thank you. I'll keep you updated. See you soon."

I wave at them as they pull into the dark street and drive off. Cam and I go to his house and I snuggle up next to him.

As I drift off to sleep, I think about how the day went. I am excited to find my father. I am scared, but mostly excited. I can't believe I finally have everything I need to find him. Despite my mum not being happy about things, I know she just needs time to process everything, and I hope that with time, she will come around and understand why I need to do this.

Chapter Fourteen

Surprise City

Over the next five days, I stay away from my house and my mum. In fact, we don't speak one word to each other. I dive into working at Boom Clap, and I focus on writing more songs. I want to avoid thinking about everything that is going through my mind. I haven't thought about when I am going to find my father, but my mum is about to end our silent treatment and drop a surprise on us all.

It's 5:00 p.m. on Thursday, and I've just finished a seven-hour shift at Boom Clap. I clock off and head back to Cam's house, where I've been staying since my mum asked me to leave. I pick Cam up, and we head to Dylan's. Dakota is due to fly back to Sydney on Sunday, so my siblings and I decide to have a family night, although Cam and Justin join us. They are practically family anyway.

Darci keeps questioning me. She doesn't know about me finding our father. Everyone agrees it's best to keep her out of it, so she doesn't understand why I'm not at home anymore.

"When are you coming home? I miss you and Mum's always out, so I've got no one to talk to."

"Darci, what are you talking about? You've been spending time with Dylan."

"Dylan's boring. All he does is talk about houses and sport, and I don't like either of those things."

I look at Cam, who is trying to hide his laughter.

"I'm sure it's not that bad. Come on, let's go pick a movie to watch."

We head into the lounge room and sit on the couches. As Darci chooses a movie, we chat, but everyone tries to avoid the elephant in the room.

My siblings and I get a message at the same time. We pull out our phones and read it. Mum has sent the same message to the five of us.

I need you all home tomorrow night for dinner. Family only. No excuses. Be home by 5:30 p.m. We need to talk. Mum x

I hand Cam my phone so he can read the message. The room goes quiet. No one makes a single sound. Finally, Darci speaks up.

"I know something's going on. You're all acting strange, and Mum's been acting weird all week. What is it?"

We don't know what to say to her. I wonder if I should tell her the truth, but I don't know how she would take it. She wasn't old enough to remember our dad when he was around, so maybe she would react differently. We had all agreed to keep her out of it, but would it really make a difference if she knew?

Dakota looks at me. "It's your decision whether to tell her or not. We all know, so it's only fair if she knows too."

"Well I have to tell her now that you've said that. Bloody hell, Dakota. Do you ever think before you speak?"

Her face turns sour.

"Do you really want to go there? You're the one who was sneaking around, lying to everyone."

Now it is my turn to be sour.

"Well, half the family wouldn't know if you'd kept your mouth shut to begin with. Thanks for that, by the way. I'm glad I confided in you just for you to turn around and tell Declan and Cam everything you promised me you wouldn't repeat."

"Oh excuse me, miss perfect. I probably shouldn't have told them, but I wouldn't have had to if you didn't lie."

"Excuse me, you're the one who told *my* boyfriend about my emotional breakdown. And you know I already feel bad for lying, so what are you trying to prove? I get it. I stuffed up!"

Suddenly Darci jumps up and yells.

"Stop fighting! I wouldn't have asked if I knew this would happen. Now someone's going to have to tell me. Don't I deserve to know?"

I take a much needed deep breath.

"I've been looking for Dad, and I found him. So, I told Mum and she didn't react very well, that's why I haven't been home. I don't know how to explain it to you or to anyone, other than saying that it's just something I need to do."

"You found Dad? It doesn't feel right saying that word. I don't even remember him. I've always questioned if he left because of me. I mean, he did leave as soon as I was born."

"Darci. Please know he never left because of you. He didn't leave because of any of us. He was going through a lot, and he had to leave to try to deal with everything. He just never came back."

She looks at me with tears in her eyes.

"Did he ever love us? I don't like having a life without a dad in it. I know we have Uncle Derek, but it's not the same."

"Of course he loved us. I don't think he's ever stopped loving us. He just couldn't be a father to us at the time, but maybe now he's ready. I know it's been hard without him, but we do have a pretty special family, even when we fight. Look at me and

Dakota: we fight like we hate each other, but I love her more than life itself, and I'd do anything for her. Uncle Derek has always been there for us, and he always will be. I know we've all looked at him as our father figure and he loves us like we are his own kids. But I know we miss our real father, so I'm trying to bring him home."

Dakota gets up and sits between Darci and me.

"We're sisters. We're always going to be here for each other, we're always going to love each other unconditionally, and Darci, we're always going to protect you."

"Can we watch the movie now? I don't want to talk about this anymore."

No one says another word, we just sit back on the couches, and Dylan puts the movie on.

~

The next day flies by. I work all day, so I'm distracted: probably a good thing since I have to face my mum tonight, and I'm not looking forward to it. I know at some point we have to face each other and talk, but I'm not sure if it's a conversation we need to have with everyone there. Maybe it will help clear the air. She wants us home by 5:30 p.m., but I don't finish work until then, so she'll already be pissed that I am late.

I'm still staying at Cam's, and I ran out of excuses to tell Anna when she kept asking me why I wasn't going home. Since I've told her the truth, she keeps encouraging me to go back, but I'm not ready, and neither is my mum. So, I resort to asking Dylan and Declan if I can stay with them until things have cooled down. I hate putting Cam in an awkward position, and I can't take much more of Cam's family questioning me, so it's easier to stay with my brothers.

At 5:30 p.m. I clock off and head to my car. I hop in and turn the engine on as my phone beeps. I open up a message from Dakota.

I hope you're on your way. Mum's not happy you're late, but we told her you don't finish until 5:30 p.m. We're starting dinner without you. I'll save you some food.

My mum really is angry. It's not like her to start dinner without somebody, and it's certainly not like her to hold a grudge like this. I turn my music up and sing along to the songs on the radio as I drive to our house. I pull into the driveway twenty minutes later, and I spot three cars: Mum's, Dylan's and another car, a blue Honda Civic that I've never seen before. *I thought it was a family dinner,* I say to myself.

I get out of the car, approach the door, and hear everyone chatting and laughing. I think about turning around and going back to Cam's, as I suddenly feel unwanted and I know the mood will change as soon as I go inside.

I stand by the front door for another five minutes, arguing with myself about leaving or staying, until I finally decide to go inside. I take my keys out, unlock the door, and head for the kitchen. As I walk in, my eyes are drawn to the stranger sitting at the table.

"Who the hell is that?"

I meant to say that to myself.

Everyone at the table goes quiet and turns to face me.

"Oh Delilah, you're finally here. How are you, honey? Come and sit down."

Wait, why is my mum suddenly in such a good mood? A few days ago she kicked me out of home. From what Dakota's told me, she still isn't happy with me, but now she's acting like nothing happened. I sit down between Declan and Darci, and lean over to my brother.

"Seriously, who is that?"

He shrugs, so I turn to Darci, knowing she won't be able to hold back from telling me. Just as I am about to ask her, my mother puts a plate of food in front of me.

"Eat up, you must be starving."

"So, are we going to sit here and pretend there's not a stranger sitting here with us? Or would someone like to tell me who he is?"

Mum sits next to the stranger and grabs his hand.

"This is Evan. My boyfriend."

I feel my eyes widen. Boyfriend? What the hell? Since when did she have a boyfriend?

"So, all those 'meetings' you were going to weren't meetings at all, were they? You were going on dates. How long have you been keeping this from us?"

Evan stretches his free hand out and offers it to me to shake.

"Hi, Delilah. I've heard so much about you. It's nice to finally meet you."

I look at his hand and I know I should shake it, but I can't bring myself to do it. For some reason, I feel angry, plus everyone is ignoring my question, again. Mum looks at Evan's extended hand before looking at me.

"Delilah, don't be rude."

I quickly shake his hand before putting my hands in my lap and turning my attention back to my mum.

"Are you going to answer my questions or are you just going to pretend like I didn't say anything?"

Everyone at the table looks embarrassed.

"No, I wasn't going to business meetings. They were, in fact, dates. I wasn't keeping anything from you, I was just waiting until I knew it was serious. Like what you did when you decided to start looking for your father, which is what we need to discuss now."

I raise my eyebrows.

"I'm not discussing Dad in front of someone I don't know."

"Delilah, your mum told me about your father and you looking for him. I'm sure you're doing it with the best intentions, but is it a good idea?"

I look at him and feel my anger building up again.

"No offence, Edgar, but you don't know the first thing about my father and I'm certainly not going to open up to a stranger. He's *my* father, and if I want to see him, then I will. I'm an adult, I can make my own decisions, thank you very much."

I know I've used the wrong name. I'm deliberately pushing the limits, and I can feel the tension building up. My siblings are becoming increasingly uncomfortable, and so is my mum, and Evan for that matter.

"Delilah, it's Evan, and don't talk to him like that. I've been thinking about it, and I think we need to see a therapist. It's about time we talked about your father and it's about time we faced the fact that I'm ready to move on. I'd like to do it in a healthy way, with a therapist who can help us work through everything in a safe environment. Someone who is trained to help people in situations like this."

"Sorry, Evan. Mum, I really don't think we should be discussing this now, and I doubt therapy will help. Isn't it a bit too late for that?"

I don't want to be rude or even argue with her, but this has come from nowhere, and I don't know how to take this news. I've always known that one day my mum would move on, and I want her to be happy. But, for some reason, this guy reminds me of my dad when he was younger; they have the same shaped face, the same eyes and even their noses look similar. I don't know why, but I feel like my mum is trying to replace my dad, like she is trying to give us what we always wanted: a father. But nothing can replace our father.

I feel more uncomfortable than I've ever been before, and I desperately want to leave, so I decide to go to my room, pack some more clothes, go to Cam's to get the rest of my stuff, then go to my brothers' house. After I've made my decision I get up from the table.

"Where are you going? You haven't eaten anything, and we haven't finished talking. Sit down, please."

"I'm not hungry. I'm going to get some more clothes and then I'm going back to Cam's. I'll talk to you later. Nice meeting you, Evan. I'm sure I'll see you around."

I walk out of the kitchen, run up the stairs and go into my room, closing the door behind me. I grab one of my big suitcases and start stuffing clothes into it. When I've finished, I sit on the bed and look around my room. This has always been one of my favourite places. It is *my* room, *my* other safe place, yet it suddenly feels cold, and empty. I feel my emotions taking over my body, so I get up to leave. As I stand up, my door slowly opens and my mum peeks in.

"Please don't go. I haven't seen you for almost a week."

"That's not my fault. You asked me to leave, so I did."

She closes the door behind her.

"Just talk to me for five minutes. Please?"

I reluctantly agree. I know we'll have to face each other eventually, but I just don't have any energy to talk about everything now. We sit and wait for one of us to end the silence. I look at my palms, focusing on every line that's delicately connected to another. I notice how they run in different directions. I've never looked at my hands like this, and I'm actually quite fascinated by them.

My mum finally ends the silence.

"You're not going to take my advice about not seeing your father, are you?"

I continue to look at my hands.

"Mum, I know how you feel. Believe me, I've taken that into consideration, but regardless of what anyone tells me, it's not going to change my mind. I'm going to see him. If it turns out to be a mistake, then that's okay, but it's a mistake I'm willing to make. Please understand that I'm not doing this to hurt anyone. I'm doing this for me. I need to see him, so he can forgive himself and so I can get the closure I need. If he doesn't want to be a part of my life, then there's nothing I can do about that, but I need to hear it from him. I hate that people have kept me away from him. Everyone says if any of us were going to find him it would be me, so why is everyone so surprised?"

I peek through my eyelashes, trying to see her reaction. She looks sad, but I also notice that it looks like she might finally understand where I'm coming from.

"I knew this day would come, and I knew it was going to be you. I'm not mad that you found him, I'm mad that you didn't tell me."

"Would you have been less angry if I'd told you straight away?"

"No, probably not, but I could have tried to stop you."

I stretch my hands out in front of me.

"Honestly, Mum, no one could have stopped me. I would have done it anyway. I know you might not fully understand, but it's going to be all right. I'm choosing to be honest and tell you the truth. He was my best friend; I need to see him. Please, just let me do this."

"I'll let you do this, on one condition: you come to therapy with us. Your siblings have agreed to it. Dakota is going to see someone in Sydney, and the rest of us are going to see a lady here. I've already found someone; all I have to do is book an appointment."

I hate the idea of talking to a therapist, but if this is the only way I can see my father, I'll do it.

"Okay. I'll go. But no more arguments about me seeing Dad."

My mum nods.

"I don't know if I can have you back here yet. It's not out of spite. I understand this is something you have to do, but I still need time."

"I understand. I'm staying with the boys anyway, so take all the time you need."

She leaves and I sit on my bed for a few minutes, trying to gather my thoughts before grabbing my suitcase and heading downstairs. When I reach the bottom I hear everyone laughing again. I look over my shoulder to see everyone sitting around the table with smiles on their faces, and I instantly notice how I feel like an outsider in a stranger's home. *I hope he's worth these sacrifices*, I say to myself as I walk through the door.

~

After another long Saturday at work, I decide to go to my uncle's. I go into his office, where he is focusing intensely on some paperwork. He looks up from his pile of papers as I sit down.

"Hey, superstar. I'm glad you're here. I spoke to Melody today, and we've got big plans ... hey, what's wrong? You look terrible."

I have the worst headache. No matter how much water I drink or how much I rub my temple, nothing seems to help ease the pain and tension I am feeling.

"Has Mum told you? I assume she has."

I can see from my uncle's expression that he knows what I am talking about. He sighs and takes his glasses off.

"What do you want to talk about first? Your father or Evan?"

I shrug.

"It doesn't even sound right putting them into the same sentence. I just don't know what she wants me to do. I knew she wouldn't like me finding him, and I'm tired of explaining it to her. Why can't she just see I'm missing him? I mean I'm so grateful I have you, you've stepped up for five kids who needed a father figure, and that's exactly what you are to us, but ..."

"But, I'm not your father. Delilah, I know that, and I have never wanted to fill that void. I have tried my best to be there for the five of you, and I know you all appreciate it, but nothing can replace a father in a child's life."

Finally! Someone understands where I'm coming from.

"Do you think it's a good idea?"

"Delilah, you have to do what's best for you. Your mum loves you, she just wants the best for you, and she just wants to protect you from the unknown."

I feel myself getting emotional again, so I change the subject.

"Have you met Evan?"

"No, I haven't. I've heard about him, and I look forward to meeting him on Sunday."

"Sunday?"

"Yeah. Didn't your mum tell you? He's coming to dinner. I assume by the look on your face that you didn't know. And what's this business about you not living at home anymore?"

My family seriously has an issue with asking too many questions at once.

"One question at a time, please. She didn't tell me, although with the way I reacted when I met him, I don't blame her. She asked me to leave when I told her about going to see Dad. She wasn't comfortable with me living there, so I left. I don't really know if I'll go back. I'm thinking about looking for a place of my own."

My uncle looks surprised.

"I didn't think you'd react positively straightaway. It'll just take time to get to know him. You need to go home though, my love. I know your mum said she isn't ready for that yet, but that's your home. You're allowed to live there."

"She made it very clear that I'm not welcome back home until I've seen my father. Anyway, what did Melody have to say? Did she tell you anything about my contract? Did I get it?"

"One question at a time, please."

My uncle winks at me before he answers my questions.

"She sat down with the panel. They watched your video and listened to your demo tracks. She said they all reacted positively. Congratulations, Delilah Walker, you are now officially a part of Brooke House Entertainment."

"Seriously? I got the contract?"

"Yes, superstar. You got the contract."

I jump up from my chair and hug him.

"This is amazing! I can't believe this is happening."

"You've got a new contract to sign. Melody e-mailed it to me this morning, you've just got to sign it and I'll send it back in the morning. Also, we discussed the next few steps for you. We want you to start working on your debut album. You need fourteen songs, which we can record here. Melody wants you to film some more covers and post them to your MusicNow account. She wants you to build a strong following, so that when your album drops you've got a support network to help get it off the ground."

I nod, trying to take everything in as I read the contract. I sign it without hesitation before handing it back to my uncle. I now have fourteen songs to prepare, but I already have four ready to go, and my uncle tells me that Melody wants to use the three I used on my demo track, so I only need seven more. I am excited to write more songs; it is something I am so passionate about. I am ready to get my life moving. I am finally on the path to creating something magical, and the thought of writing and recording more songs means the start of the most amazing journey, one that I cannot wait to get started on.

Even though my music's going well, my mum and I have to work on getting our relationship back on track, and its nearly time to see my father. I just hope things don't come crashing down.

Chapter Fifteen

Back to Basics

Despite all of the stress I've been under over the last few days, I am on cloud nine. I have secured a contract, and now I am recording and preparing songs for my first ever album. I can't believe how much things have turned around. I hope they continue to stay that way.

It is 7:30 p.m. on Monday evening, and I have spent the day in the studio recording songs with my uncle.

"How are you feeling about that session? I'll send parts of the songs to Melody to make sure she's happy with them and if she is, I'll go through them and put the finished product in the file. How are you going with writing more songs? We still need seven more, correct?"

I yawn as I walk out of the recording booth. It's been a long day. I sit down in one of the chairs, stretch my arms and legs, and start answering my uncle's questions.

"I feel pretty happy with how it went. I mean, I'm still getting into the swing of things, and I need to work on my confidence, but I think the songs will be good. I've started working on more songs too. So far I've got another one ready to go, so I only need six more now. I don't know why but I find it relatively easy to write songs and I seem to write them fairly quickly too."

"It's because you're a natural!"

I yawn again. I hadn't realised how tired I was.

"I think that's it for today. You look exhausted. Go home and get some sleep, and we can pick up in a few days. Don't force yourself to write anymore tonight, have a night off. Good job, kiddo. I'm proud of you."

"Thank you, for everything. I really couldn't do this without you."

"No need to thank me. It's an honour to help you. I'll see you in a few days."

I grab my bag and water bottle, and I'm walking towards the door when my uncle stops me.

"Delilah, please call your mum. Last night wasn't pleasant. The two of you need to talk."

"Don't remind me. I'll call her later, I just want to sleep right now. I'll see you on Thursday."

I walk out of the studio and stand by my car, allowing the breeze to cool my face. I hug my jacket closer to my chest, get in, and pull my phone from my bag. I have two messages: one from my mum and the other one from Cam. I am trying to avoid Mum, so I open the message from Cam.

Hey beautiful, I hope everything's going well in the studio. Keep tomorrow free. I've planned something for us, but you need to be up and ready by 5:45 a.m. I know it's early, but it'll be worth it. Pack a day bag, bathers, clothes and a towel. I'll see you in the morning. Love you
x

5:45 a.m.? I try to think of where we could be going so early in the morning when I realise I don't have any bathers with me, which means I need to go home to get some. I quickly reply.

Studio session went well. I'll tell you about it tomorrow. I'll be up and ready by 5:45 a.m. I can't wait to see what you have planned. Love you xx

I hit send before I decide to read the message from my mum.

We need to talk about last night. Call me, please.

I don't reply or call her. I'm not ready to talk. I think we both need more time apart. Last night's family dinner was awful, and we got into another fight. I sit in my car thinking about it. My mum decided to bring Evan over to meet my uncle and his family. She proceeded to tell us that she'd been seeing Evan for almost a year. I really don't care; in fact, I am more than happy for her. I want her to be happy and in love, but it seems like she sprung it on us straight after I told her about finding my dad. I always knew Mum would move on and I've prepared myself for this day, but what she said last night has stuck with me:

"Whether you like it or not, Evan is now a part of this family. He's exactly the kind of person you need in your life; you need a father figure, and that's what he's going to be for you. You can stop your silly little search now."

I sat there, shocked. Everyone in our family now knows I have been searching for my father and that I've found him, but no one knew how to react or respond to her comment. If they had sided with me about it, my mum would have got upset and vice versa; it put everyone in such an awkward position. I feel bad for involving our family like this. I thought that by telling my mum the truth and trying to explain things, she would be able to see why I've been doing this. But she is determined to fight me on it, even though she told me she understood. She even said I could go ahead with everything, so I am beyond confused. I continued to sit there in silence until I couldn't take it anymore. I got up from the table, grabbed my keys, and tried to leave.

"Where do you think you're going, young lady? You can't keep running from this. You're looking thinner. I know you're not eating properly. Sit down and finish your dinner. This is family night, I won't have you ruining it."

I looked directly at her and heard Darci shift in her chair.

"Oh shit, she's about to lose it. I know that face."

My mum turned to face Darci.

"Darci, don't use that word. They might be your sisters, but you don't need to copy them, especially with language like that."

Darci mumbled an apology.

"Delilah, sit down. Your sister is leaving very early tomorrow; this is her last dinner with us for a while."

I suddenly snapped.

"Oh, so now you want to play happy families? Evan here can take my spot. I'm sick of talking about this. I told you about Dad because I wanted to be honest with you. I never wanted to hurt you, or anyone for that matter. I don't know how many times, and ways, I can explain it to you. I need to see him and now I don't care what anyone else thinks. I'm going to see him. I don't live with you now, so you can't tell me what to do. Speaking of not living at home, now would be a good time to tell you I'm looking at moving out permanently. I'm really happy for you, Mum. I'm glad you found someone who makes you happy, and I'm glad that you see the potential for him to be a father figure. Maybe you two can have a child together, because he will never be *my* father, no matter how much you try to make it happen."

My mum stood up from her chair.

"Your father doesn't want you, Delilah. He doesn't want any of us. Why won't you listen to me?"

I glared at her.

"Well, I guess I'll wait to hear that from him then. Have a good night."

Without waiting for anyone to say another word, I turned on my heels and walked through the door. I stopped as soon as I made it outside. I was shaking, my head hurt and the familiar feeling of tears building up in my eyes had hit me once again.

~

I open my eyes, desperately trying to stop thinking about that dinner, and how it made me and my family feel. I know I have to give Evan a chance and get to know him, but I'm scared. I just want my dad back. Other than being a singer-songwriter, that's all I've wanted from life. If I do what Mum wants and allow Evan in, then where does my dad fit in? What am I meant to do if I see my dad and he wants a second chance? Question after question floats through my mind. I am overwhelmed by scenarios that probably won't even happen, but I can't help thinking about them anyway.

I put my phone down and start my car, heading for my mum's house. I don't know if she is home. If she is, I'll have to talk to her, and if not, well that's fine by me. She has scheduled a family therapy session for Wednesday afternoon, which everyone but Dakota is going to, so I know I'll see her then. Maybe that will be the only place we can talk without fighting.

I pull into the familiar driveway, get out of the car and check the garage. I'm relieved to see that her car isn't there. I unlock the door, turn the hallway light on and call Darci, but she doesn't reply. After checking the house, I realise no one is home. I start walking towards my room when a picture on the wall stops me. It's a photo from Darci's sixteenth birthday. My mum is standing in the middle with the boys on the left side of her, and my sisters and I are on the right side of her. We are all smiling, and despite the fact that our dad missing, we look like a family. A happy family full of love. Seeing the picture makes me miss living at home.

As soon as I walk in to my bedroom, I feel a sense of home: one that feels entirely different from the last time I was here. I want to snuggle up in my bed and go to sleep and I want to wake up and watch the sunrise from my window. I want to go downstairs in the morning, go into the kitchen and smell the sweet aroma of coffee and pancakes. But more than anything, I want things to be back to normal.

I move towards my chest of drawers, and pull out my favourite pink and white striped bikini before I grab my pink beach towel. I pack a few more clothes and shoes before throwing the bag strap over my shoulder. I turn my light off, gently close the door, make my way downstairs and leave the house, hoping it won't be long before I return again.

I arrive back at my brothers' place at 8:30 p.m. I'm exhausted, so after a light dinner, a quick shower and a glass of water, I hop into bed, set my alarm and pull my sleep mask over my eyes.

Before I know it, my alarm is going off. I sit up in bed, yawn and rub my eyes, while I contemplate going back to sleep. If I do, I won't be ready in time, so I stumble out of bed and go to the bathroom. After washing my face, I get out of my pj's. I still don't know what Cam has planned, but I know we will be close to water, so I don't bother styling my hair or doing my makeup. After putting my hair in a high ponytail, I put my bikini on, throw on a white singlet and a pair of denim shorts, and tie my favourite jumper around my waist.

I check the time on my phone, it's 5:40 a.m., so I grab my keys and head outside to wait for Cam. At exactly 5:45 a.m., he pulls into the driveway. I jump in the car and he kisses me.

"Where are we going?"

I try to hide a yawn.

"I asked Paul if I could borrow his boat for the day. Remember I got my skipper's ticket a while ago? I haven't really used it, and I thought we could both do with a break. We can spend some quality time together. I planned the whole day. We're going to go out now, so we can see the sunrise. We can snorkel and swim. I've packed food and I have my laptop, so we can watch a movie. Then I thought we could end the day watching the sunset."

"That sounds perfect, and well worth the early morning start!"

I look over at him and smile. I appreciate the effort he has gone to so we can enjoy a well-deserved break together.

After a fifteen-minute drive we arrive at the dock, where Cam parks his car. We get all of our things and head towards his godfather's boat, which has the name *Skye Sailors* splashed across the side. I stand by the boat and look at the name when Cam stands next to me.

"It's named after his daughter."

He climbs onto the boat.

"Come on. We've got a big day ahead of us and I want to get out onto the water before the sun rises."

He holds out his hands to help me onto the boat. Once I'm on board Cam turns the lights on before he tells me to go and look around. He goes up the ladder to the steering system, which has two small windows on either side of the wooden shelter. He starts flicking switches as I look around. The boat is fairly big - at least eighteen feet, if not bigger. I remember Cam telling me about Paul's boat when he got it. William had practically begged Anna to let him get one of his own, but she said he could just use Paul's since they were best friends. Paul is a nice guy, so he always lets Cam's family use the boat whenever they want to. I've never been on it before, but I've heard all about it.

I walk around the decking at the back of the boat; there is a table and a row of chairs that join together under the roof. The back of the boat itself is pretty big, there is enough room for at least eight adults to lie down comfortably. I wander into the inside cabin where there is a lounge area and a small kitchen with a television on the wall. Tucked away towards the front of the boat are two bedrooms, both connected to the bathroom, which has a shower and a toilet.

After looking around, I grab the stuff from the deck, put it in the lounge area and head up to Cam.

"We'd better get going. We're probably going to miss the start of the sunrise, but we can catch part of it."

He starts the engine and I sit down. We head towards Rottnest Island. When we arrive, the sun has already begun to rise, but we see it reach the top of the sky.

Cam finds a spot and lowers the anchor before he takes my hand and leads me to the back of the boat. He wraps his arms around my waist and rests his head on my shoulder as we watch the blue sky come to life. The sun lights the clear water, and a light breeze floats through the air, taking loose sand and leaves with it. Cam and I don't say a word to each other; we just stand there in silence. There is something so peaceful and calming about being on the water. The sound of waves crashing into the sand is incredibly relaxing. I've always loved the ocean; it is a world of incredible beauty.

When the sun has risen, we head inside and decide to have some breakfast before going for a swim. We sit at the table and watch as local tourists begin their mornings on the island. More boats begin making their way in and a ferry carrying visitors soon arrives. Autumn has officially begun in Perth, and that means the hot days are limited until the end of the year. Cam and I both know this, so we want to make the most of this day together. We turn our phones off and put them in the safe that is hidden in one of the cabinets.

We finish our breakfast and watch people exploring the island. I notice a young family, a mum, dad and three kids: two boys and a girl. The little girl sits on her father's shoulders, giggling as he chases her brothers around. They find a spot on the sand and put their towels down before heading towards the shallow water, smiling and laughing.

That moment makes me miss my family. I know they are still here, but with my mum and me not talking, things feel different. I long to have a relationship with my father again, but it really is costing me everything. I start to think about how my writing has been hindered lately. Writing songs comes naturally to me, but I've been much more distracted than usual recently. The more I think about my parents, the more I struggle to put my pen to the page and write.

I continue to watch the family as my thoughts run through my head like the waves run through the water. Cam scoots closer to me.

"Hey, what's going on? You look sad."

I snap out of my thoughts and meet his eyes.

"Sorry. I'm not sad, just thinking about everything. I don't want to ruin this day, what should we do now?"

I force a smile.

"It's okay to talk about things, you know. I'm here for you, so let me in."

"It's not that I don't want to talk to you about things. You're the only person I want to talk to right now, but I hate being such a downer. I don't want to keep dragging you into this, you must be so sick of hearing me going on about everything."

I lift my legs and place them over Cam's lap as he puts his arms around my back.

"I could never get sick of listening to you talk, even if it is about the same thing. I'm your boyfriend, and I'm happy to listen to you. You can say whatever you want. I'm not going to judge you or push you away, I'll just listen and help you work through things as best as I can. Plus, it's healthy to talk about things. So tell me, please."

I look into his blue eyes and smile. I know I can confide in him, and he is right: talking about things is healthy, and it will help. I try to swallow the lump that has formed in my throat.

"I knew that finding my father came with risks. I've said from the get go that I'm willing to risk everything, but now I'm questioning if it's really worth it. I want a relationship with my father so badly. Even if I don't get that, seeing him and hearing his side of the story will help put my mind at ease, but I really don't know if it's worth losing my mum over it. I hate fighting with her and, despite what people might think, I really do want her to be happy. I knew she wouldn't like me finding him but I thought she would eventually understand, she even told me she did. I just don't know how I'm meant to get through this without her."

I rest my head on Cam's shoulder and he tightens his grip around my back.

"I know it's hard and you've sacrificed a lot, but look how far you've come. You didn't think you'd ever find your father, but you have. I know you've heard it a million times before, but you're allowed to want a relationship with him. Every child deserves that, no matter how young or old they are. Things with your mum will work out, but for now she just needs time. You do need to accept that she's in a serious relationship with someone now though. I know you want her to be happy, but it's hard not to feel like she's trying to replace the void that your father left. You'll get through it, I promise. You just need to take it day by day."

He is right. I always focus too far into the future and I always struggle with overthinking everything. I just need to take it one step at a time. I know deep down that things with Mum will work out when the time is right, but until then I just have to focus on my music and let everything else work out around that.

I lift my head up from Cam's shoulder.

"Okay, no more depressing chats today. What should we do now?"

He picks me up, carries me in his arms and walks towards the edge of the boat.

"Cameron Collins, what are you doing?"

He doesn't answer me, but continues walking towards the water, grinning from ear to ear.

"Cam, don't you dare throw me into the water! I mean it."

I try to sound as serious as possible, but I can't stop giggling. We reach the edge of the boat and he looks straight into my eyes.

"I love you."

He lifts me into the air and releases me. I fall into the water and try to push off from the sand at the bottom of the ocean to get myself back up to the surface. It's too deep, so I kick my feet in the water as I spring towards the top of the water. I surface and look at Cam leaning against the edge of the boat.

"How's the water?"

"Well, why don't you get your ass in here and be the judge of that yourself?"

I push my arms through the water and watch Cam as he takes off his shirt before he hops up onto the barrier of the boat and dives in without a second thought. When he comes up to the surface, he looks over at me.

"Perfect swimming conditions. The water is the perfect temperature."

I laugh at him as we swim around. We float on our backs, allowing the cool water to completely relax us. After an hour of being in the water, we climb out and get back onto the boat. After getting our towels and a bottle of water, we head to the front of the boat. We put our towels down and lay back on them, allowing the sun to dry us as we look up at the fluffy, white clouds in the blue sky.

Without taking my eyes off the sky, I focus on my breathing, and I suddenly start getting ideas for a new song. It is a song that focuses on Cam and love in general. Idea after idea keeps popping up and I feel the urge to run and get my phone so I can note everything down. I'm just about to ask Cam if he minds me getting my phone when he looks over at me.

"Isn't it crazy how clouds look like objects? Look at that one, it looks like an elephant."

I follow his gaze. "Please tell me how that's an elephant?"

"Oh, come on. You're stirring me up."

"I am not. Scouts' honour."

Cam looks at me and smirks before he focuses his attention back to the sky and tries to explain what he's seeing.

"There's the head and the trunk and there's its little legs."

I look at the cloud again.

"Well, look at that. I guess it does look like an elephant," I say as I smile at Cam.

At midday, Cam goes inside the boat and comes back out with the picnic he has prepared.

"I've made chicken and salad sandwiches, with aioli on yours since I know it's your favourite, and for desert I made fruit salad. It's just watermelon and berries, but that counts as fruit salad. Oh, and I have some apple cider, too."

He hands me a sandwich and a cup.

"Thank you."

This isn't something he usually does. He's a romantic, but he doesn't like preparing food, he is more of a Subway and bottled water kind of guy. We sit on the front of the boat, eating our lunch and watching the waves float through the water. When we finish, we sit back against the boat's frame.

"You know, I'm so proud of you. I know it's taken a lot for you to get into the studio, and you've really put yourself out there. Seeing you blossom into the artist that you're meant to be is honestly the most humbling thing I've ever seen. You were born to do this, and I'm so lucky to be a part of this journey with you."

I try to fight back the tears. *All I do is cry these days,* I say to myself.

"Thank you. I really couldn't do this without you. Your love and support means so much to me."

He suddenly sighs, and I notice a look of guilt take over his face.

"What? What's wrong?"

He looks down at his hands.

"I saw your mum yesterday. I knew you were out with your siblings so I went to your house and sat down with her. Evan came over after we had lunch and I got to know him a bit and he seems like a nice guy."

I bite my bottom lip as he continues.

"I know it's an adjustment thing for you and your siblings, and they know that too. I just worry that you're never going to give Evan a chance. Your mum is concerned about that too. We only want what's best for you. We know you're going to see your dad regardless of what anyone tells you, but if you give Evan a chance you might actually like him."

I am still biting down on my lip as I watch Cam out of the corner of my eye. He shuffles on his towel. I know he is doing this for my benefit, but something feels off about him talking to my mum and Evan. I release my lip before letting out a puff of air.

"I know I haven't been the nicest person to him, it's just hard for me to see someone come in and try to do all the things my dad should be doing. I know he's trying to be there to help my mum, and I guess he's doing it to help us too, but I just can't be in that situation right now. Not when I know there's a chance my dad could be a part of my life again. At some point I'll give him a chance, but I'm just not ready to do that yet. As long as my mum's happy, there shouldn't be any problems, right?"

"Delilah, you know your mum wouldn't stay with him, or any other man for that matter, if you or your siblings really didn't like him. She values you guys more than she values any potential relationship."

"I know that. I want her to be happy. She needs time to get used to the fact that I'm going to see my dad, and I need time to get used to Evan. I'll get there, it's just not going to happen right away."

"I know. Take all the time you need ... just try not to be a bitch to him all the time."

I look at him seriously, and the smile disappears from his face. I have him right where I want him.

"Gotcha!"

I lunge at him and he laughs.

"Shit, you had me worried then."

~

Cam and I spend the afternoon watching a movie, playing a game of scrabble, chatting and listening to music. At roughly

3:00 p.m. the sun starts to disappear behind grey clouds that have come out of nowhere.

"Babe, I think it's going to rain. I wanted to watch the sunset with you, but I don't think that's going to happen."

He looks disappointed. I approach him and wrap my arms around his waist.

"You know, I've always wanted to swim in the rain."

"Really?"

He puts some loose strands of hair behind my ears.

"Yeah."

"Well, in that case, I guess we could go for a quick swim. Or have a quick dance. Don't judge me, but I've always wanted to dance in the rain."

"Cam!"

I'm not sure if he's joking, but I tighten my grip around his waist anyway. The first drops of rain fall from the sky and, before we know it, the rain becomes heavier. We exchange smiles and allow the rain to run over our bodies. He grabs my hands and pulls me into him. We sway our bodies in the same directions, at the same time, and he twirls me around a few times. We dance on the deck for a while, then head towards the edge of the boat. The rain has intensified and it has created a thick grey curtain in front of us. We jump into the water holding hands, hit the water, let go of each other, and swim back up to the surface.

We swim in circles in the water, splashing and laughing. There is no other person in this world I love the way I love Cam, and I know that nothing can ever take this moment away from us. It will be a memory I will never forget. Cam swims towards me before grabbing a hold of my waist.

"I love you, so incredibly much."

"Not half as much as I love you," I say as he helps me back onto the boat. I plant a kiss on his soft lips and he hugs me.

"As much as I don't want this day to end, we should head back. The rain's picked up and it looks like there's going to be a storm soon. We need to get back to the dock before it hits."

I nod and follow him up to the steering system. I stand between his legs and rest my back on his chest as he directs the boat back.

After one of the most magical days of my life, Cam and I secure the boat and load our stuff into his car. I can't stop smiling. Not only have I spent an incredible day with the love of my life, but I've managed to write down enough notes to write another song. Cam and I are finally back in the place we once were, and - as much as I don't believe in perfection - I know I am pretty close to it.

Chapter Sixteen

Too Good to be True

The last forty-eight hours have been nothing but incredible. Cam and I are in the best place we have ever been in, and things with my mum are getting better, even if it is happening at a snail's pace. My music is constantly improving, and my confidence and self-esteem are growing. Everything feels a million times better, but I have a feeling it is all too good to be true.

On Wednesday afternoon, Dylan, Declan and I hop into Dylan's car and head off to our first family therapy session. My mum and I have spoken through countless text messages, and we both agree we need to sit down and work through our issues. Otherwise, things will get worse and we don't want our relationship to completely deteriorate. As we head towards the therapist's office, I can't help but feel all kinds of emotions. I am anxious, nervous, and a part of me is scared. I know we will have to face everything we have avoided, which basically means we will be discussing my father. I know my mum will try to convince me not to see him, and I also know we have to discuss her relationship with Evan. Despite knowing I'll eventually have to give him a chance, I don't feel ready, and it scares me that my siblings have already started to make the transition with him. I can't even sit down with him without being rude.

I put my headphones in and hit play on my Spotify playlist. As the music hits, I look out the window and watch the world go by as we drive through a busy street. The breeze is flowing through the trees, and the leaves have begun to fall onto the ground. There are people enjoying a late lunch and coffee at the cafés we pass, and there are a few people running on the pavement.

I sit there in my own little world as I start to think about what I'm going to say to my father when I see him. A million different things cross my mind, but none of them feel like the right thing to say. I know deep down I'll have to prepare myself to be rejected by him. I hope that doesn't happen, but I know there is that possibility. I know that if that does happen, nothing will stop me from breaking into a million pieces. As I let my mind wander, I lose track of time and, before I know it, Dylan has parked the car.

We have arrived, and there is no turning back now. I take a deep breath, get out of the car and follow my brothers into the office where my mum is filling out some paperwork. Darci is sitting in one of the chairs, reading a book. When she sees us walk in, she puts down her book and waits for us to join her. Mum joins us after she hands the completed paperwork back to the receptionist. Although we've been texting, it still feels awkward to see her, so I put my head down and focus on the patterns on the dark blue carpet.

A lady walks into the waiting room.

"The Walker family?"

She has short brown hair and big brown eyes, although her oversized glasses take away from her facial features. She is quite thin, and she doesn't look very old. She's wearing a black top, a grey pencil skirt and black heels.

"Yes, hello. I'm Deidra."

Mum gets up and shakes her hand before signalling us to do the same.

"Hi, I'm Mandy King. Nice to meet you."

We introduce ourselves and follow her to her office. She points her delicate hand towards five chairs.

"Please, have a seat."

Mum sits in the middle, with Dylan and Darci on her left and Declan and I on her right. I look at Declan, who looks as nervous as I do. Mandy sits across from us and puts a notepad and pen in her lap before explaining what is going to happen.

"Your mum called me about setting up a session. I want you all to feel as comfortable as possible. This is a safe place where you can say what you like without being judged. I'm aware there are some things you all need to work on, so that's what we're going to figure out today. We will make a plan and nut out exactly what it is that we need to focus on. After that, we will set up a regular day and time for the next few months so we can work through all of these issues. My job is to sit here and listen to you all and help you figure out productive and positive ways to deal with things. Your job is to be as honest as possible, otherwise this is pointless. You're probably going to be scared about being honest, but please know you can say whatever you want, as long as it's said in a respectful way. It's okay if it's not a positive thing, it will help us work through things thoroughly. Deidra, do you want to start off? Maybe you could explain to your children why you wanted to come here."

My mother shifts in her seat before trying to answer the question.

"Well, my ex-husband, their father, walked out on us a while ago, and we've never really talked about it. I think it's time we discussed that. I've also moved on, and I've recently gotten into a new relationship. Most of my children have seemed to take the news quite well, but some haven't."

I clear my throat.

"I'd hardly say a year is a new relationship, and we all know that's aimed at me. I'm the one who hasn't jumped for joy over you getting into a relationship. If you're going to say something like that, you may as well just be honest."

"Okay, fine, I'll rephrase that. All of my children except Delilah are happy I'm in a semi-new relationship."

I roll my eyes as Mandy turns to face me.

"Delilah, is this true? What is it that makes you not want to be happy for your mum?"

"It's not that I'm not happy for her. I am very happy for her. It's just happened so quickly. We were told about him, and then we met him, and now she's always with him. It hasn't been a transitional thing."

Mandy listens to me answer her question.

"Tell me how you honestly feel about your mum's new relationship."

I look between Mandy and my mum.

"I honestly feel like she's trying to fill the void that has been impossible to fill since my dad left. Do I like Evan? I can't answer that, I don't know him. All I know is that it's going to take time for me to adjust to it. Eventually, I'll get to know him, but right now I just can't."

"Can you tell me why you can't do that yet?"

"Because she went on a mission to find her father, and now she's found him, and she's determined to see him, even though I've told her it's not a good idea."

"Mum, I can answer for myself. Part of it is because I have found my dad, but most of it is just an adjustment thing. I'm used to going to my uncle and my boyfriend's dad when I need a father figure."

Mandy is scribbling notes on her notepad as she tries to keep up with what we are saying.

"I think we've made significant progress already, and I think that the biggest issues lie between you, Deidra, and Delilah. I'd like to talk to the rest of the family now to see where they stand, but I think it's going to be more beneficial to have sessions with just you and Delilah, if that's something you're happy to do."

I agreed to Mandy's plan, mostly because I know I don't have a choice. I agree we need to fix things, but I don't know how we can move forward until Mum accepts that I am going to see my dad. I guess she can't move on until I give Evan a chance too. I get up and leave the room while Mandy speaks to my mum and my siblings.

While waiting for my family, I pull my phone out of my bag and find I have two missed calls and three text messages from my uncle. I open up the first message.

Hey, darlin'. Call me when you can please.

I hit the call button and wait for him to answer.

"Hi, love. I was just about to message you again."

"Why? Is something wrong?"

"No, everything's fine. I just wanted to let you know I got feedback from Melody about the song samples we sent her."

I feel my heartbeat quicken.

"She loves every song so far. She asked if you could record some more covers and post them online. She wants one this week and then one to two a week until the album drops. You know she wants you to build a following, so we need to get the ball rolling. You can pick whatever songs you like, just make sure you have a wide variety so people can see what you can do."

I take in everything my uncle says, I even start thinking of songs I can cover.

"Okay, I've got the day off tomorrow, so I'll film a few covers then. Can I come to the studio, though? Things are still pretty tense between Mum and me so I don't want to film them at home, and the boys make too much noise when they're at home."

"That's fine. The studio is free from ten to half past one, so you can have that space. Do you have any new songs ready to record?"

"Actually, I wrote one last night when I couldn't sleep. I can play it for you tomorrow, and you can help me decide if we should use it."

"Sounds like a plan. I've got to help your aunty with the shopping now, so I'll see you in the studio tomorrow. Bring your guitar if you can, you always play better with your own one. Love you."

"Love you, too. See you in the morning."

I hang up the phone and put it back into my bag. I sit back in the chair and watch the minutes tick by on the clock behind the reception desk. A few minutes later my mum walks out with my siblings and Mandy.

"Delilah, your mum is going to come back next week. I'd like you to come with her. Her appointment will be at the same time and day as today, so please try to keep it free. I think we've got a lot to work on, and I want to help the two of you solve these issues that are causing problems in your lives. How does that sound?"

Mum looks concerned. I just sigh.

"That's fine. I'll make sure I don't have work."

Mandy books in the next appointment, and we head out to the carpark. I go to Dylan's car and wait for him to unlock it. My mum unlocks her car before turning to us.

"I was going to cook some carbonara for dinner. Would the three of you like to join us?"

I really don't want to go. I want to go home and figure out what songs I'm going to cover, as well as make the final edits to the song I am going to sing tomorrow, but Dylan doesn't give me a chance to answer.

"We'd love to."

"Great. I'll meet you at home."

We get into the car and my brothers start talking about Declan's upcoming soccer game as I text Cam.

Hey, can you come and pick me up from my mum's in about thirty minutes?

Of course. Is everything okay? How did the therapy session go?

I'll tell you about it when I see you. Everything's fine; my brothers want to go over for dinner, but I've got a ton of work to do so I need to go back to the house.

No worries. I'll be over soon.

I know my mum won't be happy with me not staying, but right now my focus is on my music, and I have a lot of work to do before tomorrow morning's studio session.

We pull into the driveway and head inside. Darci takes my brothers into her room to show them her new bed, and I go and find Jessie. As I sit out the back with her, my mum calls out to me. "Delilah, will you come inside for a second?"

I kiss Jessie's forehead before heading inside.

"Sit down, honey."

I pull out one of the seats at the table and push one of the placemats around with my hands.

"When are you going to see your father?"

I look up from the placemat. She is watching me intensely as she tries to prepare dinner.

"Um, I don't know. When I have time, I guess."

She starts cutting up some mushrooms.

"Well, since you're so determined to see him, I want you to move back in. I know things are still tense, but this is your home, and it doesn't feel right not having you around. You need to focus on your music, and I know your brothers can be distracting. At least you've got some privacy here."

I consider her idea. As much as I want to be stubborn, I really have missed living here, and as much as I love the time I've spent with my brothers, I am ready to be back in my own room, with the comfort of my own things.

"Is Evan going to be here much?"

She puts the knife down.

"Yes, Delilah. He will be here quite a lot. At some point you're going to have to see him, you may as well just get it over with now."

I know she is right. At some point I'll need to face him, and after our last few encounters, it can't get any more awkward than it already is. I just don't know how to talk to him; I don't want him to come in and try to replace my dad. I'm not sure if he feels like that, but I know Mum wants him to be a father figure for us, and that makes me feel uncomfortable.

"Delilah, are you listening to me?"

I look up from the table.

"Mhmm, yep, I'm listening. If I agree to move back here, I don't want to be pressured into getting to know Evan straight away. You need to respect that it's going to take time for me to adjust to him being around, and you need to remember I'm going to see Dad. Nothing's going to change that."

"Yes, I know that, and I know you're going to see him. I've had time to think about it and after I talked it through with Evan, I made peace with your decision."

"You spoke to Evan about it? What did he say?"

My curiosity is getting the better of me, but I want to know what he has said.

"He said I should support your decision. He helped me realise how much you need to do this, for you. He's the one that changed my mind about the whole thing. I was very uncomfortable with the whole situation before Evan helped me see your side of it."

"That's nice of him."

"Yes, it is. Maybe you could give him a proper chance now."

I nod my head and look at a new message from Cam.

I'm here.

I tell my mum.

"Tell him to come inside, he can have dinner with us."

I relay her message.

Mum wants you to stay for dinner; I hope you're hungry. The door's unlocked.

A few seconds later the front door opens and Cam strolls into the kitchen with his hands in his pockets. He is wearing black jeans and a grey top, his hair is freshly washed and secured under a black cap. After hugging my mother, he joins me at the table. While we wait for dinner, I fill him in about moving back home, and I excitedly tell him about my upcoming session in the studio.

"I have to be in the studio until 1:30 p.m. tomorrow. If you're free, do you want to come with me?"

"Of course. It's one of my favourite things to do."

I kiss his cheek, knowing that he will get a big surprise when he hears the song I wrote for him. I am bursting with excitement, but I try my best to hide it. Thankfully dinner is ready, so once my mum calls my siblings down to set the table, I don't have to worry about explaining the goofy look on my face.

After dinner, Cam and I head back to my brothers' place. Dylan and Declan want to stay and spend time with the girls, and while I want to do the same, I have a lot to do before tomorrow. I tell Mum I'll move my stuff back in after my studio session, which she is happy to hear. Once Cam and I get back to the house, we head inside and sit on the couch.

"So, basically, I've got to start putting up covers every week to build a following. I want to write a list now so I can just pick songs and go for it. I'm going to film a few tomorrow, so I need to pick two now. Any ideas?"

We go through our music lists, trying to find songs I can use.

"I've got one. What about *Hold Back the River* by James Bay? You love that song, and it would be perfect!"

I find the song on my phone and play it, singing along when I feel confident enough.

"You're right, it is perfect. One down, one to go."

We continue searching until I find *Nobody Love* by Tori Kelly.

"This has higher notes, and it's not like my first cover. It'll show my range."

"I like it. It's a good song for you."

"Thank you. Now that I've got my two songs, what should we do?"

He checks the time on his phone.

"I should probably go home. I've got a few things I've got to do tonight, but I'll see you in the morning. I'll meet you at the studio at 10:30 a.m."

I nod and walk him to his car before he drives away. I wish he didn't have to leave so soon, but it's probably a good thing, at least now I'll have time to go over the song I wrote for him. I make myself a cup of tea, then head into the guest room, where I've been staying since leaving home almost a month ago. I put my cup of tea on the bedside table and begin to pack my stuff. I hum the tune of the song I've written for Cam while I fold my clothes. Once I am ready, I start to sing the lyrics. After going over it three times, I sit on the bed and finish the last of my tea. I take the cup to the kitchen and clean it, take my makeup off, shower, and get into my pj's. I pull the blanket back and climb into bed, snuggle into the mattress and focus on my breathing as I fall into a deep sleep.

My alarm soon sounds. After going for a quick jog around the park near my brothers', I head back. I quickly shower and put my bathrobe on. I have breakfast, brush my teeth, straighten my hair and put on a bit of makeup. I put on my black ripped skinny leg jeans, my black ankle boots and a white and black striped oversized top. I grab a jacket, my guitar and my handbag before heading back into the kitchen, where I make my usual pre-singing drink.

For some reason, green tea with honey always helps coat my throat. It seems to work wonders when I warm up my voice, and it helps with the tension put on my vocal cords from singing so much. Once my tea has brewed, I put it into my travel cup and make my way outside. I arrive, park my car, grab my things and head inside to find my uncle, who is setting up the camera to record my covers. After hugging him, I sit down and pull my guitar out. I drink half of my green tea and warm up my voice.

"So, what's the plan, superstar?"

I drink the last of the tea.

"I want to sing this new song to see what you think. We can record it now if you want. Then we can record the covers. I know what two songs I'm doing today so we don't have to worry about trying to find anything."

"Sounds good. What's this song about?"

I start to blush as I hand him the lyric sheet.

"Cam?"

"Yup. I know it sounds a bit cheesy, but I was inspired to write a song about him. This album is all about being honest and showing people who I am and what I've experienced, and well, my love for him is so strong that I want to share it with the world."

My uncle finishes reading the lyrics.

"It's written in such a beautiful way that even I'm feeling emotional from it. Your talent honestly continues to surprise me."

I can't help but smile.

"All right, let's get you in the recording booth."

He starts adjusting some of the switches. I check my phone to see if Cam has messaged me. He hasn't turned up yet, and I want him to be here so I can sing the song to him.

"Delilah? Are you ready?"

"Yeah, sorry. Cam's supposed to be here, and he hasn't texted me."

"We can wait for him if you want."

"No, it's fine. Let's start recording it now. Do you have the music I sent you?"

I head into the recording booth and secure the set of headphones.

"Yes, love. Just loading it now."

I go over the song quietly while I wait for my uncle to give me the all clear. As he gives me the thumbs up, indicating that I'm good to go, Cam walks in.

"I'm so sorry I'm late. I overslept and then I raced here, but the traffic was ridiculous. Have you started yet?"

He tries to catch his breath.

"I've got a surprise for you," I say as my uncle starts playing my backing track, then I close my eyes and start singing the words. When I feel comfortable enough, I open my eyes and finish singing the song, putting as much power into it as I can. I look over at Cam to see if he has realised the song is about him. I take the headphones off and walk back into the office.

"So, what did you think?"

I suddenly feel nervous.

"Was that song about me?"

"Yeah. I wrote it after our day on the boat."

"It was beautiful. Thank you."

"You're welcome. Thank you for inspiring me."

We sit down and tell my uncle about our day on the boat before I film the covers I've picked. When they are ready to go, we edit them before uploading the first one. We leave the studio at 1:30 p.m. and go to my brothers' house, so I can get the last of my things before I move back home. Cam follows me back to Mum's and helps me put my stuff back into my room. While we're unpacking, my mother comes in.

"It's good to have you home, honey. We're going to have a family dinner tonight, Evan's going to be here, and I want us to start making some progress, so please be respectful. Remember this is new for all of us. I'll do my best to make this transition as easy and comfortable for you as well."

"I'll try. Can Cam stay?"

"That's fine. I'm going to go to the shops now, so I'll be home later."

She waves and heads back down the stairs. I turn to Cam.

"Something's up, I can feel it. Do you know anything?"

"I swear I don't know a thing."

His cheeks start to go red, which makes me think he's hiding something, but I decide not to push it.

At 4:30 p.m., Cam and I head downstairs and decide to make mango smoothies in the kitchen. Darci yells out from the living room.

"Delilah! Come here, quickly!"

Cam and I run into the living room, worried that something is wrong.

"What is it? Are you alright?"

"I'm fine. Mum and I were just watching this show, and then we saw you. Look! You're on the TV!"

What? Me? On TV? I look at the television and, sure enough, there I am.

"Turn it up," I say as Cam and I sit next to her and watch. The reporter is sitting at a desk talking about my music.

"To local news now: twenty-one-year-old Perth native Delilah Walker is going places in the music world, with MTV naming her as one of the upcoming talents to watch. She rose to fame after posting a cover of the hit song *Nothing* by Irish band, The Script. Since then the video has had close to a million views. She recently uploaded a new cover, which is now going viral. Her first album is expected to be released within a few months."

I put my chin in my hands and stare at the television. Did that really just happen? Darci looks as shocked as I am.

"Delilah, that's amazing! MTV said you're one to watch!"

I shake my head.

"Let's not get ahead of ourselves. I've just got to focus on my album right now."

I try to play if off like it's nothing, but secretly I am screaming with excitement. Darci, Cam and I sit in the lounge room, flicking through multiple channels while my mum and Evan prepare dinner. When Evan arrived, he hugged Darci before shaking Cam's hand. He went to hug me but backed off, feeling the tension between us. I quickly said hello to him before pretending I was watching a show.

When my brothers arrive, we sit at the table and eat our dinner. Evan makes another attempt to talk to me.

"So, how's your music going, Delilah?"

"Good."

I know I'm being blunt, but I still don't feel like taking my guard down.

"That's good. What is it about music that you like?"

I know he is making an effort with me, so I look up at him.

"I like that you can tell stories through music. Writing songs is something which comes pretty naturally to me, and it's my favourite art form. It's just what I do, and it's really the only thing I'm good at."

My mum looks relieved that I'm finally being polite.

"That's wonderful. It seems like you're very passionate about it."

"I sure am."

The conversation dies down, and my mother looks nervous. She suddenly fills the silence.

"I need to Skype Dakota in."

She pulls her phone out.

"Um, why?"

I look between her and Evan.

"You'll find out in a second, honey."

She's frantically trying to get a hold of Dakota, and when she's finally gets her on the phone, she hands it to Darci.

"Evan and I have an announcement. Firstly, I love you all very much."

"Oh shit, this doesn't sound good."

Darci giggles at my comment. Our mum shoots us a dirty look, before continuing.

"You know that Evan and I have been seeing each other for a year now. I obviously didn't want to tell you guys until we knew it was serious, but it is. I am the happiest I've ever been, and I'm head over heels in love with him. With that being said, we want to tell you all that we're now engaged."

My shoulders drop in shock.

"I'm sorry, what did you just say?"

Dakota is screaming through the phone.

"This is amazing. Congratulations, Mum! And welcome to the family Evan!"

Everyone gets up to congratulate my mum and Evan while I sit in my seat. How did I not see the signs? I mean she practically said she was getting engaged when we had our first meeting with Mandy. How had I not noticed? I finally get up and hug my mum, then quickly shake Evan's hand.

As everyone sits down, I excuse myself and head outside. I find a quiet spot and look behind me to make sure no one has followed me. I pull my phone out of my pocket and find Adrian's number. I quickly type up a message, asking him for my dad's mobile number. Once I hit send, I look out into the dark backyard, focusing on the row of fairy lights in our neighbour's yard, while breathing in the fresh air.

When my phone buzzes, I quickly read Adrian's reply. I have the number and I dial it straightaway. It rings five times before I hear the most comforting voice.

"Hello, Tony speaking."

It's him. I can't believe it. *It's actually my father.* His voice sounds familiar, yet strange. I want to tell him who I am. I want to be honest and tell him how I've spent months looking for him. I desperately want to tell him I'm coming to see him, but I can't. I try talking to him, but nothing comes out.

"Hello? Is anyone there?"

I finally manage to get a few words out, although I instantly regret them.

"Sorry, wrong number."

"No worries. Have a good night."

The line goes dead. I pull my phone down from my ear.

"You too, Dad."

I look at my phone. Hearing his voice is all I need, it is the final push I am searching for to make this whole thing real. It hasn't felt this real until now, until I heard his voice. It brings a sense of relief over me, I can't even try to describe it. Now I just have to get in my car and go and see him, but all of that will have to wait just a little bit longer, at least until I have dealt with the shock of this engagement news.

Chapter Seventeen

Broken Hearts

I sit on my bed, thinking about everything that happened last night. My mum announced her engagement, and I heard my father's voice for the first time in fourteen years. I have given myself some time to adjust to the news of the two of them getting married, and I am willing to get to know him, but not until after I've seen my father.

I have been trying to contact Cam all morning but, for some reason, he isn't responding to me. I feel like something is wrong, but I keep telling myself he is just busy. After I sang him the song, he was so happy. He even shed a few tears, which he doesn't usually do. Since then, though, there's been something off with him. No matter how hard I try to fight it, I can't shake the feeling that something is wrong. He still hasn't got back to me, so I decide to message him again.

Hey. Is everything okay? It's not like you not to reply to me. I have this horrible feeling that something's wrong. Please tell me I'm just overthinking things. I love you.

I hit send and stare at my phone, hoping he will reply, but he doesn't. I need to distract myself. I look out the window at the grey clouds that have filled the sky: at least the weather's matching my mood. I open my bottom drawer and pull out a pair of full-length workout leggings. I throw on a sports bra and put my hair in a loose ponytail. I secure my phone armband, attach my headphones, pull my hoodie over my upper body, put my headphones into my ears and hit play on my workout playlist. I quickly stretch before heading downstairs. I grab my keys and shove them into my pocket, then I head through the door.

I walk out into the rain and stand there, allowing the cold drops of water to fall onto my makeup-free face. I close my eyes and take in the smell of the rain. When I feel ready, I open my eyes and start jogging. When I reach the end of the driveway, I pick up the pace and start running. I try my best to clear my mind, but my thoughts run with me. Despite my mind working overtime I find a sense of calmness from running in the rain. There is only one other thing that can bring me this same sense of calmness, and that is music.

I continue to run through the rain, listening to every word in every song that plays through my headphones. No matter what, I just keep running, even when I don't think I can keep going, even when my body becomes weak, I just keep pushing. I am becoming exhausted, but I can't stop. I want to keep running. I want to run as far away from home as I can. I even think about running to Cam's, or my dad's, but my legs won't let me.

After running for thirty minutes, I finally stop, and I instantly notice that I don't know where I am anymore. I have run away from home, not keeping an eye on how far I've actually come. I look over the unfamiliar territory, wondering where I am. The rain has picked up and the streetlights are now on. The amount of running I have done suddenly catches up to me. I put my palms on my knees as I bend my back down to try to catch my breath. When I feel better, I start running back the way I came.

Cars are driving down the streets with their headlights on, and a few people are walking with umbrellas. I have finally reached a familiar place, but suddenly I need to stop. I find the closest tree, run over to it, put my right hand on the tree trunk and arch the front side of my body towards the floor as I start to throw up. I don't know where this has come from, and I feel the most unsettling feeling. Every inch of my body hurts, and all I feel is sadness. My gut is telling me something is wrong, and now my whole body is doing the same.

After throwing up, I lean against the tree, watching as my vomit disappears into the grass as the rain clears it up. I finally lift my head up and feel warm tears roll down my cheeks. I have no idea why my body is reacting this way.

When I feel a bit better, I start to slowly walk back towards my house. Once I feel strong enough, I start jogging. I reach my house, feeling another sense of weakness in my legs. I unlock the back gate and go out the back, ripping the headphones out of my ears, removing my armband, and taking my soaking hoodie and leggings off. I throw my shoes and socks by the back door and open the gate that runs along the length of the pool. I jump into the pool with my sports bra and a pair of undies on. I kick my feet in the water before lifting my legs up to the surface. I float along the water and watch the sky as the raindrops continue to fall from the clouds. The water makes my body weightless, and the pain I feel from running so intensely suddenly disappears. I try to think of why my body has suddenly reacted so badly, but the more I think about things, the worse I feel.

After floating for what feels like forever, I finally emerge from the pool. I grab my soaking clothes and pull a towel off the undercover washing line. I secure it on top of my hips before unlocking the back door. I go into the laundry and put my clothes into the washing machine. I drink a bottle of water, go to the bathroom and turn the shower on and when the water is warm I step inside the cubicle. I wash my face before washing my body and my hair. Once I'm done, I grab my clean towel, go to my room and find my favourite pair of tracksuit pants. I pull a grey singlet out of my drawers and throw it on. I lie down on my bed and try to control my breathing. I rest my head against my pillows and within a few minutes, I'm fast asleep.

~

"Delilah, honey, dinner's ready."

I slowly open my eyes. My mum's standing over me, smiling as I wake up.

"Hi, sleepy head."

I yawn and ask her for the time.

"It's nearly seven. You've been asleep all afternoon. I didn't want to wake you. You looked so peaceful, and exhausted. Are you all right?"

She looks worried, again.

"Yeah, Mum. I'm fine." I say it as positively as I can, even though I know I'm not.

I think about telling her what happened when I was running, but I know she will just worry, so I keep it to myself.

"Come on, honey. Come downstairs and eat before your dinner goes cold."

She waits for me as I pull the covers off my body and get up from my warm bed. I follow her downstairs and head into the kitchen, where Evan is sitting with Darci.

"Hello Delilah. How are you?"

I force a smile.

"I'm fine, thank you. How are you?"

He smiles back and starts to tell me about his day. My mum puts a plate in front of me. She's made steak and salad, and as I look at the food, I realise how hungry I am. With every bite, though, I feel worse than I did before. Evan continues to talk to me, but I don't hear much of what he says. I occasionally look up and smile so he thinks I'm listening. I feel bad, and I'm certainly not trying to block him out on purpose. I just can't concentrate on anything other than this feeling that keeps intensifying. After eating half of my food, I push the plate away.

"Is that it?" Mum examines how much is left on my plate.

"Yeah, sorry. I'm not hungry anymore. I think I'm getting some kind of flu or something, I've got the worst headache. I'm going to go back to my room and relax if that's all right?"

I flash a smile at her so she doesn't worry.

"Okay, honey. I'll bring you some Panadol and a cup of tea once I've finished eating."

I check my phone once my bedroom door is closed. Cam still hasn't replied to my message. I try calling him, but he doesn't answer. After leaving him a voicemail practically begging him to call me back, I sit on my bed and listen to the rain as it continues to fall.

I get up and sit at my bay window. When my mum built her dream home, she said we could design our rooms however we wanted. I wasn't too fussed about how my room looked, as long as I had a bay window. I love sitting down while looking out at the world. I lean my back against the wall and watch the raindrops hit the glass. I feel my eyes become heavy with tiredness again, so I lean over and pull my leopard throw over the bottom half of my body.

My mum walks in, holding a freshly made cup of Earl Grey tea. She hands it to me with a packet of Panadol.

"I've got a bottle of water here for you as well. Let me know if you need anything else. I love you."

She hands me the bottle of water.

"Thank you. I love you too, Mum."

I carefully take out two pills from the packet, throw them in my mouth, and swallow them with water. I pick up my cup of tea and lean back against the wall. I'm watching the rain and drinking my tea when my phone starts to buzz.

"Hey, finally. I've been trying to get a hold of you all day." I say as I answer Cam's call.

"I know, sorry. It's been a long day. Can you come over?'"

There's something different about the tone of his voice, something doesn't sound right.

"Of course. I'll come over now."

I wait for him to reply, but he hangs up. Something really isn't right. I don't bother changing, I just grab a clean jumper out of my drawers before slipping my Converse on. I run down the stairs, pulling my jumper over my head.

"Where are you going? I thought you didn't feel well?"

"I don't, but Cam needs me."

"Needs you for what? What's going on?"

"I don't know, Mum. I'll be home soon."

I jump into my car and turn the key. The sick feeling has come back, stronger than it was before. I try to ignore it, but the closer I get to Cam's house, the worse it gets.

It's 9:00 p.m. when I pull into Cam's driveway. I turn my car off, jog up his driveway, knock on the door and wait for him to answer. He lets me in and I step inside. I hug him, but his usual warm, welcoming hug feels cold and forced.

"Where is everyone?"

"They've gone to Gavin's for the night."

A look of fear and sadness is plastered on his face.

"Hey, what's going on? You're acting weird and you've ignored me all day."

He leads me to his room without answering.

"Have a seat, please."

He signals for me to sit next to him on his bed. I sit down. I know something is wrong, but I don't think I am ready to hear what it is. A silence falls upon us, and it isn't a good silence either. It's like the silence and calmness that falls over the sky before a storm. I take a deep breath and look at him. He has his head in his hands as he starts to speak.

"I hope you know how much I love you, I've always loved you and I will always love you. Nothing will ever change that."

He stops and there's silence for another thirty seconds.

"But?"

I'm desperate for him to finish his sentence.

"But I can't do this anymore. You can't do this anymore. We can't do this anymore. I have no doubt in my mind that you're the one for me, and I know you feel the same, but the timing isn't right. We're both going in different directions at the moment. We want different things, and right now we just need to be by ourselves. I know one day, when the timing is right, we will find our way back to each other. We will find our way back home."

I don't know what to do. I'm trying to make sense of what he is saying, but I can't, all I can do is feel my heart breaking. Before I know it, I feel the tears rising in my eyes. His words hit me in the worst possible way. It feels like a knife has pierced through my skin, and is slowly twisting into my delicate heart. I can't get any words out. I want to scream; I want to cry; I want to fight to save our relationship. But when I look at his face, I know it is over and no amount of fighting will save it.

"All right. If that's what you want, then I guess we're over."

He meets my eyes, and suddenly he is irritated beyond belief.

"Why aren't you trying to stop me? Why aren't you fighting for this?"

I look at him closely. Is he serious? He can't be serious. Oh wow, he's serious. I can feel the anger building inside of me as I answer his stupid question.

"What the hell do you want me to say? And what do you want me to do? It's not going to change anything! I don't want to take a break or end things or do whatever the hell it is that you suddenly want to do. I can beg you or try to change your mind, but what's the point if you're just going to turn your back on me and watch me walk away from you? Where has this come from? I thought you loved me!"

"That's the point, Delilah. It's because I love you that I'm doing this! You need time to work on things in your life and I need time to focus on myself. So much has happened over the last few months. We both just need time and space to be alone and focus on ourselves."

He tries to hold my hand, but I get up.

"Where are you going?"

"Home. Obviously."

He shakes his head.

"Why?"

"What do you mean *why*? Why would I stay here after you've broken my heart? There's no point in staying if we're seriously breaking up. Being around you is too hard, I don't know how to be anything other than your girlfriend. I'm sorry for whatever I've put you through. My heart will always belong to you."

I turn to walk away, but he grabs my arm.

"No, I'm sorry. Please stay, one last time."

He stands in front of me, blocking my way so I can't leave.

"Don't do this to me. I can't be here with you. Not now."

I'm trying desperately to stop the tears from leaving my eyes.

"I know this is hard, but please, just stay. You can stay in the guest room. Just don't leave tonight."

I nod and, without saying a word, walk to the guest bedroom with Cam following close behind. I open the door and turn the light on. Cam watches me as I look around the room. He kisses the top of my head and closes the door behind him. I turn the light off and walk over to the bed, carefully getting into it. It feels cold and unwelcoming, it isn't comforting or warm like Cam's bed. In that moment all I want is to be with him in his room, falling asleep to the sound of the pouring rain and his soft breathing.

Instead I am in the guestroom of my now ex-boyfriend's house, trying to find a way to come to terms with the fact that I am now single. I put my head against the unfamiliar pillows and the tears escape my eyes. *Holy shit, I'm single.* The love of my life, the person I have shared my life with for close to five years, has broken up with me. How the hell has this happened? He is my soulmate, he is the love of my life, and now he doesn't even want to be with me. My tears become stronger and soon I am crying into the pillow, trying desperately to muffle the sound of my pain.

The door slowly opens, and Cam walks in. He turns on the light and sees the mess I am in.

"Shit! Delilah, please don't cry."

He turns the light off and approaches the bed. He climbs in and pulls me to his chest, trying his best to comfort me and calm me down. I try to push him away, but he's too strong. He puts my head on his chest and starts to rub my back as I try to stop the tears. I finally relax, and we snuggle up together one last time. Without looking at him, I start to tell him how I am feeling.

"I know this is what you want, but it sucks. I can tell you a million reasons why, but I'll give you the ones that mean the most. I'll never be able to call you just to hear your voice when I'm having a bad day. I'll never be able to surprise you with your favourite foods when you're having a bad day. I'll never be able to go for long walks with you where we just hold hands and smile at each other. I'll never be able to hug you. I'll never be able to feel so fiercely loved and protected by you. I'll never know what it's like to be your wife. I'll never be the mother of your children. I'll never be able to kiss you. But Cam, do you know what the worst part is? I'll never be able to love you for the rest of our lives, through thick and thin, till death do us part. I know you say we will end up together, but I think we both know that won't happen. You'll move on. You'll find someone else to love, and that will just about kill me. My heart is broken, and I don't know how I'm meant to pick the pieces up and fix things. How am I meant to move on from the one person I love more than anything in this world?"

He lies there in silence, so I decide to continue.

"I don't want to go to sleep. Why? Because when I wake up, I know it'll all be over for good. I'll have to leave, and I know I won't be coming back. I'll give you one last hug, get into my car and watch in my mirror as you disappear. Please tell me how I'm meant to do that?"

I feel like there's this stigma around men, about them not being able to show their emotions or cry as much as women do, but I disagree with that. I think men should show their feelings just as much as women do, and I want Cam to show his. I want him to show the pain I can see in his eyes when the small amount of light in the room hits them. I don't think he will, but then he does. He pulls me closer to him, and he tilts my head up the exact way he did when we first kissed. He kisses my head again, and then the tears escape his eyes too.

"Don't you ever think for a second that I won't be there for you, or that I'll ever stop loving you, because I won't. Delilah, the time just isn't right, but that's not to say it won't ever be right. I know you're the one for me, and I know you feel the same, but for now we need to get our lives sorted. We need to live as individuals. You need to finish your album, go and see your dad and get to know Evan, and I need to figure out what I'm going to do once I finish my degree."

I want to argue with him, but I don't have the energy. It's been drained from me, and I am beyond exhausted. I no longer care if I cry. I allow the pain to escape from my body through my tears.

Eventually, I fall asleep, but all too soon the sun begins to rise behind the dark clouds that remain in the sky. The realisation of what has happened hits me again as I wake up in Cam's arms for the final time. We lie there for fifteen minutes, just staring at each other. We don't say a single word. Eventually I pluck up enough courage to move. I know it is time to leave. If I stay any longer, it will just make things worse.

Cam walks me to my car, and we hug one last time. I get into the car without looking at him, pull out of his driveway and drive off. He disappears in the rear-view mirror. When he is no longer in sight, I completely break down. I haven't felt pain like this since my dad left. I suddenly feel infuriated: with my dad, and myself. If he hadn't left us, I wouldn't have lied and started looking for him. He has cost me everything. I don't even know if I want to see him anymore.

I pull into my driveway and park my car next to Evan's. My mum's car is gone, so I am hoping he is with her. I walk inside and Evan steps out from the kitchen.

"Oh, hi Delilah. I thought you were your mum and Darci."

I walk into the kitchen.

"Where are they?"

"They went to do some food shopping, and Darci had a doctor's appointment. Are you okay?"

I'm trying not to cry. I don't want him to see me like this and I certainly don't want to explain what has happened, but before I know it I have my head in my hands as the tears fall from my eyes.

"Oh no, don't cry. What's wrong?"

He approaches me and offers me the tissue box. I take it from him, then I hug him. I don't know why I do it, but I need to cry, and I need someone to hold me while I cry, and well, he is the only one here. He wraps his arms around me and pulls me closer to his chest, gently patting my back as I hysterically cry. He doesn't tell me to stop crying, and he doesn't push me away. He just holds me until I feel I am strong enough to let go. He is being so nice to me after I've been so rude to him. When I feel ready, I let go of him. I stand back and wipe my eyes with a tissue. Something about hugging him feels right, and I can't believe I've been too stubborn to allow him to be a part of my life. I sit down at the table, and Evan pulls the seat out next to me.

"Do you want to talk about what's caused you to have this reaction?"

"Why are you being so nice to me? I've been nothing but rude to you ever since I met you."

"Delilah, I know you need time to adjust to this, and I know we need time to get to know each other. I'm not coming into this to replace your father. I know you need him too, and I know nothing will ever change that. I support your decision in seeing your father; regardless of the outcome, it's something you need to do for the sake of yourself, and there's nothing wrong with that."

He hands me another tissue.

"I'm sorry for not giving you a chance. I'm sorry it's taken something bad to happen for me to realise you're a good person."

"I accept your apology. I only want the best for you, and I only want to become a support system for you. Our relationship will develop naturally and if that takes years, then so be it. I'm willing to wait until you're ready to take that step, there is absolutely no pressure for it to happen immediately. I've said the same thing to your brothers and sisters. I won't ever force this onto you guys. I promise."

I get up from my chair and hug him again.

"Thank you, for everything. I think we should start over, and I'd like to get to know you."

I start to walk out of the kitchen.

"Delilah. What happened? If you don't mind me asking?"

"Cam and I broke up."

I head towards the stairs.

"Oh, I'm so sorry. I'm here if you want to talk."

I thank him and go to my room. I snuggle into my bed and stare at the ceiling. How much can one person take? Why is this happening?

I fall asleep, and when I wake up, it's night time. I check the time on my phone, it's 1:00 a.m. I wipe my eyes before putting my head back on my pillows. I try desperately to fall asleep again, but my body has slept for the past fourteen hours. It doesn't surprise me that I slept for so long since I haven't slept much over the past week. I am mentally and physically exhausted. After multiple failed attempts I finally give up on going back to sleep.

I get up from my bed, turn my light on, find my Ugg boots and slip them on. I am still in the same clothes that I wore to Cam's, but I don't care. I put my phone in my pocket and head downstairs. The house is quiet and dark, but I follow the light from the moon into the kitchen. I close the door behind me, turn the light on and adjust the setting to the lowest one. I go over to the table, where I find a note.

"Delilah, Evan told me what happened. I'm so sorry honey. I don't want to wake you, but if you get up before me, please don't hesitate to wake me up. There's some dinner in the fridge if you're hungry. We're here for you. Mum and Evan xx"

I put the note back on the table and head to the fridge. I look inside and spot a plate with a chicken burger patty and some salad next to it. I take it out, heat up the patty, place it in between a fresh sesame seed bun, and put some lettuce, avocado, tomato and aioli on it. I boil the kettle, make myself a cup of tea, and put it in my travel mug.

I pick up the burger, my tea and my keys, turn the light off and go outside. I start my car and head towards Cottesloe Beach. As I start to drive, I notice a storm has formed above me and, before I know it, the rain hits. Lightning lights up the sky and the thunder echoes through the clouds. I chase the storm all the way to the beach, where I park my car.

I eat my burger and drink my tea, looking out at the ocean, which is black. The only time the ocean's colours are visible is when the lightning hits the sky. I sit there for an hour, just watching the lightning hit where the ocean and the sky meet. No matter how hard I try, I can't take my eyes off the sky. I finally pull my eyes away to check the time on my phone. It's 2:30 a.m. The storm is raging and I don't feel like going home. I know I won't be able to sleep, so I sit here, continuing to watch the storm as it intensifies. As I sit here listening to the rain hit the roof, I watch the lightning flash across the sky as the booming sound of the thunder gets louder. I'm focusing on the horizon when I start getting ideas for a new song.

I grab my phone, find the notes section, open a new page and start writing my ideas down. I do what I always do when I need something to get me through tough times: I write a song. I finally look up from the screen, and open my window to let some fresh air in as the rain starts to calm down. I take a breath of fresh air before I look back at the screen. I go over it multiple times before I am happy with it. I sing it over and over, trying to focus on the words and not the pain that has inspired them. The more I go over it, the worse I feel, so I finally stop. I put my phone down and try to focus on the horizon again, but my attention span is limited, and I suddenly feel exhausted. I turn the key and start my car; I take the long way home and, after parking the car, I quietly go back inside. I head upstairs and climb back into my bed, where I focus on my breathing and nothing else, which helps put me back into a deep sleep.

I wake up to the sound of someone talking. I put my arms to the sides of my body and sit up, leaning on my arms for support. My two best friends are sitting at the edge of my bed.

"Good morning, sunshine!"

I try to smile at them, but I want to burst into tears. I know I have to tell them about the breakup, but I have a feeling they already know.

"What's the time? And what are you guys doing here?"

"It's 11:30 a.m. We got a call from your mum."

I look at them and I know they know.

"She told you, didn't she?"

Rosie nods.

"She didn't tell us anything specifically. She just told us that you and Cam broke up. We're here for you, we're going to spend the day with you. You can talk to us about it, or you don't have to say a word. It's up to you. Either way, we're sticking by your side all day."

Hadi leans over and grabs my hand.

"The weather's pretty bad today, but your mum said we could go into the spa, and we brought your favourite movies over. We were thinking about having one of our old school sleep overs. How does that sound?"

I squeeze her hand.

"That sounds perfect."

I know they will be there for me, and as much as I don't want to acknowledge the truth, or even talk about it, I know I can tell my friends what has really happened, and I can certainly vent to them too. When I feel ready, I tell them everything that has happened. I tell them about finding my father, I tell them about Ryan - who I really must message or call - and I tell them about the breakup.

We sit in my room and spend the next two hours discussing everything. I tell them everything there is to know, and answer every question they ask. I am brutally honest and I apologise for keeping the truth from them. Once I explain that it was to protect them, they understand. They don't hold anything against me, they don't blame me for anything, and they don't push me away. They embrace me and understand why I've done what I have done, and why I have been so distant recently. They do everything in their power to be here for me and help pick me up when I am at my lowest.

After I tell them everything, we head downstairs to find Evan and my mum in the kitchen. They have been to the shops and bought all of my favourite food. I hug and thank them. I know it's hard to feel so down, but having a support system like this around me really helps lift my spirit. I feel like I am going to be okay, even if I don't feel it now.

My friends lead me outside, and we hop into the spa. I rely on them that day. They help pull me through one of the most difficult days I've ever faced, and I know with them by my side I'll be able to be honest about my feelings. I can cry in front of them, I can vent my frustrations and anger, and I can be brutally honest. They stick by my side, not just on that day, but for the week that follows, when all I want to do is stay in bed and cry. They help me get out of bed, and they keep me moving.

I'm certainly not coping with the breakup very well. I keep finding myself going to call Cam. I am desperate to talk to him, even though I know it is wrong. All I want to do is talk to him, but I can't, and my friends make sure they stop me in those moments. I am so appreciative for everything they have done. Without them I don't know how I would have made it through the breakup.

I know there is only one thing I can do to turn all this around: see my father, face to face. I have heard his voice, and now I need to physically see him.

A week after Cam broke up with me, I know the time has finally come. I know it is time for my dad to face the music. It is now or never. I have decided that when I wake up in the morning, I will get in my car and go and see him. This time he won't turn his back on me. This time he won't be able to run away.

Chapter Eighteen

Falling from Grace

The last six days have been hell, to say the least. I certainly didn't think I'd ever have to face days like this. I have cried myself to sleep almost every night, and I have found myself running every single day. It has become an obsession: one I can't give up on. It is consuming me, and I love it. It is the perfect distraction, and in those moments when I'm running, my world stops.

I'm not eating much, I'm not drinking enough water, and when I can pull myself out of bed it's so I can run. My family and friends are becoming increasingly worried about me, but I've stopped caring about my wellbeing.

The first few days following the breakup, I managed to stay active. My friends tried to keep my mind off things, but there were times when they had to work and couldn't be with me. In these moments my mind destroys me with dark thoughts, and I know the only thing that can change that is being in Cam's arms.

Exactly a week after the breakup, my mum convinces me to go and help her with the food shopping.

"Delilah, honey. It's time to get up. I know you're not ready to face the world but you can't stay in bed forever."

She pulls the curtains back. I try to shield my eyes as the sunlight beams through my room. She comes over to my bed and sits down next to me, gently pulling the covers back.

"I've got some food shopping to do. Why don't you come with me? We can get a coffee and some lunch when we're done."

I see the concern on her face. It's the same look I've had to see all week. As much as my body longs to stay in bed, my mind tells me it is time to get up and face the world, at least for a few hours anyway. I try my best to smile back at her.

"Sure, Mum. I'd love that."

I let the words slip out of my mouth, knowing it isn't the truth, but what can I do? It's not like I can tell her the truth. The pain I'm in isn't going to stop, or go away, until I face the world. I just don't know if I am ready to do that. Although I instantly see the relief on my mum's face when I agree to go with her.

"Fantastic! Go and have a quick shower and get changed and then we can go."

She leaves the room and, as I get out of bed, she turns back to face me.

"It's going to be okay, Delilah. I know you might not think things can get better, but they will."

I fake a smile, something I've become accustomed to all week.

"Thanks, Mum."

I head into the bathroom, lock the door behind me, brush my teeth and turn the taps on. When the temperature is just right, I step under the flow of comforting water. I instantly feel too weak to stand, so I sink to the floor. I sit against the wall and pull my legs into my chest as the water runs over my body. I put my head in between my hands and feel the intensity of the warm water as it washes over my face. I close my eyes and all I hear are the words Cam said to me when we broke up. They keep replaying, over and over. They won't stop. I feel like I'm going insane. Why does my mind keep reminding me of this? I suddenly open my eyes and get up, desperate to forget the words that are drowning me out.

I quickly wash my hair and turn the taps off. I dry my hair and put it into a messy bun. I moisturise and decide to skip putting any makeup on; that is the last thing I feel like doing. I go back into my room and go through my drawers, settling on a pair of three-quarter-length leggings and an oversized grey hoodie. I pull my Nikes on and tie the laces up before heading downstairs.

I pass Evan on the way out, quickly hugging him as I follow my mum to the car. The only good thing that has come out of this week is my relationship with Evan. He often sits down with me while I cry, trying his best to comfort me. He tries to take my mind off things too. When I refuse to get out of bed, he tries to distract my mum so she won't worry so much. I guess he sees how much pain I am in. I think he realises I'm not ready to talk or be around anyone, so he does whatever he can to give me the space I need, and I appreciate that.

It has taken something bad happening to me to finally realise that he deserves a chance. Now I see the potential for him to be a father figure to me too, and I need that more than ever right now. It has made life easier for not just my mum, but my family as a whole. There isn't any more arguing, and everyone is getting along. As far as my family is concerned, life is good, just not that good for me.

I get into my mother's car and we head towards the local supermarket. She tries her best to chat to me, but I can't concentrate on anything she is saying. When we get to the shops, we head inside, and I push the shopping trolley around while she selects the food.

"Oh shoot. I forgot apples. Delilah, could you go and get me some? I don't mind what type they are, just get eight please."

She smiles at me, hoping I am listening, and thankfully this time I am.

"Sure, Mum."

I head back over to the fruit section when I spot a familiar person. I freeze, unable to move. Cam is standing fifteen feet away from me. I'm not paying attention to my surroundings, and a few seconds after spotting Cam, a lady bumps into me.

"Shit! Sorry, I didn't see you there."

She is on her phone and she looks guilty.

"It's fine. I should have moved," I say.

Cam turns around to see what's going on, and when he sees me he starts walking towards me.

"Delilah. Hey, um, what are you doing here?"

My heart races faster and faster with each breath.

"I'm with my mum. She wanted help with the shopping."

"You remember Heather? We're, um, I mean, I'm just helping her with something. How have you been? You look thinner."

Heather strolls over to him, grabbing his hand and kissing his cheek.

"I can't find the stuff I'm looking for. Can you come and help me?"

She looks at me, trying to figure out who I am.

"Delilah? No way! Gosh, it's been forever! How are you? You look fantastic! Very thin, I love it. How do you do it?"

I don't know what to say; doesn't she have a sensitive bone in her body? I clearly look terrible. She starts twisting her strawberry blonde hair around her finger while looking into Cam's eyes, so I answer her in the most sarcastic manner possible.

"Heather! It's so lovely to see you. I'm great. My boyfriend dumped me for God knows what reason, since then I've done nothing but wallow in my own self-pity, and look at that! He's already moved on. As far as how I got so skinny, well it's quite simple really. Just go and get your heart broken, stay in bed and don't eat for a week. Oh, and lots of running helps too. Have a great day."

I turn around and walk off without waiting for a reply, suddenly feeling incredibly embarrassed. I go to find my mum and Cam runs after me.

"Stop, please."

I turn to face him. "What do you want, Cam?"

"It's not what it looks like. We're not together. I just, I don't even know how to explain it."

"You don't need to explain anything. I'm sorry for being rude to Heather. I've got to go. I'm sure I'll see you around."

I turn to leave and he grabs my wrist.

"Please tell me you didn't mean those things you said to Heather. You know, about not eating or getting out of bed or anything."

I'd love nothing more than to tell him the truth and feel the comfort that a hug from him would give me, but I know that won't happen.

"No, I just said that because I don't like Heather. I'm fine, honestly. I've really got to go. Have a good weekend."

He walks back to Heather, looks over his shoulder, smiles and sadly waves at me. I try to force a smile as I wave back, then I walk off searching for my mum.

"Delilah, where are the apples?"

Crap! I've forgotten to get them.

"Sorry. I got side-tracked. I'll go and get them now."

"It's fine. I've got everything now so I'll get some on the way out. Let's go and find a checkout."

I follow her to the checkouts, she pays for the shopping and we head to the café next to the shopping centre. I don't feel like eating or drinking anything, but it is easier to get something, so that I don't have to get another lecture from my mum about the importance of staying healthy.

I settle on a chicken salad and a latte, while my mum orders a beef salad and a latte. While we wait for our food, she says something I've never expected her to say.

"Delilah, I know this may come as a surprise, but I think if you're going to go and see your father, you should do it now. I think seeing him is what you need right now and if it's going to help you deal with everything that's happened recently, then it's time."

This is a pretty big deal. My mother has made it very clear that she doesn't want me seeing my father. She said she'd eventually accept it, but it will always make her feel uncomfortable, so to hear her say she wants me to see him means more to me than she will ever realise.

"Are you sure? Why would you say that? You've never wanted me to find him."

"I know. If I could have it my way I wouldn't let you see him, but I see the pain you're in and it reminds me of the pain he was in. He pushed everyone away, and he refused to let anyone help him. In the end, he lost it all. I see you going down the same path, so if this is what it takes to help you, then I want you to do it. It'll be good for you, and it'll probably be good for him too. Lord knows he needs to face the past and the two of you were always so close. If anyone's going to get through to him, it'll be you. Go and see him. It's time for all of us to heal and you need to deal with everything. Maybe your father is what you need in order to do that."

This is a huge step. I really didn't think I'd see the day when she was willing to let me see him. For the first time in a week, I feel better. For a moment, I almost feel happy, but then I start thinking about Cam. Of course I have to bump into him on the one day I leave the house. Why was Heather with him? Surely they aren't together. Cam said they weren't a couple, but with the way Heather was acting, I don't know if I believe him. My mind is working overtime as I notice Cam and Heather walking in to the café. My mum looks up and spots them too.

"Cameron?"

She invites him to sit down with us. Cam thanks her, but tries to find another table. The café is packed, so he accepts her offer before heading to the counter with Heather to order.

"Who's the girl he's with?"

I glare at her. "I don't know."

I feel physically sick, and the only thing I can think of doing is running.

"I'm going to run home, I need some fresh air."

"Delilah, you haven't finished your food or your coffee. You need to eat and I'm not sure if you're aware of the weather today, but it's pouring down. You're not going to be able to see where you're going, and it'll take you at least thirty minutes to run home. Just come back in the car, please. Is this because of Cameron and that girl? I'm sorry I asked ..."

"Mum, please don't fight me on this one. I've ran through these streets before, and I know my way home. I'll be fine."

She sighs, knowing she won't be able to change my mind.

"Be careful."

I get up just as Cam and Heather join her. I head outside and notice that the rain has turned the concrete from light to dark grey. The darker clouds are beginning to roll in. I take a quick breath and start running along the pavement. As my mind races, I run faster. With every step I take, I feel I'm getting away from my mind. It's almost like it can't keep up. I keep pushing my body, running faster and faster through the darkened streets. The run home seems quicker than any other time I've ran through the area, and within twenty minutes I reach the park that's close to my house. It's completely deserted and the rain intensifies, forming a grey blanket over the streets that are now barely lit by the streetlights.

I rest my right hand on a tree branch as the familiar sting starts in my throat. I know I'm about to be sick, and I know there's nothing I can do about it. I lean my body over and bend my knees as my half eaten lunch comes back up. When I can't throw up any more, I lean down, resting on my knees, trying my best to comfort myself enough to calm down. When I feel strong enough, I stand up and walk the rest of the way home. I reach my driveway and head inside, where my mum is waiting with a towel. She doesn't question me, she just smiles as I approach her. I take the towel from her and sit on the stairs while she gets clean, dry clothes for me. After drying off and changing I sit in the lounge room with Darci, who's watching a movie. I'm barely paying attention to the movie, so I get my phone out and text Ryan. I haven't seen him in a while and I've been meaning to text him, it has just slipped my mind.

Hey, Ryan. Sorry it's taken me so long to get in contact with you, I've just been dealing with a lot. Feel like meeting up in the usual spot tomorrow? I could use some fresh air and a chat with a good friend.

I try to focus my attention back to the television, but my phone buzzes straightaway.

Hey. Of course. I hope you're okay. How does 11:00 a.m. sound?

It means a lot that he is there for me. It means a lot that all of my friends are there for me. I may not have shown it, but having them by my side made this transition just a little bit easier.

Perfect. I'll talk to you tomorrow.

I hit send again and refocus my attention on the movie that Darci has chosen.

~

At 11:00 a.m. the next day, I sit on the sand at Cottesloe Beach and wait for Ryan to arrive. It's not like him to be late, he's usually early. I look around, trying to spot him, but I can't see him anywhere. At 11:20 a.m. he runs over to me.
"I'm so sorry I'm late."
He looks distressed.
"It's fine, really. Are you all right?"
He sits down next to me.
"Yeah, I'm fine. There was just a lot of traffic."
Something doesn't feel right. There wasn't that much traffic when I drove here, but maybe he went a different way.

"So what's up?"

I tell him everything about the breakup and he holds me while I cry. I sit up and wipe my eyes with the back of my jumper sleeve.

"I'm sorry. I honestly don't know how many more tears I can shed. I feel like I've cried every ounce of pain, but then it starts again."

Ryan gently pats my hand.

"You don't need to apologise. Sometimes all we can do is cry, and there's nothing wrong with that."

I meet his eyes. I don't know why but I sense he's in pain, like he's holding something back. I want to ask him what he's hiding, but I'm scared it'll push him away. I think of how to approach the question, but I just blurt it out.

"Are you sure you're okay? I feel like you're hiding something from me. You've always been here for me. I hope you know I'll always be here for you too."

I try to hold his hands but he pulls them away from me.

"Honestly, I'm fine. I'm just tired. How are things going on the dad front?"

I know he's trying to change the subject and I know not to push it.

"My mum wants me to go and see him."

"What? Since when? I thought she was against it?"

"I did too, but since Cam broke up with me, I've been pretty down. I think she thinks seeing my father will help ease the pain and maybe get me out of this bad place."

"Do you think it will?"

"I honestly don't know. I think it might help, but I'm so scared he will reject me."

Ryan moves closer and grabs my hands.

"There's always going to be that risk, but you have to face him at some point. Maybe now the time is right. When do you want to go and see him?"

"I think if I'm going to see him, I may as well do it tomorrow. It's been exactly one week since Cam broke up with me, so maybe seeing him will make the next week of my life somewhat bearable."

"I think you might be right. I can come with you, but with it being Saturday tomorrow I've got work. I wouldn't be able to go until after 5:30 p.m."

"Thank you for the offer, but I think this is something I need to do by myself."

We spend the next twenty minutes talking before getting up to leave. After thanking Ryan for all of his help, I promise to call him after I've seen my father. I watch him disappear as he heads towards his car. I sit back down on the sand and watch the waves crashing into the shore before disappearing again. My phone begins to ring: it's Dakota.

I answer almost immediately and try not to sound too sad.

"Hi Dakota."

I've been texting my sister every day since Cam and I broke up. She has tried to call me, but every time I hear her voice I burst into tears. I long to be with her while I go through this painful experience.

"Hey babe, how are you doing? Feeling any better today?"

"A bit."

"Did you get out of bed today?"

"Yes, I did. Mum made me go food shopping with her."

I'm hoping she won't ask me anything else.

"That's good. How did that go?"

There goes that plan.

"It was going just great until I ran into Cam. He was with Heather."

"Heather Tascott?"

"Yep, that's the one."

Just saying her name makes me feel sick, and angry. I wonder if Cam has secretly been seeing her. The thought makes my stomach, and heart, hurt more.

"You know I've never liked that bitch, with her stupid hair and her stupid face. I heard she had a nose job and Botox. Who gets Botox at twenty-one? I mean, she's not even old enough to have wrinkles! She's always been phoney though, so it matches her fake, boring personality. I don't know what Cam would see in her. Not that he would see anything in her. I didn't mean it like that. Shit, I'm so sorry."

"Yeah, and then Mum invited them to have coffee with us."

I instantly regret saying it aloud, I don't want to discuss it again.

"What? Sorry, you got cut off there."

I feel a sense of relief knowing she didn't hear what I had said.

"Nothing. You know I don't like saying mean things about people, but I've never liked Heather either. We can sit here and whinge about her, but it's not going to change anything. Sure, I'd feel better for a bit but, at the end of the day, she's the one who's with Cam and I'm the one who's sitting here trying to deal with everything."

"I know. I'm sorry. What else has been going on?"

"Funny you should ask that. When Mum and I were having lunch earlier, she told me she wanted me to go and see Dad."

I tell my sister about the conversation with our mother, and she's almost as shocked as I was.

"Wow, that's a huge step. When are you going to see him?"

"Tomorrow. I'll call you after I've seen him. I don't know what I'm going to say, I'm just going to see what happens."

~

The rest of the day goes by quickly and, before I know it, I'm back in my bed preparing myself to finally see my father. I decide to message Adrian, to make sure my dad is still at the same place.

Hey Adrian, it's Delilah. I was planning on going to see my dad tomorrow, and I was just wondering if he is still at the same place, the one you gave me the address for?

Ten minutes later my phone alerts me to a new text message.

Hi, love. I just called him. He's still in the same place. Good luck! I'm sure he will be really happy to see you.

~

I get up at 9:00 a.m. on Saturday morning. I have spent the majority of the night trying to sleep, but every memory of my dad floated through my mind. It reminded me of everything we did together and everything he has missed since he left. I feel too nervous to eat, so I make myself a banana smoothie.

I sit down at the table and drink it while my mum tells me that she is going over to Anna's house with Evan and Darci. She tells me I'm welcome to go too, but with Cam being there, we both know it wouldn't be a good idea. She hasn't brought up our awkward encounter with Cam and Heather, and I've been trying to avoid her.

"What are you doing today, honey?"

"Not sure yet. I might go and see Declan."

"That sounds like a good idea. Maybe you could stay there tonight? We probably won't be home until late, and I don't want you staying here by yourself. It'll be good for you to be around someone like your brother."

I want to tell her where I'm really going, but I know she will worry all day. It's going to be easier to tell her about it after I've actually seen my dad.

"Yeah, maybe."

I go to my room and spend the next six hours going over what to wear, what to say and what to do. I fight with myself about getting into the car and going. For some reason I can't find the courage to do it. At 3:00 p.m. my mum comes into my room.

"We're off now. I spoke to Anna, and Cam's not going to be there. He's going to a friend's house tonight, so if you want to come you won't have to see him."

Friend? What friend? Heather? My mind starts running wild again and I find myself on the verge of a panic attack.

"Delilah? Did you hear me?"

She's watching me closely.

"Yeah, sorry. I'll give it a miss. Thanks, Mum. Have fun though."

"All right, honey. Call me if you need me. Go and see your brother, the company will do you good. See you later. I love you."

"Love you too."

When I hear Evan's car leave the driveway, I jump up. I go to my closet and get changed before I grab my keys. I head to my car and pull out of the driveway, heading towards my father's house. I don't stop to think and I don't stop to worry about what I'm going to say. I just drive, knowing that if I don't do it now, I won't ever do it.

Fifteen minutes later I pull up outside the house. It's an older style house. The grass is brown, showing signs of being abandoned for months, and the letterbox has broken off the stand. I turn my car off and slowly get out. I start walking towards the door, trembling as my feet slowly lead me up to the rusted frame door.

I reach the door and curl my toes in my shoes. I lift my right hand, which is now shaking like a leaf, and ring the doorbell.

A few seconds later a man opens the door and leans against the frame. He is wearing blue jeans and a black singlet. He is tall and lean, but he looks tired and sad. His green eyes show signs of someone masking pain. Is this him? Is this my father? He continues to look at me, blinking a few times before he speaks.

"Yes? Can I help you?"

He doesn't recognise me. I feel a sudden pain in my chest.

"Are you Tony?"

"Yes, I am. Do I know you?"

Oh my God, it's him! It's my father. The first genuine smile in a week suddenly appears on my face.

"This is going to sound completely insane, but I'm ..."

He cuts me off.

"Delilah? It can't be. W-what are you doing here? How did you find me?"

He does recognise me! I can't stop smiling. I have found my father and he recognises me. Everything is going to be okay, I just know it.

"Ummm, it's a long story. I've been looking for you for a while now. I was hoping we could talk."

Without saying a word, my father opens the door, signalling me to go inside. I smile at him as I walk in. Within seconds of stepping inside I smell an all too familiar smell. Whisky and cigarette smoke fills the air like it did when I was little. I look back to my father, who is staring at me. I slowly approach him. When I get close enough, I throw my arms around him and hug him as tightly as I can. Tears roll down my cheeks as he gently wraps his arms around me. He quickly pulls away from me.

"What are you doing here?"

"I came to see you. You left me. You left all of us with no explanation, nothing. You promised me you would come back for me, but you didn't. You lied to me and now it's time to sit down, talk about everything and move on. I want you back in my life. Please listen to me."

He looks at me as if he has seen a ghost.

"No. I can't do this. I'm sorry. You need to leave."

What? No, I can't leave. Not after all of the searching, all the sacrifices I have made.

"No. I'm not leaving. You're going to hear me out. Dammit, you're not going to push me away again."

"Delilah, you don't understand. Things aren't that easy, I can't just sit here and explain everything. I've moved on, I'm sorry if that hurts you but I can't be in your life and you can't be in mine."

I look at him, feeling the same heartbreak I've felt all week.

"Don't pull that shit with me. I'm not seven anymore! You say I don't understand? Well, make me understand. I'm your daughter, I deserve an explanation."

He shakes his head, not saying a word. All the pain I have felt over the past fourteen years finally hits me.

"You abandoned your daughter when she needed you the most. You left all of us when we needed you. Do you not realise that?"

"Of course I do. Don't you think I feel bad?"

I step closer to him and try to remain calm.

"Then why didn't you come back?"

"I don't know. I just couldn't."

I can see him shutting down, but I've worked too hard for it to end this way. I've had to fight for this, for him.

"Dad, please. Don't turn your back on me. I see the pain in your eyes, please, let me in. You were my best friend. We can have that again; you just need to talk to me. I know you've been hurting. I know you haven't been able to forgive yourself, but that's why I'm here. I forgive you, I still love you and, dammit, I still need you. I've never stopped needing you. We need to heal, together. Let's work through this, just you and me. Then, when you're ready, you can see the rest of the family. Please, just let us in."

I feel the tears roll down my cheeks, and he finally sees the damage he has caused. He steps towards me and I see his walls fall down. He drops his guard completely. He grabs me and hugs me, letting go of years of anger and guilt as he cries with me. I know in this moment that we are going to be okay. This will be a fresh start for all of us, and we finally have the second chance we have been looking for.

He suddenly pulls away from me. His walls are back up, and I see nothing but fury in his face.

"Leave, now, and don't ever come back."

I feel my heart break into a million pieces, but I can't let him see that. He doesn't deserve to see that. He has pushed me away for the final time. I realise I can't save him, or the relationship we once had. The man I knew is gone. I start to walk towards the door, then turn around to face him one last time. I use my last ounce of strength to tell him one more thing.

"You can ignore me all you want. You can pretend you don't know who I am, or that I don't exist, but I exist. I *still* exist. No matter what you do or where you go, I will always be your daughter, and nothing will ever change that. You made the right decision walking out on us. You never deserved us. I've learnt something recently, here and now is all we have, and you can't buy time. You can't make up for all the things you've missed, and I have finally realised that. I looked for you, I found you and I was willing to forgive you, but you still don't want me. Everything you've ever said to me was a lie. I walked through your door hoping you would see the pain you'd caused, but you just don't get it."

He points to the door and I slowly walk towards it. I hope with every ounce of my body that he will stop me, but he doesn't. He waits until I walk through the door and then he slams it behind me. Just like that, everything is over. My father has shut me out. He has pushed me away, and this time it's for good. I fold my arms, pull them to my chest and walk to the car. When I get in, I stare into the distance. I know I shouldn't, but all I want to do is talk to Cam. Somehow it's the only thing that makes sense. I wipe the tears from my eyes as I find his name in my phone. My finger shakes as I hit the call button. I listen to the phone ring three times before he picks up.

"Hello?"

It isn't him. A familiar, high-pitched voice answers instead. "Hello? Who is this?"

"Is Cam there?"

The voice snaps back at me. "He's in the shower. Why are you calling my boyfriend?"

My boyfriend? *He's not yours, he's mine*, I feel like screaming. That's what he used to be anyway, he used to be mine. I feel my heart break again, I can't believe he lied to me. He said he wasn't dating anyone, but he is, and she is *his* girlfriend. I know it's Heather, and I know she is proud of herself for finally getting the guy she's always been desperate for. I try to hold back the tears.

"No one, sorry. My mistake."

I hang up the phone and throw it onto the passenger seat. The tears flood my face, but my tears are the least of my concern. I look back at the house and see my father watching me through the dirty window. He closes the torn curtains when he notices me looking, and I drive off, knowing I'll never see him again.

This pain is unbearable. I can't take it anymore, I just want it to stop, to go away, to leave me alone. My own father, the man who's supposed to love me unconditionally and protect me from the pains of the world, has shut me out for good. He doesn't want me. I don't want to be me. I want to escape. I want to disappear. I want to be anyone but me.

I speed home and when I reach the house, I run inside and throw up. When I'm done, I go into the bar my mum has set up off the front room. I don't usually go in there, but tonight I'm making an exception. I grab a bottle of vodka and go to my room. I sit in the middle of the floor and cry while drinking the liquid which practically burns my throat. It tastes disgusting. My body isn't reacting well to it, but I don't care, and I certainly don't want to stop. The more I drink, the more the pain intensifies. I try so hard to numb it, to make it go away, just for a moment or two, but it won't go away. I drink half the bottle before I can't take the pain anymore.

I go into my mum's room and find the bottle of sleeping pills the doctor has prescribed her. Without thinking, I take them back to my room. I rip the lid off and take some out. I throw them into my mouth and drink more vodka. The pills are gone, and I feel ill. My whole body has started to become weak. I fall to the floor and finally the pain is slowly fading away. My eyes start to close and soon, everything goes black.

To be continued...

About Meagan Dux

Meagan Dux is a twenty-something proud Aussie who was born and raised in Perth, Western Australia. She graduated from Murdoch University with a Bachelor of Arts degree, where she majored in Theatre and Drama in 2017. During her time at university, Meagan was an actor and stage manager.

After spending her life as an avid book reader, Meagan decided to pen her own novel. She wrote her debut novel *The Rise of Delilah* within a few months in 2015/16. She then spent a year preparing it to make its graceful debut into the world.

While recovering from an ankle reconstruction in 2016, Meagan decided to pursue her dream of being an author, and she is now in the process of editing her third novel, as well as working on writing her fourth novel.

As a passionate fan of the AFL, Meagan often goes to games, where she proudly cheers for her two teams, the West Coast Eagles and the Richmond Tigers. When not watching football, Meagan can often be found drinking copious amounts of coffee, reading, writing, taking photos of the sunset, and walking along the stunning beaches in Perth's south with her beloved Labrador, Marley.

Meagan lives with her parents, her two brothers, their three dogs, a cat, and a bird named Bailey in Perth.

Keep in touch with Meagan on her social media channels:
Facebook: www.facebook.com/authormeagandux
Instagram: www.instagram.com/authormeagandux
Twitter: www.twitter.com/meagandux
Snapchat: authormeagandux

Acknowledgements

When I wrote this novel, I had a dream of where it would end up, and that dream was to have it published. I didn't think this day would come, but alas, here it is, and now it's my turn to thank the people who worked tirelessly behind the scenes to help make my dream a reality. I have thanked these beautiful souls a million times in person, but without them, this novel wouldn't be in your hands right now.

To my family, thank you for encouraging me to keep going when I thought about quitting, multiple times. Your love and support helped me get through the times when I didn't think I could write anymore.

A special thank you to my mum. You are my rock; I wouldn't be where I am today if it wasn't for you, I love you to the moon and back.

To Karen McDermott, who is the very reason my novel is where it is today. Words are not enough to thank you for everything you have done for me. You made my dream a reality, and I'm so happy that I was encouraged to contact you. Your passion for this industry is inspiring. You are an angel, and I thank you so very much.

To my editor, Georgina Gregory. Your invaluable words of encouragement and your advice when I had a million and one questions for you has never gone unnoticed. You helped me make the transition from aspiring author to author much more enjoyable, and I'm thankful it was you who was there for me when I needed a fabulous editor! Your brutal honesty was the best thing for me, and I'm forever thankful that you're still by my side.

To Dani Orlando, from Orlando Media, who happily came on board to help me with the social media side of this job, thank you. Your guidance and constant comfort was a blessing when I was at my wit's end. And a special thank you goes to you for helping make my vision for my cover come true.

To my beautiful friends, in particular, Kieran, Kelsie, Alex and Nashy. Thank you for supporting me and being so passionately excited about my dream. I'm lucky to have friends like you in my life.

To Danielle Paparone, Jessica Ialeggio and Philippa Travia. You girls are my angels. Thank you for reading my novel before I had an audience to read it. Your invaluable feedback and words of support, encouragement, and pride means more to me than you'll ever know.

To Bobbi Cooper, my Gossip Gregson buddy. Our drives to get coffee or food are some of my favourite memories. Your love for this novel helped me get through the days when I wanted to quit. Your belief in me has also never gone unnoticed. I'm lucky to have someone I can laugh with over the silliest things like I do with you. And this comes with the medieval meal. Thank you for your friendship.

To BJ Woodford, one of my oldest, and dearest friends. Thank you for being a positive light in my life. You were so passionate about my novel, and you have since continued to do everything in your power to help me get to where I am today. You were the first person to read my novel, and you blew me away with how much you loved and related to it. Thank you for sticking by my side when everything went wrong.

To Claire Tebbutt, one of my best friends. Thank you for never giving up on me, and for never getting sick of me venting to you about my writer's block. Your friendship means the world to me.

A special thank you to Hannah Summers. You never complained when I messaged you at 2 in the morning to complain about the mess in my head, and you did everything in your power to make me feel better. Thank you.

A very special thank you to Dr. Singh, who went above and beyond her duty of care to help me get through the darkest moments of my life. Some people make such an impact on your life, and you are one of those people for me. Your reassurance and constant care for me has never been overlooked, and I am eternally grateful to have such a caring person in my life.

To anyone who picks this novel up, whether it is through an online store or a bookstore, thank you. Without you, I wouldn't be living my dreams. I sincerely hope you enjoy reading this novel as much as I have enjoyed writing it.

And finally, to my guardian angel, Rolly. This is for you. I love you.